TENDERLY, YALE TOUCHED HER FACE

"I always thought you were the most beautiful thing I'd ever seen on ice."

Kira flushed. "That was a long time ago, Yale."

"Maybe so, but the other night when I saw you skating, it was as though the past fifteen years had never happened."

"We can't recapture the past, Yale."

"No, we can't," he agreed, and with that his arms went around her. And his eyes never left her face as he pulled her gently to him. "But maybe we could find a future together...."

She wanted to say that they couldn't, that too much had happened, but the words refused to come. And when his lips touched hers, she forgot all her doubts. All their differences fled her mind, and there was only the pressure of his mouth on hers....

ABOUT THE AUTHOR

Risa Kirk's literary repertoire includes several romantic suspense novels, two historical romances, and with the publication of *Dreams to Mend*, three Superromances. Between books this California author loves spending time with her husband, Ray, a professional horseshoer, and her menagerie of cats, dogs and horses.

Books by Risa Kirk

HARLEQUIN SUPERROMANCE
200—BEYOND COMPARE
238—TEMPTING FATE

Risa Kirk

DREAMS TO MEND

Harlequin Books

TORONTO • NEW YORK • LONDON
AMSTERDAM • PARIS • SYDNEY • HAMBURG
STOCKHOLM • ATHENS • TOKYO • MILAN

Published August 1987

First printing June 1987

ISBN 0-373-70273-6

Printed in Canada

PROLOGUE

"GOOD AFTERNOON sports fans, and welcome again to our coverage of World Cup skiing. We're here at Lake Placid, New York, the site of the 1980 Winter Olympic Games, and the Men's Downhill has just been won by the Austrian, Franz Bauer. The women's competition should be even more exciting, with the U.S. in strong contention for a first. Here to tell you why is Chad Devane, our expert commentator on the scene. Chad...?"

Chad Devane's handsome face filled the television screen, and Kira Stanfield glanced up impatiently from a desk piled high with reports. She was working at home this Sunday because no matter how diligent she was at the clinic with all the paperwork, she still fell behind. This was the weekend she had set aside to catch up, but her flurry of guilty zeal on Friday had somehow vanished the moment she walked in her front door. Now the weekend was almost over, and she couldn't put it off any longer. She had planned to watch *SportsSunday* while she worked, but the program was proving too distracting, so with a sigh, she got up to turn off the set.

Halfway across the living room, she glanced out the big bay window and exclaimed with pleasure. It had started snowing again, and after moving to Vermont only a month ago, she was still thrilled at the sight. It was such a change from Seattle's seemingly endless rain that she went to the window to watch. A fresh snowfall made everything seem so new again that she almost hated to go outside and disturb that pristine covering of white.

Smiling at her fanciful thoughts, she caught sight of her reflection in the window—a slender young woman of thirty-two, with green eyes and dark hair that just grazed her jawline. Dressed in jeans and a heavy sweater, she hardly looked older than some of her patients, young athletes such as she'd once been, who came for treatment to the famed Stonebridge Sports Injury Clinic in the little town of Stonebridge, Vermont. She had always looked younger than she was, and in her youth it had been a constant source of annoyance. Now that she was older, of course, she could be amused when someone mistook her for an assistant at the clinic, especially when they discovered that she was the head of the physical therapy department.

Remembering her original errand, she turned back to the television. She hadn't been paying attention to what the announcer was saying; his shrill enthusiasm was irritating, and she was about to turn off the set when he said, "As anyone who's read the paper or listened to the news is aware, the newest superstar in woman's skiing is our own Mimi Duncan. Today we're fortunate to have with us the father of that fifteen-year-old wunderkind, Yale Duncan. As I'm sure many of you know, Yale was the first American man to win a medal in Alpine skiing—a silver—in the year…uh…" The announcer hesitated, then gave an embarrassed laugh. "I'm sorry, Yale. I just… What year was that?"

"Nineteen seventy-two," Kira whispered, unable to take her eyes off the screen.

"Nineteen seventy-two," Yale Duncan answered, sounding amused. From his height of six-foot-three, he looked down at the commentator, who seemed to have shriveled. Waving away the man's awkward apology with a lift of his hand and an older version of the grin that had set feminine hearts fluttering fifteen years ago, and probably still did today, he said kindly, "Don't worry about it, Chad. It was before your time."

Devane looked even more embarrassed at his faux pas, and Yale seemed amused again as the commentator fumbled with his next question. Kira groped for a chair. She had seen pictures of Yale recently in the sports section of the paper—who hadn't? Ever since his daughter had won the Giant Slalom last month in Austria—where she came in an unbelievable full second ahead of the runner-up—the Duncan family had been in the public eye. That was the second race Mimi had won this year, and with her skis firmly pointed in the direction of a World Cup title, she and her father had become "news."

But this was the first time Kira had seen Yale on television, and she realized that the newspaper prints hadn't done him justice. As hard as it was to believe, he was even more handsome now than he'd been fifteen years ago when they had known each other.

She blinked, shaking her head against old memories. It was so long ago, she thought, and until all this recent publicity about Mimi, she had completely forgotten about Yale. After all, they'd both been so young, and so much had happened since. She hadn't thought of him in years.

Now, despite herself, recollections came flooding back. She and Yale had been in the news, too, all those years ago; in an Olympic year when excitement was running high, an enterprising reporter had discovered that they were...involved. Just a youthful romance, she thought quickly, and then knew that wasn't true. She had been in love with Yale—or thought she was—and she had believed he loved her, too. But it was so difficult then; with both of them training for the Olympics at Aspen—she with her coach and he with his ski team—they rarely had time for themselves. Days were filled with hours of practice, and nights were spent trying to stay awake over neglected study books. Then, after that article appeared in the paper, whenever they did manage to sneak away for a while they were hounded by the press. Some wit had dubbed them the sweethearts of sports: the skating queen and the skiing star. It had been so romantic that they'd believed it themselves.

But then she'd gotten hurt, falling on a simple axel that she'd completed flawlessly thousands of times in practice, and her whole life changed. Suddenly, she wasn't anybody's sweetheart anymore. Her chance at Olympic glory passed her by while Yale went out and captured his. He won an unprecedented silver medal in the Downhill that year while she went home to cry over the unfairness of it all. Yale became a national hero, but her skating career was over. Her dreams had been shattered by one careless moment on the ice.

Restless, Kira stood again. She hated thinking about the past; she had trained herself not to dwell on what might have been. It didn't make any difference now. She had carved a new life for herself since then—*two* new lives. One with her husband Gil before he died last year, and another trying to give injured young athletes the second chance she'd never had. She hadn't skated since the time of her injury, but she didn't care. She was happy with what she was doing, satisfied, fulfilled. Yale was only a name from the past, a face she barely remembered, a man she wanted to forget.

She was just reaching out to snap off the television set when the camera switched abruptly back to Chad Devane's picture-perfect face. He had obviously recovered from his earlier embarrassment, for he said smoothly now, "That was Yale Duncan, ladies and gentlemen, the father of our first competitor, Mimi Duncan." He put his hand to his ear. "I just received word that we're ready to begin this exciting competition, so we'll switch now to our cameras at the starting gate."

Kira couldn't turn off the set now, just when Mimi was going to race, and she perched on the edge of the rocking chair to watch. As Mimi's red-suited, slender form filled the screen, helmeted head down, her body tense with concentration as she balanced over her skis behind the starting wire, Kira felt herself tensing, as well. How often had she felt this way right before Yale was going to race! She could remember how her heart had pounded, how her palms would become clammy. Downhill was so dangerous, even then; now, with the new, faster skis, it was even more so. She'd heard it said that Downhill skiers were either the most courageous of athletes or the most foolhardy, depending on one's viewpoint, and she believed it. Waiting tautly for the clock to start, she wondered what Yale was thinking right now. Could he see his daughter poised for that perilous sixty-mile-an-hour run down the mountain? Unconsciously, she clutched the arms of the rocking chair.

"Three . . . two . . . one . . . and go!"

Mimi was a blur of crimson as she shot out of the starting gate, and as the camera followed her down the first steep incline, Kira tensed even more. Crouched into an "egg" position that was designed to minimize wind resistance, Mimi sped down the mountain like an arrow shot from a crossbow. Accompanied by a running commentary from an unseen announcer, she tucked her arms tightly against her sides and flew over one section at such speed that the commentator's voice rose a full octave.

"Oh, oh! Did you see that?" the announcer shouted. "Now we know why this girl has developed a reputation on the circuit for being absolutely fearless! She was almost out of control on that one, and— That was *another* close one!" he shrilled, interrupting himself as Mimi shot over a mogul, this time thrown slightly off balance because of her tremendous speed. "She took some air there so she'll have to make up for it on the next section! "These downhillers go at tremendous speeds, ladies and gentlemen, and— Uh, oh!" he shouted, as the camera followed Mimi flying down another section, forced to half stand this time to keep her balance. For a heart-stopping instant, it looked as though one of her skis was about to slide out from under her, and Kira gripped the chair arms tightly, willing that slight figure to stay upright. Mimi was one of the smallest women competitors, barely five-foot-four and only a hundred and fifteen pounds, she remembered reading, and sports writers had marveled that anyone so slight was strong enough to hold on against these tremendous speeds. Somehow she managed. Mimi got her skis under control again, and Kira was just sitting back in relief when another camera took over and caught Mimi flying around a curve.

"Wow!" the commentator cried. "Listen to those skis chatter! But she's making even better time on this than she did on any of the practice runs, and if she can— Oh! Did you see that? She almost lost it again! She's really going all out today, ladies and gentlemen, and if she can—"

He never finished his sentence. On a section the skiers had ominously dubbed Flyaway, something happened. One instant Mimi was speeding down the mountain in that tuck position, her arms pressed tightly to her sides, her poles thrust out behind her...the next, she was in the air, flailing to keep her balance.

"No!" Kira cried, leaping to her feet. "No!"

Before her horrified eyes, the red-suited figure catapulted into space and came down hard again, her tremendous speed cartwheeling her over the snow. Ski poles flew in two different directions, and one ski broke in two, the pieces flying away like spokes snapped from a wheel. She was going too fast to stop, and she cannoned down the mountain, careering off the bales of straw that had been placed along the perimeter of the run, coming finally to rest in a tiny little heap of crimson, the leg with the ski still attached bent grotesquely under her.

The camera held on the scene and Kira was unable to turn away. Frozen, she watched as people ran from all directions to help, until finally Mimi was hidden from view by the press of the crowd. The show cut away then to a commercial, and after an endless, tense wait, the program returned, the screen filled this time with a solemn new face.

"For those of you who have just tuned in, this is Kent Braedon of *SportsSunday* reporting to you, live, from Lake Placid, where the United States fifteen-year-old wonder, Mimi Duncan, has just fallen during the Women's Downhill on this race toward the World Cup title. A preliminary examination by physicians on the scene indicates that it will be some time, if ever, before Mimi will be able to ski again. We'll have a more extensive report later on *SportsUpdate*, but for the time being, I'm sorry to say that it looks like America's hope for the gold in Women's Downhill has just evaporated. This is Kent Braedon of *SportsSunday* reporting. And now, Chad, back to you.''

After witnessing such a tragic accident, Kira couldn't listen to the toothy Chad Devane. Reaching out, she snapped off the set. Her work still awaited her, but it was a long time before she went back to her desk. Try as she might, she couldn't erase the sight of Yale from her mind. The camera had caught him at the last, bending over Mimi, and the agonized look on his face as he gathered his injured daughter in his arms was a sight she knew she would never forget.

CHAPTER ONE

KIRA WAS IN HER OFFICE reading an article on the latest developments in sports equipment when the head of the Stonebridge Clinic, Dr. Miles Gentry, knocked on her door. As chief of the physical therapy department, Kira tried to keep abreast of the latest innovations in case one of her young patients asked her opinion, but she had to shake her head wryly at the thought of honeycomb-disc wheels on racing bicycles and digital catcher-pitcher communication systems for baseball players. Glancing up as Miles came in, she gestured with the magazine and said ruefully, "Whatever happened to hand signals and ten-speed bikes?"

Miles looked blank. "I beg your pardon?"

She pointed to the article she'd just set aside. "It says here that in the future, engineers and computers are going to be the ones to design and test sports equipment."

"Really? That's nice," he replied vaguely.

She could see he was preoccupied and couldn't resist teasing him a little. It wasn't often that he went around in a fog, but when he did, he was absolutely oblivious to anything else. He reminded her of the absent-minded professor at such times, and she said innocently, "Yes, I thought so, too. Soon we won't have to worry about humans playing sports at all. I was just reading that games will be between computers, so we'll be out of jobs. Won't that be wonderful?''

''Oh, yes. Absolutely.''

She laughed aloud. ''Okay, I give up. Do you want to tell me what's on your mind?''

He looked blankly at her again, a slightly balding man of thirty-eight, with brown hair and kind blue eyes behind gold-rimmed glasses. The receding hairline made him look older than he was, but he claimed not to mind. He believed his young patients had more confidence in a father figure, especially when he was the head of a clinic as prestigious as Stonebridge. Athletes from every sport came here for treatment, and the clinic's reputation surpassed most others in the country. Stonebridge had, on occasion, even treated athletes from outside the United States.

When Kira had come here three months ago for her interview, she'd been impressed—not only with the equipment, which was the most up-to-date she'd ever seen, but with Miles himself. As the clinic's owner and administrator, he was involved with every facet, and it was clear that he ran Stonebridge efficiently. What was even more important was that both his patients and his employees obviously loved him. She had liked him instantly herself, and when after that single interview he had offered her the position of head of the therapy department, she'd been thrilled. She had instituted a pilot program in sports therapies at the Seattle hospital where she had worked for the past four years, and Miles had been impressed with her success. She had always wanted to work with athletes because she identified so strongly with their special medical problems, but Stonebridge was the first sports medicine clinic to which she had applied, and the fact that he wanted her to head the department here was an honor.

When she'd first obtained her license, she'd spent five years as a therapist in a small Seattle clinic because she was busy studying for her advanced degree. By the time she had received her doctorate in exercise physiology, her husband, Gil, had already established his accounting business. There was no question of them moving, so she had applied to one of the hospitals in the city and had spent her time reorganizing the department. She was just starting to build a name for herself as a specialist in sports injuries when Gil was diagnosed with kidney disease. Life after that became a nightmare of doctor's visits and dialysis treatments and hoping that *something* would work. Helpless to prevent it, she had watched him slowly taken from her, and the strain had been crippling. It had taken her months to get over his death; sometimes she wondered if she ever had. After watching him suffer and struggle so bravely, she felt so sterile inside at times, so incapable of really feeling anything again.

If she hadn't had her work, she didn't know what she would have done. There were times when she was sure she would have—as her sister Jilly might have said—gone right around the bend. Jilly had been so patient with her after Gil had died last year; even though she had her own husband and her job as a high school teacher at Seattle Union High to keep her busy, she'd always been available when Kira needed a good cry.

But after a few months of moping around, she had finally realized that she couldn't lean on her sister forever. Jilly had already suggested that a change of scene might help, so when Kira had heard of the opening at Stonebridge, she had applied before she gave herself a chance to think about it. When Miles hired her, there was no turning back. She had returned to Seattle only to sell everything: the house, the car—even most of her furniture—before she moved to Vermont. Jilly had advised her to start a new life, and she had. She had come to Stonebridge with only a few clothes, a rented car, and her cat.

It seemed so long ago, she thought now, even though it had just been three months. She'd been a different person when she first moved to Vermont—so unhappy, so sad . . . so lonely. Even after she had settled into her new job and found the cottage and started to furnish it, she couldn't keep busy enough. She loved her new home, but it seemed at first that she constantly found excuses to stay away from it. The echoing rooms and the sounds of her own footsteps seemed to increase her loneliness, and when Miles had found her working late, again, one night, he had asked her out to dinner. After that one date, they had both known there could never be anything between them, and they had settled into an easy friendship that she had come to value greatly.

"Kira, what's your schedule like for the next few months?"

Her reverie interrupted by Miles's question, Kira blinked and leaned forward to check her calendar. When she first came to the clinic, Miles had been running himself ragged trying to organize every detail from ordering fresh towels to scheduling patients. As his new second-in-command, Kira had relieved him of many responsibilities, and now she was the one who designed individual therapy programs and scheduled patients. As she flipped through the pages of her calendar, she said, "Well, we have Jimmy Rodriquez still coming in daily for that soccer injury, and I'm afraid we'll be treating Linda Kent, our gymnast, for quite awhile on that Achilles tendon. Then there's—''

''Noreen and Betsy can manage now with those two, can't they?'' he asked, mentioning two of the three other therapists Stonebridge employed.

''Well, yes,'' she said, surprised. Miles rarely interfered with scheduling, and she looked at him curiously. She saw his excited expression and couldn't help teasing, ''Don't tell me your mysterious basketball player from last year is going to check into the clinic again!''

Just for an instant he looked almost wistful. Miles was an avid basketball fan, and one of his prized possessions was the white-framed eyeglasses the athlete had deliberately left behind. Kira hadn't been here then, of course, but she had heard the story several times: how the famous athlete had checked in under a false name, how he had arrived in the dead of night. Miles still grew excited when he told the tale, even if the press had found out the next day. But then, Kira thought with a smile, it was a little difficult hiding someone who was over seven feet tall.

Looking somewhat downcast, Miles shook his head at her question. ''No, it's not him. Fortunately, he's doing well. This is someone else...someone you'd never expect in a million years.''

Mentally, she ran down the list of athletes who had been hurt or injured lately, but no one sprang to mind. It was January, and thus far the winter sports season had been mercifully accident free. She had no idea who could cause his excitement. ''I don't know. Who?''

He paused dramatically. ''Mimi Duncan.''

She looked at him blankly. Remembering that terrible fall Mimi had taken only six weeks or so ago, she said faintly, "Mimi Duncan is coming here?"

He was too excited at the thought to notice her dismay. "I know, I didn't believe it at first myself. I mean, everyone said she'd never ski again, but when her father called last night for an appointment, naturally, I said we'd see her right away."

"Right away!" Wondering why the thought of seeing Yale again filled her with such dread, she heard the shrill note in her voice and tried to pull herself together. "I mean," she said hastily, "the last time I heard, she was due to have surgery. Has she recovered enough to begin therapy already?"

"That's what we're going to find out," Miles said, and then looked at her curiously. "Is something wrong?"

"No, of course not," she denied, too quickly. What was the matter with her? What difference did it make whether Mimi had chosen Stonebridge or another clinic for her therapy? She was an athlete, just like anyone else.

No, she wasn't, Kira thought grimly. Other athletes didn't have Yale Duncan for a father. She didn't want to have to deal with Yale, not when she'd had more than enough of the Duncan family after Mimi's accident. It seemed then that everywhere she looked she saw one of their faces. They seemed to have become more popular than Prince Charles and the Princess of Wales; it was exasperating. After that first week, she'd resolutely ignored it all.

Or tried to, she thought irately. Because she knew the reason behind all the publicity, and if she allowed herself to think about it, she became outraged all over again. Yale had always been able to manipulate the press, and he'd obviously been having a field day over this.

Now that Miles had brought him to mind again, she thought angrily that Yale hadn't changed at all. He was the same person he'd been all those years ago when all he could think about was using sports for his gain, and she didn't want to have anything to do with him. Oh, the fights they'd once had! He had called her a purist about sports and athletics, and maybe he was right. But he was an opportunist and always had been. He'd told her long ago that he'd parlay winning a gold medal into making him a wealthy man, but even though he'd fallen short of first place, his silver medal had still enabled him to keep that promise. Boise had been too small for him after that; he had moved almost immediately to Los Angeles, where the action was, and now he was one of the country's most successful sports agents, with a stable of star athletes as dazzling as the deals he made for them. Oh, she knew all about Yale! In a business where multimillion dollar salaries for superstar athletes were almost commonplace, the contracts Yale negotiated were legendary. He had done well for himself, all right, and this latest publicity hadn't hurt his business at all. She could almost picture him rubbing his hands together in glee as athletes lined up outside his door begging to be represented by him. How like him to turn a tragedy like this to his advantage!

Realizing that Miles was still staring at her curiously, she looked down at her desk and told herself that she couldn't believe that Yale was glad his daughter had been hurt. As much as she detested him, even she couldn't grant him that. But he obviously wasn't above turning a profit from it, and that's what made her so angry.

Was that why she was so reluctant to see him again? Hastily, she said, "I'm sorry, Miles, I was just surprised. I thought that Yale—Mr. Duncan—would take his daughter to one of the clinics in California. They have perfectly adequate facilities there, you know."

He looked pleased. "But none of them are Stonebridge, and we have treated Olympic skiers before. I think it's reasonable that he bring his daughter here. After all, she is America's hope for a medal in the Women's Downhill."

She gave him a sharp look. "According to those endless conjectures in the paper, Mimi is hardly going to ski again, much less win a medal."

"That's why I asked about your schedule. I thought you would take over Mimi's case personally."

"Me?"

"Who else? You're the head of the department. Don't you think an athlete of Mimi's caliber deserves the best we have to offer?" He smiled. "In case you hadn't noticed, that's you."

She refused to be swayed by the flattery. "But we have an entire department of therapists who are just as qualified as I am to handle Mimi's therapy, Miles. Why don't we assign one of them?"

"Because inevitably the press will find out she's here, and then there will be all sorts of questions. If they discover she's not getting personal attention from the head of our therapy department, well... With that fund drive for the clinic coming up, we really don't want any adverse publicity, do we?"

She knew he was talking about the winter carnival the clinic sponsored every year, the proceeds of which were used to modernize the facilities with the latest equipment. Machines like isokinetic computers weren't cheap, nor were even less esoteric pieces of equipment like back tables and gravity machines. Because of Miles's administrative capabilities, the clinic did quite well, but innovations occurred every day, and Stonebridge had a reputation to maintain.

"You've never worried about that before," Kira said, trying not to sound sullen. Miles had a point and they both knew it.

"We didn't have a Mimi Duncan here before," Miles countered, and leaned forward again. "Now, under normal circumstances, I don't believe in interfering with the way you run your department, Kira. You've done a wonderful job these past few months. But this time, I'm afraid you're going to have to accommodate me. Mimi Duncan deserves special treatment, and she's going to get it, don't you agree?"

She didn't agree at all. "I just think—"

He glanced at his watch and shook his head. "I'm afraid we don't have any more time to discuss it, Kira. Yale and his daughter have an appointment today."

She bolted upright in the chair. "Today! When?"

"Unless they were delayed by weather, Yale promised to have Mimi here by three."

Kira's glance flew to the clock. She almost groaned when she saw that it was two minutes to that now. Whatever else he might be, Yale had always been maddeningly punctual, and she knew that he wouldn't be late.

"OH, LOOK!" Mimi Duncan exclaimed, craning to see out the plane window as the jet began its descent toward the airport at Rutland, Vermont. "Isn't it beautiful?"

Her father leaned over his seat and glanced down. "I guess so," he said. "If you like snow."

"Oh, Dad!" Mimi rolled her eyes and he smiled as she pressed her nose against the window in an effort to see better. "Why don't we come to Vermont sometime to go skiing?" she asked, turning her head so that her cheek rested against the Plexiglas as she looked down. The plane banked to the right just then and she gave up and sat back with a sigh. "It has some of the best skiing in the world, you know."

"I know," Yale said dryly. "But we haven't come here on vacation because you prefer Squaw, or Mammoth, or Colorado—remember?"

The plane leveled out, and Mimi immediately sat forward again. "Yes, but it's so pretty here," she said, looking down. And then, without warning, "Dad, do you think I'll ever ski again?"

Yale immediately reached out and took his daughter's hand. "Of course you will," he said with quiet assurance. "As the doctor said, it's just a matter of time."

"Yes, but how *much* time?" she asked intensely, and turned to look at him, her blue eyes wide.

Yale resisted the impulse to reach out and touch that soft cloud of red hair that framed her face. Sometimes he marveled that he'd fathered such a beautiful child, and he had to hold himself back from spoiling her completely. She was so vivacious, so energetic . . . so alive. Everything seemed to vibrate when Mimi was around; it was as though she infused the air around her with her limitless energy. Even as a small child she had never entered a room so much as burst into it, and he had taught her to ski when she was very young just so he would have some way to channel all that momentum of hers.

Now, as he looked at her, he almost wished that he'd never bought her that first pair of tiny skis. Then he shook his head. It was pointless to blame himself for her accident; he knew that Mimi would have learned to ski even if he'd forbidden it. It was something she had to do, just as it had been for him.

So he looked into those eyes she had inherited from him and said, "I don't know how much time, darling. That's why we've come to Vermont, to find out."

Mimi leaned back with a sigh. "Boy, I hope it's soon," she muttered, and then bolted upright again. "Dad, you won't make me use that wheelchair, will you?"

Yale hesitated. The airline had offered Mimi the use of a wheelchair when they landed, and because he hadn't known how far it would be from the plane through the terminal, he had accepted. Mimi had been appalled when she found out. Her crutches were bad enough; she absolutely would not be wheeled through the airport like an invalid. Besides, she already had to wear a leg brace. Did he want her to be humiliated completely?

Involuntarily, he glanced down at the appliance. Because it wouldn't fit under her good slacks, Mimi was wearing a detested skirt today, and he marveled at the simple complexity of the brace's design. It was the latest in orthopedic technology, composed of fiberglass and plastic, so lightweight it felt like a feather, so strong and durable that it could be worn scuba diving or skiing. Wincing at that last thought, he raised his eyes and looked into his daughter's expressive face.

Trying to be reasonable, he said, "We don't know how far it will be from the plane to the rental car, darling, and I don't want you to get tired before your appointment at the clinic. Don't you think it would be easier if you had a wheelchair?"

Mimi's jaw set in the obstinate way Yale knew so well. Sighing, he admitted that she had inherited her stubbornness from him, too, and for a moment was indecisive. He knew he was often too lenient with his daughter, but in the five years since his divorce from Marissa, he'd been so glad to have Mimi with him that he couldn't help himself. Marissa hadn't fought him on custody; she'd been too involved with her latest in a series of young lovers to be bothered taking care of a then ten-year-old daughter. By the time of the divorce, he hadn't cared what his wife did, or with whom, just as long as he could have Mimi with him.

Her expression still rebellious, Mimi had turned to look out the window again as the plane banked to the left this time and began another descent. The beautiful snow-covered terrain of Vermont rolled by beneath them, but Yale didn't see it. He was watching Mimi and thinking, as he had so often, that his daughter was the only good thing to come of his marriage.

Sometimes it seemed incredible to him that he'd married Marissa Dexter in the first place. Looking back on those days now, when he'd been the captain of the ski team and Marissa was one of the legions of "snow bunnies"—those girls who followed the team everywhere hoping to get noticed—he could hardly believe he was the same person. Oh, he'd been so arrogant then, so cocky. He'd loved the attention, the adulation; he'd thought it was his due. Everyone had believed he'd take the gold in the Downhill that year;

he'd believed it himself. After all, he was the best, wasn't he?

But in the end, it was the Swiss, Bernard Russi, who had been just a micro-millisecond faster, and because of him the gold had slipped from his fingers. Just like that, he'd gone from being a winner to an also-ran. It hadn't mattered that everyone—the team, the crowds, the press, his hometown of Boise, Idaho—went crazy over the fact that he'd won the silver, because in his heart, he knew it wasn't good enough. He'd set his sights on the gold and failed. It had been a crushing blow to his twenty-year-old ego, and if he hadn't been so devastated, so unhappy, he never would have turned to the blond, blue-eyed Marissa. She'd thrown herself at him, and he hadn't been able to resist. But he never would have married her if she hadn't become pregnant, and he never would have gotten involved with her in the first place if it hadn't been for... Kira.

Kira. Lord, he hadn't thought of her in years. Kira Blair, America's skating sweetheart. The press had dubbed her the "Faerie Queen," he remembered, and she deserved the title. He'd never seen anyone—before or since—so lovely on the ice. Power and grace and speed, and such a breathtaking presence that she captivated every audience and held them in the palm of her hand.

Kira. How could he have forgotten her?

Thrusting away unbidden memories of beautiful green eyes and a smile so brilliant it could melt a judge's heart, he realized his daughter was staring at him. Anxiously, she said, "No wheelchair, okay, Dad?"

Yale sighed. He knew he should insist, but he didn't have the heart. Mimi had been through so much since the accident, and she'd been so brave, so determined to get better that her doctors had been astounded at her progress. Remembering that heart-stopping fall she had taken during the race, he shuddered. Even though it had been six weeks ago, he could still see it as clearly as if it had happened yesterday.

He'd been standing near the finish line, one part of his mind on the clock, counting the seconds; another part skiing the course with her, as he had done several days before, to get the feel of it so they could discuss strategy. When he could make the time, they always did that before a competition, for even though as a member of the Olympic team Mimi was trained by both the Olympic coach and her own coach, she still wanted her old man's opinion.

Yale smiled to himself at that, feeling flattered that his daughter so eagerly sought his advice, recalling how it felt to be that good at something that gave such joy. He hadn't been much older than Mimi when he was selected for the Olympic team; he was only twenty when he'd won the silver. As disappointed as he'd been in himself, he still would never forget the thrill of standing on that dais and seeing the stars and stripes raised in his honor. He wanted Mimi to feel that pride in herself and her country, and maybe that was really why he had taught her to ski. If he never gave his daughter anything else in her entire life, that sense of accomplishment would be enough. Because even though he'd fallen short of his personal goal at the time, he'd still achieved something no other American had before. It was good, but not enough, and as he stood there that day on the dais, he realized that if he wanted to accomplish more, he had to strive harder. He'd never forgotten that lesson; it was one of the reasons he drove himself so hard today. Never, never again, would he be an also-ran.

He glanced toward his daughter, craning at the window as the runway rushed up at them. Would Mimi ever succeed in her goal? They had talked so many times about her winning first the World Cup title, and then the gold medal, that he wondered how she would react if either opportunity was taken from her. Gazing at her profile, with the determined chin and the slightly upturned nose he adored and she detested, he felt such a wave of love for her that it almost frightened him. He'd been almost out of his mind the day she'd gotten hurt, terrified at the thought of losing her. Glancing down at her injured leg, he wanted to take the brace and hide it and pretend that none of this had ever happened. He didn't care if she never skied again, just as long as she could learn to walk again, to live a normal life. For a while, the doctors hadn't even been sure of that.

The plane's wheels skidded on the runway, and Yale felt the backward thrust of reversed jet engines. Mimi glanced at him, and he smiled. She smiled back, and once again he felt a pang. During those seemingly endless first days after her surgery, while she was lying so pale and depressed in that hospital bed, he had despaired that he would ever see that elfin smile again. Feeling a rush of gratitude that they'd come this far in so short a time, he couldn't help himself. Reaching out, he grasped her hand.

Mimi rolled her eyes in one of those half-exasperated, half-pleased gestures that so amused him. "Oh, Dad," she said, but her fingers tightened around his.

In the end, despite his better judgment, he didn't insist on the wheelchair. He knew how Mimi felt being wheeled around, and he sympathized. Even though her progress on crutches was slow, and almost painful at times to watch, he couldn't take that sense of independence away from her. The doctors had warned him that her rehabilitation would be long and difficult, and while he could, he wanted her to feel that she still had some control over her life, even if it was only hobbling from point A to B.

So he tried not to notice how white her face was by the time they climbed into the rental car, and he didn't comment when she sank down in the front seat with a grateful sigh. Heading out of the airport onto U.S. 7 toward Manchester and the smaller town of Stonebridge, he merely glanced across the seat and murmured, "Okay, honey?"

Her face still pale, Mimi nodded. After awhile, she sat up higher on the seat, watching as they passed stately old trees and homes set back from the road. Most of the houses were made of clapboard, and the majority were painted white. It was like a scene from a postcard, completely different from California, but he knew she wasn't really seeing it when she asked anxiously, "Are we going to be on time?"

He glanced at his watch. "If I don't get lost, we'll make it with time to spare," he answered, and smiled across the seat at her. "Nervous?"

She looked indignant. "Are you kidding? I can't wait to get started!"

Yale laughed and reached out to squeeze her shoulder. "That's my girl," he said, and laughed again when she rolled her eyes.

"Oh, Dad!"

When they came to the little town of Stonebridge, they both started looking for the sign directing them to the clinic. Mimi was the one who saw it first—a small placard placed just at the edge of a snow-covered village green. As they drove slowly through, Yale glanced at the wooden storefronts and hand-carved signs, and thought that they might have moved back a century in time. There wasn't even a traffic light, he noticed, and smiled wryly. It was a far cry from Los Angeles, with its clogged freeways and blazing lights.

"Maybe we should have rented a horse and buggy instead of this car," he commented, pointing out what had to be a genuine hitching post in front of the post office.

Mimi gave him one of her wide-eyed looks. "Gee, it would be great to have a horse, wouldn't it?"

Yale laughed. "I think we'll stick with the car."

The Stonebridge Clinic came into view, and as Yale drove slowly toward it, he hoped he hadn't made a mistake. Even though he and Mimi had seen pictures, and so didn't expect a giant modern building with walls of glass and steel struts, the place still didn't seem...clinical...enough now that they were here. Mimi obviously felt the same way. As he parked the car and turned off the ignition, she glanced at him skeptically before she turned to look back at the famous clinic.

The house before them seemed to be exactly that: a house. Built of red brick that had mellowed over the years to a soft rose color, the mullioned windows caught the light and reflected it back. It was two stories high, and a covered veranda ran the length of it, three steps in front, two ramps at either side. The double front doors were obviously hand-carved, and the mansard roof was dotted with no less than three chimneys. It was a wonderful old place, and under other circumstances, Yale would have admired it. Now, when he looked across the seat and saw Mimi's frightened expression, he just wanted to drive away. "Are you okay?" he asked hesitantly.

"I thought it would be...different," she said, subdued.

Yale heard the quaver in her voice and knew she was close to tears. That decided him, and he reached to open the car door. They hadn't come all this way only to drive off again without going inside; the least they could do was keep their appointment. Dr. Gentry was waiting for them now, and so he said cheerfully, using her nickname to make her smile, "Come on, Sprite. We're here. The least we can do is go in and see the place."

Mimi turned slowly from her inspection of the house to look at him. "All right," she said in a small voice. "But if we don't like it, can we just leave again?"

Yale didn't hesitate. He had already thought about the other clinics available in California, and if those didn't suit, there was always the big Sports Medicine Center in Colorado. This one was supposed to be the best for Mimi's therapy, but damn it, if Stonebridge didn't work, he'd *build* her a clinic if he had to. She hadn't gone through all this only to be stopped now.

"That's a deal," he said, and climbed out of the car to come around and hold the passenger door for her. "If you don't want to stay, we'll just turn around and go home."

Mimi nodded and took the crutches he held out. The sidewalk had been cleared of snow and ice, but he still had to restrain himself from helping her. He watched as she hobbled around the side of the house and up the ramp, but he couldn't prevent himself from opening the clinic door for her. He was just reaching for it when she grabbed his arm. "You promise?"

Yale solemnly crossed his heart. "On my honor."

Mimi sighed. "Okay. Let's get it over with."

The main door opened onto a huge entry, and right in front of them was a pretty young girl sitting at a desk. She stood up immediately as Yale introduced himself and his daughter, and she smiled at both of them. "I'm Trudy, the secretary for the clinic. If you'll please follow me, Dr. Gentry and Dr. Stanfield are waiting for you."

As the girl turned and started down the wide hallway, Mimi pulled on her father's arm again. "Who's Dr. Stanfield?"

Yale didn't have time to tell her he didn't know. Trudy opened a door just then and announced, "Mr. Duncan and his daughter are here, Dr. Gentry."

Always watchful of Mimi on crutches, Yale let his daughter go first. His attention was on her when out of the corner of his eye he saw a middle-aged man with thinning brown hair and thick glasses stand and hold out his hand. "Dr. Gentry, Mr. Duncan. I hope you had a pleasant flight."

Mimi safely seated, Yale turned to acknowledge the introduction. He was just holding his hand out when he saw the woman standing behind the desk. For a moment he was so stunned he just stood there like an idiot, his hand extended, frozen in midair. Vaguely, he felt Gentry reach awkwardly over the distance that separated them and grasp his hand, but it seemed beyond him to return the handshake. He couldn't believe it—he had to be dreaming.

It was no dream. Transfixed, he watched as she came around the desk, moving with the same effortless grace he remembered, gazing at him with those incredible green eyes. He would have known her anywhere, he thought dazedly. It had been fifteen years, but she had barely changed at all.

"Hello, Yale," Kira said, and that was all. Before he could reply, before he could even gather his wits together to say anything, she had turned to his daughter. Holding out her hand, she smiled that dazzling smile that had charmed audiences all over the world. "I'm Dr. Stanfield," she said warmly. "And you must be Mimi. Welcome to the Stonebridge Clinic."

CHAPTER TWO

"Do you two know each other?" Miles asked. Sensing something in the air, he glanced from Kira to Yale and back.

"We...did a long time ago," Kira said, and tried not to look at Yale. She had thought she was prepared to see him again, but she had forgotten how magnetic he was in person. Even after all these years, he still filled a room when he walked into it, and one glance told her that the television screen hadn't lied. He was even more attractive than he'd been before; fifteen years had given him a maturity and confidence that had been mere brashness at twenty, and his aura of assurance was definitely compelling.

Glancing quickly at Mimi, Kira saw the girl staring at her with frank curiosity, and she smiled. The grin Mimi returned gave her a start, for when she smiled like that, the resemblance to Yale was uncanny. Although Mimi's hair was red instead of her father's black, she had inherited those blue eyes—and the determined set to the chin. Intrigued, Kira sat beside her.

"You've come a long way, Mimi," she said. "You must be tired."

The grin vanished. "How could I be tired after all these weeks of lying around? Nobody will let me do anything!"

Kira smiled again. "We'll soon see about that."

Mimi immediately looked hopeful. "Does that mean I'll be able to get rid of this brace and these stupid crutches?"

Kira had automatically noted the anti-rotational brace Mimi was wearing and she approved. But even though she hadn't read the medical reports yet, she knew it would be some time before Mimi was ready to abandon either aid, and she thought it only fair to warn her. "I think we'd better run some tests first, don't you?"

"All I've *been* doing is taking tests," Mimi complained. "When will things be normal again?"

Kira sympathized. Mimi was a world-class athlete; she worked hard to attain and maintain a level of fitness that the rest of the population only dreamed about. Consequently, inactivity was more difficult for her to handle than it would be for someone else. All that pent-up energy had to go somewhere, and Kira knew from experience that unless it was properly channeled, it could be destructive. She never allowed her patients the luxury of self-pity, but sometimes it was hard for her, too. She understood all too well the frustration of an athlete who had been sidelined for the season; she had experienced it herself.

Reaching out, she touched Mimi's hand. "I understand. And I promise you, we'll try to do something about it. But in the meantime, how about a Coke or something while I go over your medical reports with your father and Dr. Gentry?" She smiled encouragingly. "I know Trudy's just dying to show you to the lounge so she can get your autograph."

Mimi sighed and gathered her crutches. Levering herself to her feet, she said, "Well, okay. But my autograph isn't going to be much good if I don't get back to skiing again. After reading those reports, will you be able to tell me how soon I can start?''

"We'll do our best," Kira said mildly. But her expression sobered as soon as Mimi turned and started out of the office. Although Mimi didn't seem aware of it yet, Kira knew it would be months before she could even think about skiing, longer still before she was cleared for competition—if she ever was. Her therapists could do a lot for her, but in the end, it all came down to physical factors and Mimi's own determination to get better. Without the right combination, she would never ski competitively again.

As soon as the door closed behind Mimi, Kira took a deep breath and turned to Yale. She couldn't continue to ignore him, so she said, "You have a lovely daughter, Yale."

"I think so, too," he replied, and then looked mildly embarrassed. "I sound like every proud father, don't I?"

"You have reason to be proud," Miles said. "Not only is Mimi a champion athlete, but she also seems to be quite a girl."

Yale's expression turned serious. "She is. I just hope she'll be able to ski again."

Kira couldn't seem to help herself. Her voice was sharper than she intended as she said, "I'm afraid it will be some time before she's ready to do that."

Both men looked at her strangely, and she felt herself turning red. She didn't know why she had spoken like that; Yale's remark had been a natural one. The entire country was undoubtedly hoping the same thing. Why should she take exception to what he'd said?

Annoyed at herself, she avoided their eyes, stood and went around to her desk. "Did you bring Mimi's medical records?"

"Of course." Yale's voice was noncommittal as he placed his briefcase on the desktop and took a thick packet from it. Kira hadn't noticed the case until now, but it was obviously genuine leather, handcrafted and fitted with dual combination locks. Her mouth tightened. The briefcase seemed the perfect symbol of all Yale stood for. She could just imagine the multi-million dollar contracts for his superstar athletes that had been placed behind those double locks, and when she thought of their old argument about the purity of sports versus the gains to be made, she had to force herself not to snatch the folder from his hand.

"Is there a copy for Dr. Gentry?" she asked.

Miles still sensed something in the air. Uncomfortably, he looked from one to the other again and said, "Er . . . Yale and I discussed the details of Mimi's case on the phone last night, so I can go over the full report later. In the meantime, why don't you read it yourself, Kira? Yale and I will have a cup of coffee in my office, and when you're finished, we can discuss the options."

Kira didn't care for that suggestion at all. She didn't want to be left alone to sort out her confused feelings about Yale; she wanted to get this over with as soon as possible.

"I really think we should discuss this before Mimi and Trudy come back, don't you Miles?" she asked. "If you'll both sit down, it will only take me a few minutes to glance through the records."

Miles glanced uncertainly at Yale, who shrugged. They both took a seat on the office couch as Kira opened the folder containing the dozens of medical reports. Mentally blessing her foresight in taking a speed reading course years ago, she went quickly through the pages. A few minutes later, she looked up.

"I see that Mimi was operated on for a torn medial collateral ligament of the right knee. What prognosis did her orthopedic surgeon give you?"

As the discussion moved into medical areas, Kira tried to relax. Surprised when Yale seemed to be acquainted with all the medical terms, she grudgingly gave him a point. It was obvious that he'd taken the time both to question Mimi's doctors and to study her file, and when they reached the end of the discussion, she wished that more of her patients—or their parents—were as well informed.

Aware that Yale was watching her, Kira stared down at the papers on her desk. Her mind had flown ahead during the conversation to the various therapies she might use in Mimi's case, and now that she had all the facts at her disposal, she made her decision. She didn't want any part of it.

She couldn't go through this charade of pretending that she and Yale were mere acquaintances; she just couldn't do it. Until he'd walked in here a few minutes ago, she had convinced herself that he was part of a past best forgotten. But seeing him again made her remember all the dreams they had spun so long ago when they were both so young. Nothing had turned out the way she had planned, but until she saw him again, she had thought she'd come to terms with all the disappointment. After all, circumstances changed and life went on, didn't it? She'd been forced to carve out a different path for herself than she had planned so long ago with Yale, and their lives had gone in completely different directions after she was injured. He'd sped away like a comet, and she had been left home alone, to cry.

But you can only cry for so long, she thought, *even when you're seventeen and you're sure your life is over.* The irony of it was that she had just begun to emerge from her self imposed isolation that summer when her father died of a heart attack. In her grief for him, she had completely forgotten about Yale—especially when her mother called a family conference to discuss her skating. Her father had been a dentist, and while he'd left a substantial insurance policy, they could manage only if her older sister, Jilly, was willing to sacrifice, too. She was leaving the decision up to her daughters.

But Kira felt that she couldn't ask Jilly to give up more than she already had. Life in the Blair family had centered on Kira's skating for years, and now that her father was gone, she didn't think it was fair to continue on. Training at her level cost a small fortune each year, and now there was only so much to spend. She couldn't ask either her mother or her sister to sacrifice everything for her.

Her mother had been proud of her, and obviously relieved, but Kira had only felt guilty at the lie. The truth was that she had been dreading a return to the ice—the endless hours of practice, the complete dedication to the sport to the exclusion of everything else. After coming so close to winning at the Olympics, and then losing it all, she couldn't summon the energy to do it all over again. So she had gone on to college and her degree. Later, she'd gone for her master's, then her Ph.D. She'd been married by that time to Gil, but even though she had never told him, the proudest day of her life had been receiving her doctorate in exercise physiology. Dr. Kira Stanfield. Somehow it made all the other sacrifices along the way almost worth it.

Almost? Now she wondered if that was true. Seeing Yale today had revived all those feelings she thought were buried, and she wondered if she could pretend any longer that she didn't wish her life had turned out differently. What would it have been like if she hadn't been injured the day before she was to perform her final program? Where would she be if she and Yale hadn't had that last awful argument?

Realizing that the silence had gone on too long, Kira closed Mimi's folder. "Miles, could I see you a moment . . . alone?"

Yale immediately sat up. "What is it? If you don't think Mimi will ever be able to ski again, I want to know right now."

Embarrassed that she'd been so blunt, Kira said quickly, "It isn't that at all, Yale. I just wanted to consult with Miles for a few minutes. There's no reason to be concerned."

Glowering, Yale sat back again. "That's easy for you to say. Your daughter's future isn't at stake."

Aware that Miles's questioning look had turned to a frown, Kira stood. "No, but I understand how you feel. This will just take a moment, Yale, I promise. Miles?"

Dr. Gentry had no choice but to follow her. With a murmured excuse to Yale, he let her lead the way to his office. But as soon as the door closed behind them, he turned to her. "What was that all about?"

"I just wanted to talk to you alone, Miles. I'm sorry."

"Sorry! I don't understand what's going on. You're acting as though you don't want Mimi Duncan here."

"It's not that, Miles, it's—" She stopped, flushing at her near slip of the tongue. She'd almost said that it wasn't Mimi she didn't want here; it was Yale. "What I meant to say was that I just don't see how I can take on Mimi's case right now. After a surgery like that, she's going to need extensive therapy, and I just—"

Miles straightened to his full height of five-foot-eight. "I believe we already discussed scheduling, Dr. Stanfield," he said as Kira looked at him in dismay. It was rare he spoke so formally to her; it was rarer still for him to look as angry as he did now. "And I recall asking you to make Mimi Duncan your top priority. Noreen and Betsy can take some of your other cases. It's time they assumed the responsibility anyway."

Kira swallowed another protest. He was right; Mimi Duncan *was* a special case. As Miles had said before, after all the media attention Mimi had received lately, the clinic could only benefit if the press found out she was here. But when that happened, she'd better be supervising the case or they'd want to know why. Americans took their athletic superstars very seriously; she could imagine the outrage if Mimi wasn't receiving the best the clinic had to offer.

"All right," she said reluctantly. "You win."

Miles hid his relief behind a wide smile. "Good, I'm glad you agree. Now, let's go back and discuss procedures with Yale. I'm sure you can appreciate how anxious he is."

Kira was sure he was. But she couldn't face Yale again right now. She had to sort out her conflicting emotions first, and she said quickly, "You go ahead. I'd like to talk to Mimi for a few minutes, and then do some testing so we'll know where we are."

He nodded. "All right. I'll show Yale around the clinic, and then we can all meet back here when you're finished."

Kira finally tracked Mimi down in the main therapy room. When she saw what was going on, she hid her amusement. It was clear that Mimi had already made friends; she was surrounded by the other therapists and their patients who had come in for treatment that morning. Like a queen holding court, she was perched on one of the treatment tables, fielding eager questions and looking like she was having the time of her life. The group around her was so enthralled that no one noticed Kira standing there, and she used the opportunity to study her new patient. Despite Mimi's animated face and expressive gestures as she described her accident, Kira detected something in her voice that didn't ring true.

Then Mimi glanced up and their eyes met. Kira saw a fleeting expression cross the young skier's face and knew she'd been right. Mimi wasn't sharing anything of herself; she was giving an interview, and it was obvious that after all the publicity that had surrounded her these past few months, she had learned how to do it well. She knew how to entertain, how to put herself in the best possible light, how to fend off questions she didn't want to answer, with a joke and a laugh. She was good, Kira thought, but then she should be. She'd had a great teacher. Yale had always known how to use his charm and charisma to his best advantage, too.

"All right, gang," she said, stepping up to the table where Mimi sat with her braced leg propped up. "I'm afraid Mimi and I have some testing to do, and—" she glanced around the grinning group "—I'm sure you have some work to do yourselves, right?"

There was a chorus of mock groans, but everyone quickly scattered. Kira was known to be compassionate and sympathetic, but she also had a reputation for getting results. Time at the clinic was too valuable to waste, and if she suspected a patient wasn't working up to potential, she would often supervise a session herself to watch what had become known, with legitimate dread, as the Stanfield Marathon.

"What's the Stanfield Marathon?" Mimi asked.

"Oh, you've heard about that already?" Kira said, amused. She took a tape measure from the drawer under the treatment table and began to remove Mimi's knee brace. Glancing professionally at the seven inch scar on the inside of the knee, she noted that six weeks after surgery, Mimi was healing well. The incision was now a reddened, slightly raised curving line, but the surgeon had known what he was doing; in a year or so, the scar would hardly be noticeable. She placed the tape measure around Mimi's calf and took a measurement. "It's just a little test I devised to see how well patients were doing. Things like half squats and side thrusts and toe springs, that's all."

Mimi saw the twinkle in her eyes. "That's *all*?"

"By the time you get to that point, you'll be able to breeze right through," Kira said with a smile. She didn't mention that the exercises were done as fast as possible, with only two minute rest intervals in-between. It was more difficult than it sounded, especially after a surgery such as Mimi had, but since it would be at least six months before she was able to do anything approaching the marathon, Kira didn't see any point in alarming her.

Mimi seemed to forget the Stanfield Marathon for the moment in her curiosity about what Kira was doing. She watched intently as Kira wrote down several calf measurements before moving upward to her thigh. "What are those for?"

Kira explained that she always took a series of measurements before beginning therapy so both legs could be compared and treatment adjusted accordingly. Even though the clinic had a computer to assess such components as strength, endurance, torque and range of motion, there were still some things that were best measured by hand.

"Why?" Mimi asked curiously. "In case the computer breaks down?"

"I suspect it's more to make us feel useful," Kira said with a laugh, and handed Mimi her crutches. "Come on. I'll show you what I mean."

Some time later, Kira had the computer printout of Mimi's test in her hand. Despite her mixed emotions about Yale being there, she was excited when she read the results. She wanted time to study them thoroughly before she designed a therapy program, but a quick scan told her what she had already suspected. For being just six weeks post-operative, Mimi was already ahead of the average person on every level. Kira knew that was due partly to her superb physical condition before the accident, but that wasn't the total reason. So eager to get rid of her brace and crutches, Mimi had given her all on every test from the stationary bicycle to the isokinetic machine, and Kira suspected that she had been exercising privately for some time.

Pleased at the idea—as long as Mimi didn't overdo it, she thought—she sent the girl ahead to join Miles and her father while she stopped a moment in her own office. Tossing the printout on the desk, she sat down and wondered why she felt so hostile toward Yale. She knew it didn't make sense, but she was resentful that he'd come to Stonebridge, especially when so many other facilities were available. Too restless to sit, she got up again and went to the window to gaze out at the frozen pond behind the clinic.

Why did Yale have to show up now, just when she had her life back together again? It had been so hard for her to leave Seattle after Gil died; even with Jilly's encouragement, she hadn't wanted to pack up everything and just...go. But she had, finally, and now she had put down new roots. She loved her little cottage of a house; she loved her job and her position here. Seattle and everything that had happened there seemed so far away. It was as though by selling everything and starting over, she had become a new person—a different person. She was more independent and sure of herself, and she had finally realized and accepted that she would never fulfill old dreams, that such things were best left behind. She'd been happy here, content.

Or at least she had been until this afternoon. But seeing Yale again made her wonder if she hadn't been fooling herself all this time. Already she could feel the old discontent stirring, that sense she'd once had of things uncompleted. Her life had turned out so differently from what she had dreamed as a girl that sometimes...

Stop it! she told herself, and clenched her fist to halt her runaway thoughts. She was being ridiculous, childish. It was absurd to become so disturbed at seeing Yale after all this time. What was he to her but a youthful romance, a fantasy she'd grown out of long ago? She was in charge of her own life now; she made her own decisions. She was no longer a lovestruck seventeen-year-old girl; she was a grown woman. Even if she wanted to, she could never recapture the past with Yale. There were too many years lost in between. His daughter was living proof of that, and on that thought, she resolutely reached for the printout of Mimi's test results and marched down to Miles's office. With a professional smile that revealed nothing of her inner turmoil, she sat down and said, "I've just studied Mimi's test results, and here's what I think we should do..."

"OH, DAD," Mimi breathed when she and her father were in the car again. "Isn't she wonderful?"

Yale knew very well who Mimi meant, but for some absurd reason, he couldn't answer directly. Avoiding her eyes, he grabbed the map to find out where the hotel was. He'd made reservations to stay overnight even if they decided not to accept the clinic, but now he wished they were taking the next flight out. Seeing Kira again after all these years had been a disturbing experience, and he didn't know why. They'd known each other so long ago; they were different people now. Why should it matter?

But it did matter, and now he wished he had never heard of the Stonebridge Clinic. He was sure by the look on Mimi's face that she was going to want to stay, and he wasn't so sure that was the best thing.

For who? You or Mimi?

Frowning, he folded the map. "Who? Dr. Stanfield, you mean?" he asked, and when he saw Mimi look at him indignantly, added weakly, "Well, there were other therapists."

Mimi sat back against the seat with a sigh. "Yes, but none like Dr. Stanfield."

Despite himself, Yale had to agree with that. Dr. Stanfield, he thought admiringly; he never would have guessed it. When he had known Kira before, her name had been Blair, and she'd been America's darling. She'd been too preoccupied with skating to think much about school then; all her energies had been focused on the Olympics. If she'd won the gold medal, she would have been a star. She could have written her own ticket because nothing was too good for another of America's skating queens.

But none of that had happened. He could still remember the day before the final programs were scheduled, that segment of the skating competition that would determine the winner. Tension had been thick enough to cut with a knife, for though Kira had already won the short program, the Austrian—what was her name? Beatrix something; God, he'd thought at the time he would never forget it—had been first in the school figures. He couldn't remember now who was in third, but it didn't matter. Between the top two skaters, the winner of the long program would be awarded the gold medal. No one doubted that the American, Kira Blair, who sailed through spins and turns and jumps, who made the audience catch their collective breaths with her grace and beauty on the ice, would win.

And then, disaster. During her practice time, the day before that final competition, Kira had landed a jump wrong. It was an axel she had done hundreds—thousands—of times before, not even the most complicated in her program. But this time something went awry. The edge of that quarter-inch blade she was supposed to land on went out from under her. Instead of coming down as light as a feather as she always did, she went sprawling.

He'd been there, watching her practice. Even now, fifteen years later, he could remember the horror he felt when he saw her go down. Kira never fell. She was as at home on skates as she was in shoes—more so, in fact, because of all those years of six, and seven and eight hour practice days.

But she had fallen that day, and when he saw that she couldn't get up, he'd rushed out onto the ice to help. So had practically everyone else in the arena. Kira had been instantly surrounded by coaches, officials, and anyone else who happened to be there, and he couldn't fight his way through the crowd to get to her. He'd had to follow the ambulance to the hospital, and it had been hours before he was allowed to see her. He'd talked to her coach by then and learned that everyone hoped the injury wasn't as serious as they'd dreaded. Kira had torn some ligaments in her ankle and was already receiving therapy for it, and the coach had contacted the Olympic committee about approved medications. If all went well, Kira might still be able to compete.

But Kira hadn't competed that final night after all. After a tearful practice the next day, her coach had to agree with her that the ankle would never hold her through her complicated program. The Austrian won the gold medal that year, and after they'd had their last furious quarrel, Kira had gone home. He hadn't seen her again until today.

"Dad?"

Embarrassed, Yale realized that Mimi had been trying to get his attention for some time. "What is it, Sprite?"

Mimi took a deep breath. "I know what I said before, but I've changed my mind."

He was still bemused. "About what?"

"About the clinic, about staying here for therapy. Could we stay, Dad?"

Although he'd expected it, Yale was still dismayed. Reaching down to start the car, he said, "I thought you didn't like it here."

"That was before. Now I know that Dr. Stanfield will fix it so that I can ski again. Please, Dad!"

Annoyed that he was still unnerved about seeing Kira again, he said, "Well, I don't know, honey. I thought we agreed to think about it. Maybe we should consider some of the clinics closer to home."

"I don't need to think about it, Dad. I want to stay here. Oh, please!"

He hesitated and told himself that it wasn't because of Kira. He'd reconciled himself long ago to the thought of losing her, and he hadn't wondered in years if their youthful romance wouldn't have died a natural death, anyway. They'd been so young, then; their heads had been turned by all that publicity, by the adulation that America gives her sports figures. They used to laugh about it, on those rare times they managed to sneak away from the watchful eyes of their coaches. He remembered one time when he'd had to catch Kira as she jumped out of a dorm window because her coach, the feared Madame Sasanova, was guarding the door. So infatuated with each other then, they had made a game of it, sneaking off as often as they could. Which wasn't as often as he wanted, he remembered ruefully, and thought of that night he'd talked Kira into jumping out the window. He'd promised to catch her, but he'd lost his footing at the last second, and they'd both landed in that snowbank, stifling their laughter in case the dragon lady came running to see. Kira had lain on top of him, and he could still remember it so clearly even after all these years: that slim body in his arms, those beautiful green eyes, that luscious mouth, parted in laughter...and then parted for his kiss.

"Dad?"

With a jerk, Yale came back to the present. The past was gone, and there wasn't anything he could do about it. He'd never had the chance to find out if he and Kira were destined for more than a youthful romance. After that last quarrel, their pride had kept them apart, and then, when he'd stupidly gotten involved with Marissa and she became pregnant, there hadn't been any point in pursuing his relationship with Kira.

And there wasn't any point in pursuing it now, he told himself firmly. Kira Blair had become Dr. Stanfield; there was obviously a husband lurking somewhere in the background. Even if she hadn't been wearing a wedding ring... Had she been wearing a ring? he wondered suddenly. He couldn't remember. Then he shook his head. It didn't make any difference anyway. Even if he wanted to recapture the past, to have a chance to make things right, to mend a few dreams, too much had happened. He and Kira were no longer the headstrong young people they once were; they were adults, with careers, responsibilities...families.

That reminded him that he hadn't answered Mimi yet, and he glanced across the seat at her. But Mimi wasn't looking at him; she had bolted forward and was clinging to the dashboard, looking ahead in delight.

"Look, Dad!" she squealed. "A house for rent!"

"Now, Mimi..." he warned.

She turned to him, her eyes shining. "Oh, Dad! Isn't it perfect?"

Reluctantly, Yale stopped the car. He took one look at the house Mimi was excitedly pointing at and knew he was doomed. Long ago, when she was small, her favorite bedtime story had been about a family in a house exactly like this: a huge Victorian, with gingerbread on the roof and two brick chimneys and a screened-in porch. Ancient trees had clustered protectively around it, and there had been a birdhouse hanging from one of the limbs, a swing on another. She had always said wistfully how one day they would all live in a house like this, and when Yale saw that except for the snow-covered lawn and the bare branches of the trees, this could have been the house in the storybook come to life, he knew he could no more drive away from it than he could have jumped over the moon.

Thirty minutes later, with Mimi hanging so excitedly on to his arm that he could hardly sign the deposit check, he handed the rental agreement to her. If he'd had any doubts about the wisdom of staying in Stone-bridge, they were dispelled when she threw her arms around him and hugged him tightly.

"Thanks, Dad," she whispered. "You won't regret it, I promise. I'll work really hard to get well. I won't let you down."

"You never have, Sprite," he said tenderly. But as he hugged her in return, he wondered why he suddenly had a vision of Kira on the ice—not as the girl she'd been, but as the beautiful woman she was now.

CHAPTER THREE

"YOU LOOK deep in thought."

Kira turned at the sound of Miles's voice. She'd been standing by the window in her office, thinking how nerve-racking the past two weeks had been. Everyone else at Stonebridge seemed thrilled that Mimi was coming to the clinic for treatment, but as much as she enjoyed working with Yale's daughter, she was still tense around Yale himself. As ridiculous as it was, she had begun contriving excuses as early as the second day, pretending to be busy during the times he dropped Mimi off for her session or came to collect her again. In fact, she stayed completely out of sight until she was sure he was gone. Thankfully, her absurd behavior would soon no longer be necessary. Mimi had mentioned the other day that their housekeeper, Mrs. Trent, would soon be coming to Vermont to help out. She had added ingenuously that though she loved the housekeeper, she was almost sorry the woman had agreed to come. Now her father would rarely be home.

"You mean he leaves you alone?" Kira was horrified.

"Oh, no," Mimi had corrected hastily. "Mrs. Trent stays when Dad's gone. Sometimes when he's working he goes away for days at a time. I used to miss him a lot, but it's not so bad now that I'm on the World Cup circuit, because I'm not home much myself."

Mimi's expression had changed then, and Kira knew that she was thinking about how long she'd been away from skiing. In an effort to divert her, she remembered how difficult it had been to keep up with her studies when she was skating, so she asked quickly, "But what about school?"

Mimi wrinkled her nose. "I thought I was going to get a vacation from that now that we're staying here, but Dad's hired a tutor. Can you believe that?" she asked indignantly. "I used to be able to send in my lessons when I was gone to a race or something, but Dad said that whether I was skiing or not, I was going to get a real education."

Thinking that that was probably the first thing she and Yale had ever been in complete agreement about, Kira had changed the subject. But the idea that Yale could go away for long periods and leave his daughter in the care of a housekeeper still rankled. Wondering why she should feel so annoyed when it obviously wasn't any of her business, she looked at Miles this morning. He was standing in the doorway holding two coffee cups and trying to balance a plate of sweet rolls on top of one of them, and when she reached for the plate with a skeptical expression, he looked sheepish. "I couldn't help myself. Trudy brought them in, and they looked so good. Do you want one?"

"You've got to be kidding," she said, and tried not to laugh as she took the cup with the black coffee. Miles's sweet tooth was a source of amusement among the staff and his young patients, who often teased him about the bad example he set. "I guess I'll have to talk to Trudy again," she said. "Doesn't she know about your diet?"

Miles sat down, protectively holding the plate. "What diet? And don't you dare talk to Trudy. This is my one source of enjoyment in an otherwise hectic day."

Kira couldn't argue with that. The routine at the clinic was frantic at times. The busy schedule was one reason the two of them had devised these early-morning visits in her office. It was the only time they had without interruption to discuss current cases or new arrivals, or any other details that needed attention. After these precious few minutes here they each went their separate ways. With all the demands and comings and goings of patients, they sometimes didn't even have time for lunch. Which was one reason why, Kira thought with a smile, Miles guarded his sweets. Sometimes a roll was the only thing he would eat all day.

He took a bite of one now, chewing with satisfaction for a moment or two before he swallowed and said, "Okay. What's on the agenda today?"

They discussed their current cases for a few minutes—the dancer who was about to be released, the hockey player who wasn't doing as well as expected—and then Kira hesitated. She was reluctant to bring up the subject of Mimi because she avoided talking about either of the Duncans whenever she could, but she had to ask his advice.

"I'd like to talk to you about Mimi Duncan."

Miles looked pleased until he saw her expression. "Why, is something wrong?"

She'd taken a seat behind her desk; now she got up and walked to the window again. If she tried, she could just make out the roof of the house Yale had rented through the outline of leafless trees. She'd been horrified when she'd found out that Yale was going to be living so close to her. The only thing that separated them was the pond behind the clinic. Frozen now at the end of January, the pond was really more of a small lake, but it suddenly didn't seem big enough.

Thinking that Lake Erie wouldn't have been large enough where Yale was concerned, she frowned and turned back to Miles.

"Nothing's wrong, exactly," she said slowly. "It's just that I'm worried about her."

"But I thought she was doing so well."

"She is, she is," Kira said hastily. "It's just that she's . . . well, she tries so hard—"

Miles laughed. "I know. I've seen her. I wish all our patients had such determination, don't you?"

Frustrated that she hadn't communicated her concern to him, Kira shook her head impatiently. "That's just it. I've had youngsters eager to get well before, but with Mimi, it's . . ." She paused, searching for a word, and ended lamely, "different."

"Different," he repeated, sobering. "How do you mean?"

Kira sat down again. "I'm not sure. Sometimes I sense that she's almost on the verge of hysteria."

"Hysteria!" Miles looked at her incredulously. "Mimi?"

Feeling foolish, she made herself plow on. "I know it sounds ridiculous, given the way she acts with everybody else, but honestly, Miles, when she's with me, she has such mood swings. One minute she's laughing about not being able to do something, the next she's so grim it's as if her entire life depended on doing the upcoming exercises, or repetitions, or whatever I've scheduled."

Relieved, Miles sat back. "Is that all you're worried about? For heaven's sake, Kira, she was a champion skier before her accident. You know how focused elite athletes can be. It's only natural for her to have ups and downs. And remember—she's only fifteen years old. At that age, everything is a matter of life and death!"

Kira recognized the truth of what he said, but she was still doubtful. Her feeling about something being wrong refused to go away. But since it was more an instinct than anything she could put her finger on, she shook her head helplessly. "I suppose you're right...."

Miles gathered the coffee cups and his empty plate and stood. Smiling down at her, he said, "I've learned to trust your instincts, Kira, but this time I think you might be looking for something that isn't there. Are you sure Mimi doesn't remind you of someone else?"

Kira looked up sharply at that, wondering what he meant. Was he referring to her at that age? But she saw by his face that the remark had been an innocent one, and now she felt even more foolish. She and Miles had never really discussed her skating career; she had made it clear at the outset that she preferred not to talk about it, and he had respected her wishes. Busying herself with the papers on her desk, she muttered, "No, it's not that."

"Well then, perhaps the best thing to do would be to talk to Mimi."

She'd already considered that. "Do you think I should?"

"If you're worried about her, yes. Besides, you always did know how to talk to these kids, Kira. It's one of your strongest assets."

She was pleased at the compliment. "All right. Maybe I'll think about it."

"Or you could talk to her father."

She'd already thought of that, too, and rejected the idea as soon as it occurred to her. Talking to Yale was the last resort. Besides, if Miles hadn't believed her, Yale would think she'd lost her mind. "No, I don't think so."

He seemed surprised at her sharp tone. "Why not? It's obvious that he's genuinely concerned about his daughter."

Oh, really? she wondered acidly. *If he's so concerned, why is he gone all the time? Why does business seem to take precedence over everything else?* She knew she wasn't being fair, but she couldn't help it. The idea that Yale could repeatedly go off and leave his daughter in the care of a housekeeper still annoyed her.

"Yes, I suppose he is concerned," she said neutrally. "But I think that if I talk to anyone, it should be Mimi herself."

"Suit yourself. I know you'll do the right thing."

But what was the right thing? she wondered, after he had gone. Sitting back, she massaged her temples, trying not to believe that Miles was right. If talking to Mimi was unsuccessful, she'd have to talk to Yale. There was no other way. She couldn't let this go; Mimi's welfare was at stake. She hadn't imagined that underlying desperation she'd sensed in Mimi, and she had treated enough athletes to know that what the teenager felt was different from the usual desire to get well. Normally she would have been pleased at such effort on the part of a patient, but Mimi was trying to do too much too soon.

"Mimi's here for her appointment, Kira."

Trudy's voice came over the intercom just then, and Kira decided to talk to Mimi today. Then, if she still couldn't make any impression, she wouldn't be able to put off a conference with Yale any longer. One of them had to make Mimi realize that healing took time, and that sometimes working too hard was just as undesirable as not trying hard enough. If she kept on this way, there was a real possibility she might do herself harm, Kira thought, and reached for her lab coat.

Mimi was waiting in one of the therapy rooms, dressed in shorts and T-shirt even though it had begun to snow lightly again outside. "I hope you didn't wear that in the car," Kira said when she saw her. She was stalling, trying to gauge Mimi's mood.

Mimi laughed, that infectious giggle of hers that was so difficult to resist. She was definitely up today. "Who said I came in the car? I thought it was time to start running again to get in shape, so I jogged over here."

Kira raised an eyebrow. She was used to Mimi's teasing; if she thought for an instant that Mimi actually had gone for a run, she would have been aghast. "I suppose the next thing you're going to tell me is that you've entered the Manchester Ten-K race this month."

Mimi's eyes widened. "Is there one?"

Kira raised her eyes heavenward. "I don't know, but if there was, I'm sure you'd try to enter."

"Not yet, but soon. In the meantime, what are we going to do today?"

Kira had brought her clipboard with the attached schedule she'd planned for Mimi: so many minutes on the stationary bicycle, so much time in the weight room, a session on the isokinetic machine. Glancing at it briefly, she set it aside and leaned against the therapy table Mimi was perched on. "What would you like to do?"

Mimi was surprised. "I . . . I don't know," she said, as though the idea was completely foreign to her. "You're the one who always chooses the exercises."

Kira had chosen this time purposely to talk to Mimi because for once they were alone in the therapy room. The half dozen or so tables would soon be occupied with patients, but for the time being, they were by themselves. She hoped that Mimi would feel more relaxed in here than in her office; unguarded, the girl might say something that would help Kira understand why she was pushing herself so hard.

"I know I usually supervise your session," she said casually, "but if you could decide what you wanted to do today, what would it be?"

"Really?"

"Really."

Mimi looked around. "Well, I guess I'd start warming up on the bike," she said hesitantly. When Kira just nodded, she gained more confidence and went on quickly, "And then I'd do some trampoline work, and some weights—oh, and the treadmill—I can't forget that! And then I'd practice on the Lido for a while, like always, and then—"

Kira held up her hand. "I think that's enough for right now."

"But I haven't finished!"

"Yes, you have," Kira said firmly. "The only step left to take after that would be the whirlpool . . . if you could crawl over to it by then. Honestly, Mimi, don't you think that's overdoing it a little?"

Mimi looked at her uncomprehendingly. "But I want to get well!"

This was the opening Kira had been waiting for. "You are getting well. But as I told you before, you have to take things a little more slowly."

Mimi didn't like the sound of that at all. "But why?" she wailed. "I can do it!"

"I know you can," Kira said soothingly. She heard that desperate note in Mimi's voice again and put her hand on the girl's arm. "You just have to give yourself time."

"I don't have time!"

Kira heard the rising shrillness in Mimi's voice and spoke sharply herself. "Of course you do!"

"But I want to ski!"

"I know you do, and you will. It just—"

Mimi clutched her arm. "Haven't you ever felt that way about anything—that you absolutely *had* to do it, or you'd *die*?"

A vision of a practice rink, cold and lonely in the black predawn hours of the morning, flashed into Kira's mind. She saw a solitary figure, dressed in two sets of leg warmers and a black leotard, repeating the same double toe loop again and again, trying to get it right. She did it so many times that the bleachers began to swim before her eyes, and her coach's voice became the only sound in the world except for the rasp of her blades on the ice. And still she fell. Again and again, over and over, determined not to leave until it was perfect.

"Yes," she said, her voice far away. "I've felt that way before."

"You can't have!" Mimi cried. "If you did, you'd know why I have to work so hard. If I don't, I'll lose my edge!"

Kira knew all about "the edge," that sometimes elusive quality that created champions. It was a keen readiness for competition, honed by endless hours of training, so that by the time an individual entered that final, all-important contest, he or she was like an anxious Thoroughbred eager to leap out of the gate and run.

But some Thoroughbreds, Kira knew, actually ran on broken bones. So fierce was their determination to win that they refused to be stopped. Only when the race was won did they pull up lame, and by then it was too late. Her expression hardened. She wasn't going to let that happen to Mimi Duncan, she vowed, and decided right then to lay it on the line.

"Mimi," she said quietly. "Please listen to me. I know how difficult it is, and how impatient you are to get back to competition, but the truth of the matter is that you will never compete again if you don't follow this program—"

"How can you say that?" Mimi whispered, her face turning pale. "How can you be so cruel?"

Kira had to reach out and prevent her from jumping off the table. Tightening her hands around the girl's shoulders, she forced Mimi to look at her. "It's not my intention to be cruel," she said firmly, "but you're old enough to understand the facts."

"But—"

"And the facts," Kira went on inexorably, "are that you have to build strength and endurance slowly. You've had serious surgery on that knee, Mimi. Do you want to take the chance of undoing all the good you've done so far?"

Mimi was silent. At last she said in a small voice, "No, but..." She looked up, her expression agonized. "But what will my father say?"

Kira was taken aback. "What do you mean?"

Mimi hid her face in her hands. "I don't want him to be disappointed in me."

Kira pulled away Mimi's hands. "Your father would never be disappointed in you. He loves you, Mimi. He's very proud of you."

Mimi still refused to look up. "Do you think so?"

"Of course I do! Why in the world do you have to ask?"

"Because he's gone so much," Mimi said, and then looked up quickly. "Oh, but I understand," she hastened to say. "I know how busy he is, how many important clients he has...."

More important than you? Kira wondered grimly, and heartily disliked Yale at that moment. How could he think of business when his daughter needed him? She was about to say something when Mimi rushed on in his defense.

"And he does come to all my important competitions," she said eagerly. "He's always there...when he can be." She smiled proudly. "Do you know we even ski the course together and he points out things my coach doesn't even see? Everybody loves my dad. He's famous, you know."

"I know," Kira said, somewhat curtly. She really didn't want to talk about how wonderful Yale was right now.

"Have you ever seen Dad ski, Kira?"

"Well, I—"

"He's fantastic!" Mimi exclaimed, her eyes shining again. "Even now. There's no way anybody could beat him if he went back into competition."

Kira had to protest at that. "Oh, now—"

"No, I mean it. If you could see him, you'd know!"

"I have seen him," Kira said shortly.

"When?"

"I beg your pardon?"

"When did you see him ski?" Mimi asked, and then sighed ecstatically. "When he won his medal?"

"As a matter of fact—"

"He should have won the gold, you know," Mimi interrupted again, nodding vigorously. "He really should have. He was good enough."

Kira couldn't help herself. "Someone should have told that to Bernhard Russi," she said, naming the Swiss who'd captured the gold in the Downhill that year.

Mimi looked up quickly, her face alight again. "You *did* see him!" she squealed.

Kira recognized her mistake too late. She never should have said anything in the first place, she thought. However determinedly she had tried to avoid it, the conversation had degenerated into a discussion about Yale, and now she knew even less about Mimi than when she'd started. What had she been trying to accomplish, anyway? she wondered irritably. She wasn't a psychologist; she was a physical therapist. It wasn't any of her business *why* Mimi wanted to ski so badly that she was risking further injury; her job was making sure she was physically fit to return to her sport.

Impatiently, she picked up her clipboard again. "I think we'll start with the bicycle today," she said, and made a check next to that column with her pen. "Five minutes—no more."

"Oh, Dr. Stanfield!"

Kira looked at her. "Five minutes," she repeated.

Mimi had calmed down enough to recognize that tone. With a sigh, she levered herself off the table. She was just hobbling over to the row of stationary bicycles, the brace strapped firmly to her leg, when Kira stopped her.

"And please don't try walking around without that knee brace anymore, Mimi," she said, looking down at her clipboard again.

Mimi's eyes widened with surprise. "How...how did you know?"

Kira hadn't known—or at least, she hadn't been sure. It had been an educated guess on her part. But when she glanced up and saw Mimi's guilty flush, she knew she had scored. "It's my job to know these things," she said. "I'm the therapist, remember?"

She saw Mimi give her several wondering glances during the rest of the session, but she ignored the girl's awed expression. It never hurt to have her patients think she had eyes in the back of her head, and after the conversation she'd had with Mimi today, it was even more important for her to keep a step ahead. If Mimi lost respect for her as a therapist, she might get impatient and start working on her own, and Kira wanted to avoid that at all costs. Mimi was volatile enough already; she just couldn't take the chance that the girl would do something rash and destroy everything she had worked so hard to achieve.

Unfortunately that meant that she was going to have to talk to Yale. She and Mimi parted on good terms when the session ended, but as her perspiration-soaked and bedraggled patient went off to take a shower, Kira realized she couldn't put off a parent-therapist conference any longer. She hadn't forgotten that almost-hysterical tone in Mimi's voice when they'd talked about skiing, and as much as she dreaded it, she would speak to Yale when he came to collect his daughter. Now that the housekeeper was coming from California, Yale would be away more, and with his frequent absences from home, Kira knew she had to take advantage of the opportunity. It might be some time before she had another one, she thought grimly, and went out to the front office to wait.

YALE WAS RUNNING late. He hated to be late for anything, but to be delayed fetching his daughter from her therapy appointment was inexcusable. By the time he finally dashed out to the car, he was in a black mood that turned even darker when he saw the snow covering the windshield. Now he'd be delayed further while he wiped the stuff off, and in the meantime, Mimi was waiting. He was never late; she'd be worried that something had happened to him. Digging the snow scraper out of the glove box, he muttered a curse as he rasped it across the glass. He never had this problem in Los Angeles; whoever thought snow in winter was a fact of life had obviously never lived in Southern California. It was ironic when he remembered that he'd spent part of the previous night convincing Hilda that winter in Vermont was a delight.

Their housekeeper, Hilda Trent, hadn't been able to fly out until now. Although she was a widow and her children were grown, there had been a family emergency that had prevented her from coming sooner. But thankfully her brother was out of the hospital and doing well, so she had called late last night to say she could come if he still wanted her.

If he still wanted her! The past two weeks without Hilda had been a nightmare. Even though the house he and Mimi had rented came completely furnished, there were still necessities like sheets and towels to buy; he'd barely recovered from that shopping expedition when Mimi remarked that unless they wanted to eat out all the time, they had to have food in the house. That meant another trip to the little grocery in Stonebridge, and naturally he'd gotten all the wrong things. Well, it didn't matter. The only thing he knew how to cook was bacon and eggs, and his daughter wasn't much better: her speciality was hot dogs and beans.

So when Hilda had called, he'd dropped everything to make arrangements for her to come. The L.A. condo had to be closed and some of the things Mimi wanted sent out, but after numerous phone calls, it was done. He'd been so busy he hadn't had time to take care of business, and he'd just been about to dash out of the house this morning when one of his clients called.

Throwing himself into the car, he started toward the clinic. But that call reminded him that he hadn't been paying as much attention to business as he usually did; he'd been too preoccupied with Mimi. Now that she was getting well, he'd have more time, and that was another reason he'd be glad to see Hilda. Several of his players' contracts were coming up for renewal, and it was essential that he meet with them before he started negotiations. He'd learned these past two weeks that things were almost impossible to do from here; he had to be wherever the action was to be effective. It was part of his job, and Mimi understood that. Hilda did, too, thank God. She'd stay with Mimi while he took care of business. It had been their arrangement ever since his divorce, and whenever he thought about it, he was proud of himself for working out such a satisfactory solution. Mimi was very fond of Hilda, and the housekeeper regarded Mimi almost as her daughter.

He smiled. Things had worked out well, after all. Now all he had to do was collect Mimi, drive to the airport at Rutland where Hilda's flight was due, and deliver his daughter and his new house into the woman's capable hands. With a sigh of relief, he turned into the small parking lot at the clinic and went inside.

KIRA SAW YALE drive up and she tensed. Now that the moment was here, she wasn't even sure what she was going to say. To make sure they wouldn't be interrupted, she had introduced Mimi to two young people her own age who had been coming in for hot-pack treatments and diathermy. Like everyone else in Vermont, it seemed to Kira, Jack and Alison were avid skiers, and the injuries they had sustained were minor ones from hotdogging—skiing gymnastics. They'd been lucky this time, and Kira hoped that a little comparing of notes between the three of them would convince them to consider skiing down the mountain the old way again. It would also give her time to talk to Yale.

But now that he was here, she wanted to change her mind. Talking to him didn't seem so important when she was watching him stride purposefully up the sidewalk. He was so good-looking even dressed in jeans and a ski sweater that she nearly whirled around and ran back to her office. She couldn't talk to him, she thought in a panic, not when just seeing him made her heart beat faster. By the time he opened the front door and stamped the snow from his shoes, she was sure she'd make a complete fool of herself.

Yale looked up just then and saw her standing there. He immediately looked concerned. "What is it? Has something happened to Mimi?"

Kira shook her head. She had herself under control now, and she was able to say calmly, "I'd like to talk to you for a few minutes, Yale."

Relieved that Mimi was all right, he glanced at his watch. "About what? Can't it wait?"

Annoyed, Kira couldn't help herself. "Why, are you late for an appointment?"

He seemed preoccupied, looking over her shoulder for his daughter. "As a matter of fact, I am. Is Mimi ready? We have to leave right now."

Mimi came down the hall just then, accompanied by her two new friends. Before Kira could protest, she had seen her father and eagerly introduced them. "Dad, this is Jack and Alison. And guess what? There's going to be a sleigh ride this weekend and they asked me to go."

"That sounds like fun—"

"Yale!" Kira said, exasperated.

He glanced at her, then back to his daughter. It seemed to Kira that he chose deliberately to misunderstand her, for he said, "Maybe you'd better ask Dr. Stanfield about that. In the meantime, we've got to get going. We have to pick up Hilda."

"Hilda!" Mimi squealed delightedly. "Oh, Dad! When?"

"Right now. She called late last night—I wanted to surprise you. So get your coat and let's go. I'll meet you in the car in just a minute, all right?"

As the trio of youngsters went off, Yale looked at the irate Kira again. "Okay. What did you want to talk to me about?"

Kira was so irked by this time that she nearly refused to answer. Yale was obviously too busy to listen to what she said, so she replied stiffly, "Never mind. I can see you're in a hurry. We'll talk another time."

He nodded vaguely and started toward the door, only to turn around and come back. "*Was* it important?"

She hesitated. "Yes."

"All right then. How about tonight? We'll have dinner and talk then."

"Dinner!"

"That's the only time I have. I've got to leave tomorrow for New York, and I'm not sure when I'll be back."

"I see." Kira was trying to hold on to her temper. "Well, if that's all the time you can give me, I guess I'll have to accept your invitation. I didn't dream you'd have to squeeze me in."

He seemed oblivious to the sarcasm, glancing at his watch again. "I've really got to leave now or I'll be late. Shall I pick you up at eight?"

"I suppose that will have to do," she snapped.

Yale looked at her for a moment. "You know," he murmured, "I'd forgotten..."

She lifted her chin. "What?"

He hesitated a moment, then shook his head. "Never mind," he said with a grin. "I'll see you at eight."

He strode out before she could reply.

CHAPTER FOUR

KIRA WAS STILL ANNOYED when she left her office that
night. She wasn't sure how he had done it, but she felt
that Yale had somehow manipulated her into this dinner meeting. Glaring in the direction of the house he
had rented as she closed the back door of the clinic, she
started down the snowy path to her own cottage. Soon
though, with her breath making clouds of vapor in the
air and her cheeks tingling with the cold, she forgot her
annoyance. The sun had already set by this time, but
with the approach of another storm, the light had that
pink and mauve quality she loved. Outlines seemed
blurred, and everything looked soft, even the glitter of
ice crystals on the frozen surface of the pond. She'd
heard that children sometimes gathered here to skate,
but the area had remained empty so far, and she
couldn't help thinking of one Olympic champion she'd
read about who used to practice on the pond near her
home in Connecticut. For a moment, she could picture...

Her foot slipped on a patch of ice just then, and she
exclaimed as she tried to catch her balance. The
tempting image of skaters darting over the pond vanished from her mind, and then she was home, stamping her boots on the back steps. Her huge orange tabby,
Purr, greeted her at the door, his purr like the rumble
of a truck as he rubbed against her legs. She had named

him Whispurr when she'd found him at the animal
shelter because his meow was so weak and frail, but
when he had blossomed to nearly twenty pounds under her care, and his purr was loud enough to wake her
at night, she decided to shorten his name. Her good
humor restored, she smiled as she bent down to ruffle
his thick fur.

"You old con artist," she murmured as she opened
the back door, and had to smile as he sashayed in ahead
of her, his plumed tail with the white tip proudly aloft.
He always had been impervious to criticism.

Because she had some time before Yale arrived,
she'd brought home a few reports to go over. But after
feeding the cat and starting a fire in the old-fashioned
wood-burning stove that was her main source of heat,
she couldn't concentrate on her work. Finally, with a
sigh, she went to take a bath and change. She had
promised herself that she wouldn't make too much of
a fuss about tonight, but when she found herself adding some of her precious bath salts to the tub, she exclaimed impatiently. What was the matter with her?
She was acting as though this was a date when in reality it was a business meeting. She had agreed to this
dinner only to talk about Mimi; for all the romantic
undertone there would be, she and Yale might as well
be meeting in her office at the clinic.

But as irritated as she was with herself, she still
dressed carefully, trying on several outfits before she
finally became so frustrated at her indecision that she
donned the cream wool slacks with the matching cash-
mere sweater she had chosen in the first place.

"What do you think, Purr?" she asked rhetori-
cally, studying the effect in the bedroom mirror. The
cat, curled into a giant ball on the bed, opened one eye,

yawned, and went back to sleep again. Kira looked back at her reflection. "You're right," she muttered, and tied a silk scarf in rusts and greens and golds around her neck for dash.

Finally ready, she was just leaving the bedroom when the doorbell rang. Surprised at the leap her heart gave, she stood where she was for a moment and willed herself to calm down. Yale was the father of one of her patients; whatever had been between them was in the past. All she had to do was concentrate on that, and everything would be fine.

She was still reassuring herself when she opened the front door. But when she saw Yale in a topcoat, with a white silk scarf casually draped around his neck, the only thing she could think of was how handsome he looked. Feeling even more helpless and exasperated with herself than she had before, she managed to invite him in. She had already decided that she wasn't going to prolong this evening by asking if he wanted a drink, so she said quickly, "I'm ready. I just have to get my coat."

"Take your time," he said easily, and went into the living room while she turned to the hall closet. She was just reaching for her coat when she sighed and dropped her hand. Now that he was here, it seemed churlish not to offer him something, and she left the coat where it was and followed him inside.

"Did you do this?" he asked, gesturing to the living room when he heard her come in.

Because she was so annoyed with herself for these ambivalent feelings, she perversely became annoyed with him. "You sound surprised."

He seemed amused by her tone. "Do I? I didn't mean to. It was just that this doesn't seem your...er...style."

She was about to reply just as sharply to that when she realized that if she took exception to everything he said, the evening was going to be even more of a strain than she anticipated. Wondering if this irritating anger she felt was a way of keeping an emotional distance, she glanced away and said, "The cottage seemed to dictate the style, I guess."

He nodded, and she covertly watched him as he looked around again. She couldn't help feeling proud, for the pine-paneled walls and the shining pegged floors with their handmade rag rugs made the room look inviting. An old spinning wheel she had found stood in one corner, and the oak-frame couch and chairs were upholstered in a colorful material. She had placed macramé wall hangings here and there, and when Yale saw an especially intricate one he went over to admire the complicated design.

"This is beautiful," he said, and glanced over his shoulder. "Don't tell me you did this, too."

"As a matter of fact, I did," she said, enjoying his look of surprise. "It started when I began prescribing macramé as therapy for some of my patients. I had to know how to do it myself, so..." She shrugged, and glanced around. "I have to admit that once I started, some of these got out of hand."

"I don't agree. These are works of art."

Now she was embarrassed. Deciding that it really was time to leave, she went to get her coat. They went to dinner at the Stonebridge Inn, where Kira had been once before, and as they walked in, she looked around with pleasure. The inn was a quaint little place with a

cheery fire blazing in the huge fireplace at one end of
the dining room and old-fashioned prints on the wain-
scotted walls. There were only half a dozen tables, but
they were set with starched white cloths, fine china and
silver. Candles flickered on every table, and as Kira and
Yale were seated just near enough to the fire to feel its
radiating warmth, she was glad only one other table
was occupied. She didn't know the couple, and she was
relieved. This way there would be no awkward explanations or speculations about why she was having dinner with the father of one of her patients, and she and
Yale could talk in private.

The waiter came, and after they had ordered, Kira
turned immediately to Yale. They were here to discuss
his daughter, but before she could say anything, he
smiled. "I want to thank you, Kira," he said simply.

She was startled. "For what?"

"For Mimi. I haven't seen her this bright and cheerful since her accident. I have you to thank for that."

She was embarrassed again, touched despite herself. "I haven't really done anything," she said awkwardly. "And you have to remember that depression
is common after what she's been through. Sometimes
I think inactivity is much more difficult for athletes to
endure than pain."

He reached for the wine the waiter had just poured.
"Was that the way you felt?"

She stiffened and frowned. The last thing she wanted
to talk about was the fall that had ended her career.
Yale saw her expression and hastily put down his glass.
"I'm sorry, Kira. I didn't mean to—"

"Forget it," she said curtly.

"But I—"

"I said forget it!" she repeated fiercely. "I thought we came here to talk about Mimi!"

"We did. But..." He stopped. "Look, don't you think things would be a lot easier if we stopped pretending that we don't know each other? I'm feeling awkward, and I know you are, too. Why don't we call a truce—for the evening at least?"

She started to answer that she didn't want a truce, that she didn't want anything to do with him at all. It was absurd to let him affect her this way, as though the past fifteen years had never happened and they were young once again and filled with dreams they planned to share. She shook her head. She was no longer seventeen, and he wasn't her handsome ski hero. Yet, somehow when he smiled...

"You're right," she said abruptly. "It is ridiculous to go on pretending when we're obviously going to be seeing each other from time to time during the next few months."

He started to smile until he realized what she had said. "Months?" he repeated. "But I thought Mimi was doing so well."

"She is," she said quickly. "But Mimi has had serious surgery, and even the most determined patient still has to deal with physical factors."

"Yes, I know. If determination was the only key, I think Mimi would have been on the slopes long before now."

She looked at him curiously. "Is that what you want?"

"Well, of course it is! Naturally, I want what she—" He broke off and looked at her. "What do you mean?"

They had arrived at the real reason she had agreed to have dinner with him. She had wondered if he was aware of how desperately Mimi wanted him to be proud of her, and since there was no mistaking his concerned expression, nor his obvious love for his daughter, Kira knew she had to say something. She was sure that once she explained her concern to Yale, he would have a talk with his impatient daughter and Mimi wouldn't push herself to the point where she did more damage than good.

"Have you ever asked Mimi why she is so obsessive about skiing?" she asked.

Yale laughed. "What do you mean? Mimi was born to ski!"

"Are you sure?" Kira pressed. "Have you ever thought that maybe she's just trying to make you proud of her?"

"Of course she wants me to be proud of her!" he exclaimed. "But that doesn't mean she's competing just to please me! Whatever gave you that idea? Mimi could no more hang up her poles than she could stop breathing!"

Angry that she had worked herself up to this only to have Yale laugh at her fears, Kira said sharply, "Mimi says differently."

He stared at her for a moment before he laughed again. "That's ridiculous. She was only teasing you. You should know by now what a little joker she is!"

"She wasn't joking, Yale."

He shook his head indulgently, refusing to believe her. "Then she was trying to get out of doing something she didn't want to do. She has a way of getting around people, or haven't you realized that by now?"

Kira looked at him uncertainly. After working with Mimi these past two weeks, she knew how difficult it was to resist that infectious grin and those big blue eyes; she'd had to harden her heart herself. Mimi hated the stationary bike, and there had been several occasions when Kira had been tempted to allow her to shave a minute or two off the required riding time. Maybe she *had* been mistaken, she thought, and decided that she would have another talk with Mimi about this.

Feeling foolish for making such a big deal about it, she watched the waiter return to serve their entrees and tried to think of a safe topic that would give them something to talk about without delving into personal things. Even though they had called a truce of sorts, she wasn't ready to dip into the past with Yale, and she was sure he felt the same way. Seconds later, she was dismayed to realize that he didn't feel that way at all.

"So tell me," he said, after tasting the excellent roast beef, "when did you get your doctorate? You could have knocked me over with a feather when I realized the Dr. Stanfield at the clinic was the Kira Blair I had once known."

She took a quick sip of water. "Oh…it's a long story," she said vaguely.

"I've got time."

Trapped, she glanced down at her plate and realized she hadn't eaten a thing. Lifting her fork, she said, "It's not very exciting, Yale. After I came home from the…from the Olympics, I decided to go to school."

She didn't mention her father dying, and that there had been very little money for her to continue training, and he mercifully didn't ask. Instead, he said mildly, "I suppose physical therapy was a natural choice, wasn't it?"

She looked at him sharply, wondering if there was some other meaning behind the remark. Then she told herself she was being ridiculous, and forced herself to answer in the same vein. "Yes, I guess it was. When you think of all the times during training that we could have used a therapist..." Her voice trailed away, and she went on quickly, "Anyway, once I got started, I couldn't seem to stop. I got my Masters in Exercise Physiology, and then went on for my Doctorate." She smiled. "Did you ever think I'd find my niche in school, of all places?"

His eyes twinkled. "Not when I remember how you hated the books! You were almost as bad as I was!"

"Yes, but you were better at getting around your tutor than I was," she said with a laugh.

"I didn't have to deal with the dreaded Madame Sasanova, either, did I?"

They laughed together, caught up for an instant in memories of younger days when skiing or skating was the most important thing in their lives...except for each other. As though the thought struck them at the same time, they sobered and Yale asked awkwardly, "What does your husband do?"

What little appetite she'd had vanished. "He has...had...his own accounting office in Seattle," she said. "He died of kidney disease last year."

Yale was silent a moment. Then, quietly, he said, "I'm sorry. I imagine that was a difficult time for you."

She reached quickly for her water glass again. "Yes, it was," she said, and marveled that she could talk about it so calmly. She had never been able to discuss Gil's dying before, not even with Miles. Not even with Jilly, she remembered. She and her sister had cried so many times together, but they had never really *discussed* Gil's illness. Glancing covertly at Yale, she wondered why she didn't mind talking about it now.

Realizing that it was up to her to lighten the moment, she forced a smile. "I ended up in Seattle, of all places, but somehow I wasn't surprised when I read that you moved from Boise to Los Angeles. I remember you saying that you always wanted to be where the action was."

He gave her a mock grimace. "Did I really say that?"

"I take it you don't like Los Angeles."

"Not particularly. If it hadn't been for my work, and because Marissa liked it there, I would have been just as happy in a place like ... like Stonebridge," he finished, and sounded surprised.

"Somehow, I can't imagine you being happy with the bucolic life for long," Kira said, and then, because she felt it was a shadow between them, had to mention his wife. "I read about your divorce, Yale."

He laughed shortly. "I think everybody did. Marissa made sure it was front page news."

He sounded so bitter that she looked at him in surprise. Tempted to reach out and touch him, she grabbed instead for the coffee the waiter had brought when he cleared their plates, and decided the wisest course was just to say nothing. After a moment, Yale reached for his cup, too.

"Sometimes I think the only good thing to come out of my marriage was Mimi," he murmured. "If I hadn't had her, I think I would have—" He stopped, and then went on with a forced smile, "It all worked out for the best, anyway, you know. I got Mimi, and Marissa got everything else."

Kira wasn't sure what to say to that, either, and when Yale saw how uncomfortable she was, he put his cup back in the saucer and reached impulsively for her hand. "I'm sorry," he said quietly. "Sometimes I . . ."

It was all she could do not to turn her palm up and entwine her fingers in his. She had become increasingly aware of his presence throughout the meal, and she had wanted him to touch her. Now that he had, she realized that she wanted more, much more, and on the pretext of reaching for her coffee again, she removed her hand and said hastily, "I understand. But you do have your daughter. She's a beautiful girl, Yale. You must be very proud."

"I am," he said, and then sat back with a sigh. "It's been difficult at times, trying to raise Mimi alone. I think it would have been different with a son, but a girl. . ." He shook his head. "Sometimes I wonder what I'm even doing."

He sounded so rueful that Kira had to smile. "Well, from what I've seen, I think you've done a wonderful job," she said sincerely. "And I'm sure Mimi thinks so, too."

He raised an eyebrow at that. "I'll be sure to tell her you said so when we have another battle over studying, or dating, or staying up late, or any of the hundreds of other things we've 'discussed' these past five years."

Kira laughed, remembering the interview Mimi had given that sports reporter last week. As Miles had predicted, it hadn't taken the media long to discover that America's skiing sensation was at the clinic, and when Kira had heard about a request for an interview, she had discussed it with Miles, and they had decided to leave the decision to Mimi. They'd both been amused when she had airily told them that she could spare a few minutes after her therapy session; she was willing to talk to reporters as long as they didn't interrupt her workout.

"That's not what she told that reporter last week," Kira said. "She thinks the sun rises and sets on you, Yale."

He gave her a grin. "I'm glad to hear that she listened to me, then. I told her to say that at least once each interview."

"You did not!"

"Yes, I did," he insisted with a twinkle in his eye.

She laughed, but she was suddenly uncomfortable again. Remembering how Mimi had rashly promised the reporter that she'd be back on skis before the end of the season, she was about to say something to Yale about it. Then she realized she was being too protective again. What had she expected Mimi to say? Naturally, she'd want to reassure her fans that she'd return to skiing soon, and as Yale had said, Mimi knew how to get around people. The reporter had still been dazed by the interview Mimi had given him when he left the clinic, and Miles had been delighted at how well things had gone.

So she decided not to mention it after all, and she was feeling so relaxed by the time Yale took her home that she invited him in for a nightcap. Yale always had been able to make her laugh, and as she went to warm the glasses for brandy, she realized with surprise that she had actually enjoyed going out with him. Remembering how nervous she'd been, how anxious to have the evening over with, she felt foolish as she went back to the living room with the drinks. Yale was sitting on the couch and when he saw her expression, he looked at her curiously.

"What is it?"

She couldn't tell him, for it didn't make sense, even to her. She realized that she and Yale were no longer the love-struck teenagers they'd been all those years ago, and yet somehow tonight, after she'd gotten through those nerve-racking first few minutes, it was almost as though the intervening years hadn't really happened at all—as though neither of them had married, as though Yale hadn't had a child. She knew that was absurd, and on that thought, she pretended to shiver. "I was thinking that it's cold in here. Maybe I should stoke up the fire."

Yale immediately set his glass on the table. "Let me..."

"No, I can get it," she said quickly. She wanted something to do, a task to keep her hands and her mind occupied. Even though Yale hadn't moved from the couch, she could feel his presence filling the room, and she wasn't sure she liked her response to it. She didn't want to remember how things had been, but as she went to the stove, she caught a whiff of his after-shave, and it brought memories flooding back. She could see them walking arm in arm on moonlit nights; she could see him hanging over the railing at the rink, winking and mugging at her before her coach saw him and chased him away to his own practice. She remembered his triumphant grin as he crossed the finish line after a race, and how proud she'd been when he would ski up to her in a flourish and grab her in a bear hug to the roaring approval of the crowd. She could still feel the thrill she'd experienced when he kissed her, his lips cold from another of those heart-stopping runs down the mountain, and how they had been linked in the press. The skating queen and the skiing star. What a romantic couple they'd been.

But no more, she told herself firmly. All that was in the past, and she was not going to get so caught up in old memories that she forgot the present. Jerking her head to rid it of those tantalizing images, she reached for the kindling box and the newspapers she kept beside it. Crumpling papers and placing the wood on top of them, she struck a match and told herself that she didn't *want* to take up where she and Yale had left off. She refused to start out on the same path again, only to be derailed emotionally, as she had been then. It had taken her a long time to get over Yale, and it really didn't matter whether it was because she'd been so young, or too blindly in love; the point was that she wouldn't go through it again.

The fire started in the enameled stove, and she had just turned back to Yale when Purr came in. He immediately jumped into the startled Yale's lap, and when Kira saw Yale's expression, she nearly burst into laughter. The cat looked so comfortable and Yale so helpless that she hid her amusement and said, "I'm sorry, Yale. Here, give him to me."

Yale stood up with the cat just as she reached for it, and as he handed the limp, purring animal over to her, their hands touched. She felt the contact through her entire body, and it was a second before she dared raise her eyes to his. When she saw him staring down at her, a strange expression on his handsome face, she drew in a breath. She knew he was going to kiss her, and she was suddenly powerless to resist him. Slowly, drawn inexorably toward each other, she raised her head and Yale dropped his. Time seemed to stop, and Kira's heart began to pound as she looked up into those deep blue eyes. Straining, she leaned toward him until their mouths were only inches apart . . .

And then the cat yowled and twisted out of her arms. As he leaped indignantly down and bounded up the stairs to the loft bedroom, the spell was broken, and Kira laughed shakily. Caught up in that breathless instant with Yale, she hadn't realized that she'd been squeezing Purr tighter and tighter, and as she watched him disappear with a flick of his white-tipped tail, she didn't know whether to be relieved or not that he had destroyed that tense moment.

Yale looked as undecided as she felt. Scowling in the cat's direction, he reached for his brandy and finished it in one gulp before he grabbed his coat. "It's getting late," he muttered. "I think I'd better go."

He didn't mention what had just happened, and neither did she. But because she still felt off balance and a little unnerved as she walked him to the door, she spoke without thinking. "Yale, will you at least think about what I said?"

Blankly, his mind obviously on other things, he looked down at her. "About what?"

Now that the moment had passed, Kira was wondering what had happened. She had *wanted* Yale to kiss her just now; despite all her assurances that she didn't want to get involved and that the past was best left forgotten, she had nearly cried out in disappointment when the cat had interrupted them. Annoyed that she wasn't able to control herself better than this, she plunged ahead. "About Mimi. I am worried about her Yale, and—"

He flushed. "I thought we settled that."

Why was she pursuing this? Before she could decide, some demon made her say, "I don't think we settled anything at all. I told you I was concerned, and perhaps you would be, too . . . if you ever stayed in one place long enough to talk to her."

Now he was annoyed. "What are you talking about?"

She had started this, now she had to go on. "Mimi tells me that you imported your housekeeper so that you could go away on business."

His expression turned stubborn, a look that she well remembered from all those years before. "So?"

"So! Don't you think you should be here to help Mimi with her therapy?"

He stiffened, and she knew she'd gone too far. "Isn't that what you're for?" he asked, his voice dangerously low.

She lifted her head. Why was she *doing* this? This wasn't like her at all, she thought desperately. "I can only do so much, Yale. You're her father, the rest is up to you."

He looked at her a moment, his eyes hard. "No, you're wrong, Kira," he said coldly, and reached for the door. "The rest is up to her."

She was too shocked to stop him, and by the time he had closed the door behind him, she was seething. Oh, how like Yale to say something like that, she thought angrily. He always had demanded so much of everyone just because he was so good at things himself. They had been through this before, during the last terrible quarrel. . . .

Jerking her head, she told herself she would not think about that horrible time. Marching into the living room, she spied the two brandy glasses on the coffee table and took them into the kitchen. She could see the house Yale had rented as she stood at the sink, and her mouth tightened as she remembered the reason Yale had asked her out to dinner tonight. His house-keeper had barely arrived, and already he had made plans to leave on business. She should have known nothing she said would have any effect on him; he always had been too stubborn to listen to anyone but himself.

Feeling grim, she went upstairs to the bedroom. One thing was certain, she told herself, there would be no more dinner dates with Yale Duncan. Her instincts had been right in the first place; she should have continued to avoid him.

"Damn him," she muttered, and saw Purr scurry under the bed as she approached. The cat obviously thought he was in trouble, but she didn't feel like cajoling him out of his hiding place. Things might have turned out so differently tonight if he hadn't interrupted them, and when she finally turned out the lights, and Purr jumped cautiously to his place at the end of the bed, she didn't know whether to scold him or not.

WHEN YALE OPENED the door, his housekeeper, Hilda Trent, was sitting in the living room, placidly knitting another of the sweaters that had been such a hit with Mimi's ski team. Mimi herself had drawers full of Hilda's beautiful designs, and he had quite a few himself. It seemed that his gray-haired, round little house-keeper either had knitting needles or cooking utensils in her hands; in the five years he'd known her, he'd never seen her sit idle.

"Did you have a good time, Mr. Duncan?" Hilda asked as he took off his coat and hung it on the rack in the hall.

Yale came into the living room. He had started a fire for her before he went out, and he automatically went over to stoke up the coals. "It was a business meeting," he said, and ignored her raised eyebrow. She knew—because he had told her when he was cajoling her into coming to Vermont—that one of the reasons he wanted her to come was because none of his contacts were here.

"I see," she said.

He'd been squatting by the fireplace to fix the fire, and he turned on his heel to look at her as she sat complacently in the easy chair. She'd taken off the sensible shoes she wore during the day and put on her worn slippers, and he couldn't help thinking that with her hair in a little bun like that and half glasses slipping down her nose, she looked like Rockwell's idea of everybody's grandmother.

"Hilda," he said, and thought how silly it was that she addressed him so formally while he used her first name. But he'd asked her before if she wouldn't call him Yale, and when she seemed so uncomfortable with the idea, he hadn't insisted.

"Hilda," he began again, and wondered why he was about to ask her this. But he couldn't seem to help himself. With Kira's accusation still ringing in his ears, he had to know. "Do you think I'm away from home too much?"

She looked at him over the top of her glasses, the knitting needles never missing a stitch. "That's not for me to say, Mr. Duncan," she said.

"Yes, but—" he started, and stopped. He knew that tone. It meant that she had decided this was one place she wouldn't step over her boundaries, as she put it. Sighing, he wondered why she didn't feel that compunction at other times, such as when she wondered aloud why he dated so many women and refused to settle down with just one. Not that she thought he should get married again, mind you, she was always careful to add. That was his business entirely, and she was sure he would marry when he was ready. Still, it would be nice to hear a name more than once. The way it was now, a body couldn't even keep track of all the new faces for all the comings and goings.

"I will say one thing," Hilda said, breaking into his thoughts.

"What?"

Carefully, she folded her knitting and put away her needles. Rocking her way to the front of the chair, she allowed him to help her to her feet. "It doesn't matter what I think," she said, her wise gray eyes on his face, "only what *you* think. Good night, now. Will you have time for breakfast in the morning?"

"Oh . . . no, don't bother. I'll probably be leaving early," he said, and watched her slowly climb the stairs to her room. Well, that was a big help, he thought sourly. The only problem was that after listening to Kira tonight, he didn't know what he thought . . . about anything at all.

His expression grim, he turned to bank the fire. But it was a long time before he went upstairs to his own room, and even longer before he climbed wearily into bed.

CHAPTER FIVE

KIRA ARRIVED at the clinic the next morning in a bleak mood that even a fresh snowfall overnight couldn't alleviate. She hadn't fallen asleep until nearly dawn because she kept replaying the evening in her mind. The more she thought about it, the more gloomily certain she became that she hadn't handled herself or Yale or the entire situation well at all. Depressed, she was sitting at her desk staring disconsolately out the window when Miles knocked on her door.

"Yes, what is it?"

He looked taken aback at her curt tone, and she immediately felt sorry that she had snapped at him. "Don't mind me," she said contritely. "Things haven't gone very well for me this morning. I guess I got up on the wrong side of the bed."

"Don't worry about it," he said with a smile. "I'm that way myself sometimes."

He wasn't; he was just being kind. She had seen him in many moods since she'd come to the clinic: preoccupied, harassed, tired, firm. But she had never heard him snap at anyone.

He took the chair opposite hers. "Anything you want to talk about?"

She hesitated. Did she really want to tell Miles what a fiasco last night had turned out to be? She had accepted that dinner date with Yale for the sole purpose of discussing his daughter's progress. She wanted his help, but instead of enlisting his support, all she had done was alienate him. Now that she'd had all night to think about it, she admitted that she'd had no right to accuse him of neglecting his daughter. It was no concern of hers how often he was away from home on business, and since neither father nor daughter had asked for her opinion, she should have just kept her nose out of it.

"I take it your conference with Yale didn't go well," Miles commented when she didn't reply.

She had told him last night before she left that she had arranged to talk to Yale, but she hadn't said that it was going to be over dinner. Wondering why she had neglected to mention that little detail, she glanced away from him. "No," she said. "It didn't."

"What happened?"

She looked at him sourly. "He just about told me to mind my own business."

"I see."

Kira wasn't sure that he did. She said shortly, "Yale seems to feel that Mimi doesn't need his help or support."

"Oh, I'm sure that's not true, Kira. I thought Yale was very concerned about his daughter."

"Then why did he shrug away my concerns?" she demanded. "Why did he leave for New York this morning?"

He looked surprised again at her tone, but his voice was mild when he said, "The man does have a business to run, Kira. Don't you think you're overreacting a little?"

She opened her mouth to protest before she realized the accusation might be true. Sitting back, she rubbed her temples. The headache that had been threatening all morning had just burst into life, and she had no one to blame but herself. Miles was right: she was being too emotional about this. She was getting too involved with Mimi, with the entire situation, and it had to stop. She'd had other patients who were just as eager as Mimi to get well; she had sensed the same impatience and frustration in them, but she had dealt with it differently. She had been sympathetic but dispassionate at the same time, and she hadn't lost her objectivity, as she was in danger of doing now. What was wrong with her? She *was* overreacting, and it wasn't like her at all.

Wasn't it? Now that she thought about it, she realized that she had always been too emotional where Yale was concerned. When they'd been seeing each other all those lifetimes ago, one word—even a look—from him could send her into a tailspin or into a state of euphoria. She frowned. She had assumed she was past that adolescent phase; after all, she wasn't seventeen any longer. She could handle herself better than this, and on that thought, she looked resolutely at Miles.

"You're right," she said. "I'm being foolish. It's just that Mimi is so talented, so bright. I'd hate to have her push herself so hard for the wrong reasons."

"And what do you think those are?" he asked curiously.

Uncomfortably, she shifted in her chair. "Well, you heard her during that interview she gave to *Sports Illustrated* when they found her here, Miles. She said she was determined to race again this season."

He waved his hand indulgently. "Yes, but she's young, Kira, and you know how these kids are. Even when something happens that proves they're not indestructible, they refuse to believe it. I'm sure she knows, deep down, that even with her formidable determination, it's just not possible for her to race again before the end of the year.''

Kira wasn't so sure Mimi was aware of that. Or if she was, she had decided not to accept it. She was working harder than any other patient she'd had before, and Kira knew as well as anyone how focused a world-class athlete could be. Their determination not to let anyone—or anything—stop them was what made them champions. But she had seen for herself the results of what such fierce resolve could do: that Japanese gymnast, for example, competing on the rings, knowing his kneecap was broken even before he nailed a superb routine and a spectacular dismount; another skier, winning the World Cup title after skiing with a broken hand, the ski pole taped to her palm because she couldn't grip it herself. The list went on and on, and so did the broken bodies that would never recover after the event was won. Too much damage had been done in the competition itself, and suddenly, nothing was left except a scrapbook of clippings and memories of how it had once been. Nothing was worth that, Kira thought fiercely: no award or prize or medal or recognition. She should know—she'd had to make that choice herself.

Thrusting away the painful memories, she looked at Miles again. ''I'm not so sure she knows that,'' she said.

Miles pushed himself up from the chair. ''Then maybe you should have a talk with her,'' he replied. ''Doesn't she have an appointment today?''

Kira glanced at the clock. ''Yes, in a few minutes, in fact,'' she said, and suddenly looked thoughtful. An idea had just occurred to her. ''I think I will have a talk with her today. Would you mind if we played a little hooky?''

''You're the therapist,'' he said, and with a wave, went off to struggle with the budget.

Feeling better than she had since she'd come in this morning, Kira smiled fondly after him. Miles always seemed to know the right thing to say, even if it wasn't what she particularly wanted to hear at the moment. But as always, their talk had helped her straighten out a few things in her mind, and she was going to take his suggestion. Checking her schedule, she reached for her coat and started out to see if Mimi had arrived for her appointment yet. She was just emerging from her office when Mimi opened the front door, accompanied by a tiny, round, gray-haired woman whom Kira rightly assumed to be the newly arrived housekeeper.

''Dr. Stanfield!'' Mimi said eagerly when she saw her. ''I'd like you to meet Mrs. Trent. Hilda, this is my doctor.''

''Her therapist, actually,'' Kira corrected with a smile, and held out her hand. ''I'm very pleased to meet you, Mrs. Trent.''

''Likewise,'' Hilda Trent said with a warm smile. ''But I know you have a busy schedule, so I'll be running along.''

''I'll be finished in an hour, Hilda,'' Mimi said, giving the woman an affectionate hug. ''But you don't have to come and get me. I can walk.''

''That may well be, Miss, but your father would have something to say about that, wouldn't he?'' Hilda said with mock severity. ''No, I'll be waiting outside in the car when you're finished, and we can go shopping together. I can't imagine what you two have been living on until now, but I intend to stock those cupboards before the day is out.''

''Oh, I can hardly wait!'' Mimi said fervently. ''I'm so tired of eggs! I think that's the only thing Dad knows how to cook.''

Her lips twitching, Hilda said goodbye and left. Mimi watched her go out the front door, then she turned to Kira with a grin. She had her backpack in her hand, and she said, ''I have to change, Dr. Stanfield. I'll just be a sec.''

''Actually, I think we'll do something different today, Mimi.''

Mimi had started down the hall toward the dressing room, but now she stopped and looked over her shoulder. ''What?''

''How about just going for a walk instead of working out?''

''Really? You mean it?''

Trying not to smile, Kira said, ''I would have suggested it sooner if I'd known you dreaded your workouts so much.''

''It's not that,'' Mimi said quickly, her eyes sparkling as she pulled her coat on again. ''But did you see all that new snow? I always like to be the first to make a trail—''

''I bet you do,'' Kira said dryly, and gestured. ''Come on, then. I'm not sure about forging new trails, but a slow walk around the block won't do any harm.''

''Maybe we could make some snow angels!''

Without warning, Kira was swept back in time to a snowy night in Aspen. She'd just finished four hours of practice, and even though she'd stood under a hot shower in the locker room until the water ran cold, it seemed that every muscle in her body ached. She'd been learning a new series for her long program, and she'd fallen again and again on the double toe loop, double axel, single toe, double flip combination. Her coach had been relentless, shouting and screaming instructions at her until she was in tears and sure that if she fell one more time she'd never get up again. Yale had surprised her by being outside when she finally came out, but she'd been so dejected and discouraged that he couldn't even get her to smile. It had snowed earlier that night and as he walked her back to the place where she was staying with her coach, their footprints were the only ones to disturb the new snowfall. The air was suffused with that soft pink light she liked, but she was so tired she hardly noticed. Yale did his best to cheer her up, but it was no good. After such a disheartening practice session, she was sure that she'd never make it through the Olympic trials. She was almost in tears when Yale, America's skiing sensation, the handsome athlete who had captured so many feminine hearts that he even received fan mail, threw himself down in the snow.

She thought at first that he'd hurt himself, and all she could think of was how disastrous an injury so close to the trials would be for him—for the team. Yale was the captain; the best skier they had. "What's wrong? What are you doing?" she'd cried as he began to flail his arms and legs—up and down, back and forth. She didn't know what was the matter with him, and she was in a panic, ready to run for help.

Then she realized he was laughing. When he stood up again, covered with snow, and gestured proudly at the giant snow angel he'd made, she had to laugh, too. They'd both laughed so hard that they clutched at each other, their mirth ringing out over the quiet neighborhood until they knew someone was going to come. With their hands over each other's mouths, something changed in his eyes. Slowly, their hands dropped and their lips met, tenderly at first, and then with the swiftly rising passion of youth. They were both breathing hard when they parted, and she would never forget the look on his face as he gazed down at her. Snowflakes glinted in his hair and on his eyelashes, and she thought he was the most handsome man she had ever seen. His arms went around her and he hugged her tightly to him.

"I knew I could make you laugh," he whispered, and gestured toward the angel with his chin. "Whenever you're down, just think of that, and if you need me to make another one, just call...."

Remembering that incident so long ago, Kira closed her eyes. She hadn't thought of Yale and the snow angel in years, but that night in Aspen seemed as close to her now as though it had happened yesterday. Why was she remembering all these things now? Why was she torturing herself with memories of another life? It served no purpose except to make her think of what might have been.

Mimi looked at her anxiously. "Are you all right?"

Kira blinked and returned her attention to the girl. "Of course. Why?"

"You looked so funny for a minute. Are you sure you still want to take a walk?"

"I'm sure," Kira said, and led the way out to the porch. The ever-efficient Stonebridge residents had already cleared the sidewalks, and she glanced up and down the quiet street. "Which way would you like to go?"

"Can we go look at the pond?"

Kira hesitated. Mimi had made such good progress that she'd been allowed to abandon her crutches, but she was still wearing her brace. The last thing either of them needed was for her to slip on a patch of ice lurking under the snow, so she said dubiously, "Well, I don't know. I don't think a path has been cleared out there yet."

"Yes, there has," Mimi said earnestly. "You made one this morning on your way to the clinic."

Kira looked at her in surprise. "How did you know that?"

"Because I saw you. Dad and I both did. We always watch you walk to work."

Startled, Kira exclaimed, "You watch me?"

Mimi flushed. "Well, we don't exactly *watch* you," she said hastily. "It's just that we can see you when we're having breakfast. It's not like we're spying or anything," she added quickly. "But you're just across the way, you know, and..."

Her voice trailed away on a painful note, and when Kira saw how embarrassed she was, she couldn't be upset. She wasn't sure she liked the idea of Yale sitting at his kitchen table and watching her walk to work, but when she thought about it, she didn't know why it should bother her. As Mimi had said, it wasn't as though they were spying on her. And the pond was public access. Why should she care?

"I didn't think you were spying," she said. "I was just surprised, I guess. Most of my patients don't even know where I live." Then, without thinking, she added, "Maybe you could visit me sometime."

"Could I?" Mimi seemed delighted with the idea. "Dad says you make the most beautiful wall hangings and that you have them all over the house!"

Kira glanced at her, thinking that if Yale had mentioned the macramé to Mimi this morning before he left, he would have had time to talk to her about what they had discussed last night. "What else did your father tell you?" she asked cautiously.

They had started walking in the direction of the pond after all, and Mimi bent down and scooped up a handful of snow. Shaping it absently into a ball, she said innocently, "Only that you used to be a wonderful skater. He said that he's never seen anybody as good as you."

Kira didn't know what to say. For some reason, she had never expected Yale to mention her skating career to his daughter, and she felt so flustered that she muttered, "Oh, well, I... That was a long time ago."

Mimi tossed the snowball up and down without looking at her. "He has a picture of you, did you know that?"

Dismayed, Kira gave her a quick look. "No. I didn't. What picture is that?"

The snowball went up and down again, up and down. Absurdly, Kira couldn't keep her eyes off it. "When you won the World Championships," Mimi said absently. She took aim at a tree and let fly. The snowball splattered against the trunk, causing the laden branches to release a shower of snow. "Ah..." she murmured in satisfaction, and reached down to grab another handful. She'd just started to shape that into another missile when she stopped abruptly and turned wide blue eyes on Kira. "How come you quit skating, Dr. Stanfield?" She saw Kira's startled expression and added hastily, "You don't have to tell me if you don't want to."

Kira knew she had to say something, but speech seemed beyond her. *Damn Yale,* she thought, and then knew that it wasn't his fault. As much as she wanted to, she couldn't hide that part of her past; whatever she had accomplished in skating was part of sports history, there for all to see.

Mimi's cheeks were red, but not from the cold. "I'm sorry, Dr. Stanfield," she said. "You don't have to tell me, honest. Dad says that sometimes I talk before I think, and he's right. Can you forgive me?"

She looked so miserable that Kira had to smile. Placing an arm around Mimi's shoulders, Kira hugged her and said, "Don't worry about it. My father used to say the same thing to me when I was your age."

Mimi was still embarrassed. Glancing down at the new snowball she had made, she crumbled it in her fingers and let the particles fall to the ground. Then, typical of a fifteen-year-old who was trying to make things better, but who only succeeds in making them worse, she looked at Kira and said, "It's just that I was curious. How could you get all the way to the Olympics, and then quit?"

Kira was tempted to say that it hadn't been quite that simple, but she wasn't sure she wanted to go into all that now. They had stopped by the edge of the lake, and as she glanced out over the wintry setting, she wondered how to explain. She had to say something, she knew. It was like the macramé, in a way: she couldn't expect her patients to give their all for her if she wasn't willing to give something in return herself. She couldn't allow Mimi to think that she had simply given up after she'd been injured; Mimi would lose confidence in her as a therapist. Sighing, she made up her mind. There was a wooden bench nearby, and she gestured toward it.

"Why don't we sit down for a minute and talk?" she said.

After they had cleared the snow off the bench and sat down, she asked, "Did your father tell you I was injured at practice during the Olympics?"

Mimi nodded. "Yes, it was the day before your final program, wasn't it?"

"Yes, it was," she managed to say calmly, and tried to thrust away the pictures that leaped into her mind. But the reel unfolded despite herself, and as though she were outside looking on, she could see herself on the ice that morning at practice.

She hadn't wanted to go that day; she was feeling the strain of the previous competitions. The pressure on her had been enormous: Peggy Flemming had won the gold medal four years before in Grenoble, and after Sjoukje Dijkstra of the Netherlands had ended United States domination of Women's Singles in 1964, the Americans were determined that the title would not be wrested away again. Everyone's hopes rested on her—America's skating darling, their Faerie Queen.

She closed her eyes briefly again. She could even see what she'd been wearing that day: two sets of leggings and her old red leotard for luck. Her ankle had been giving her trouble and she'd wrapped it, but halfway through the practice, she had skated over to the side and removed the support. Her coach had been annoyed, but when she had tersely explained that there wasn't enough room for the bandage inside the tight leather of her skate, Madame Sasanova had reluctantly agreed. Her movements were constricted, and she had to practice as she was going to perform. Both tense that day, they had compromised on relacing the skate. A quarrel was very near the surface, but there was enough stress without that. Everyone knew that the final program would determine the gold.

So with the skate relaced as tightly as it could be, she had started her warm-up again. The ankle felt tender, but she had skated under much more painful conditions, and at any rate, she was so keyed up that she hardly noticed.

Now she knew that had been the problem. Oh, she had gone over it a thousand times in her mind since then, seeing it again and again until she thought she would scream. Years ago, she'd had nightmares about it. They always started with her coming around that curve and going up into the air in a simple axel she'd done countless times since she'd learned to skate. But that time something had gone wrong. She could feel herself over-rotate as she went up, and even though she managed to correct it by the time she landed on the ice again, she was at such an odd angle that her ankle simply couldn't hold her. If the ankle had been strong and well, she might have pulled it off; sheer strength and endless hours of practice sometimes defied the laws of physics. But her ankle hadn't been strong, and her leg couldn't hold her. She could remember even now the sense of absolute disbelief as she landed and felt her blade slip out from under her. She'd been so shocked that at first she didn't even feel the pain of the ankle ligaments tearing away. This couldn't be happening to her, not now, not when she'd sacrificed so much and come so far. It wasn't fair!

But life wasn't always fair, and by the time the doctors poked and prodded and X-rayed and debated, her ankle was the size of a balloon and she knew she wasn't going to skate. If it had only been the pain, she would have done it. Or at least she would have tried. But she knew, as soon as she attempted to stand, that she'd never get through her complicated final program, no matter how determined she was. Physical laws could be bent only so far, and the doctors told her privately that even if she managed to get out on the ice, she wouldn't leave it under her own power.

Realizing that Mimi was looking curiously at her, she blinked away the memories and said, "It happened the day before my final program, while I was practicing. I tore the ligaments in my ankle and couldn't finish the competition."

"Gee," Mimi said somberly. "That must have been tough."

"It was."

"How did it happen?"

Kira smiled a sad little smile. "Like most of these things, I guess—a stupid accident. I fell out of an axel and my leg couldn't hold me." She didn't say that she'd hidden the problem with her ankle from everyone except her coach, or that they had both prayed it would hold together until after Sapporo; it would have sounded too much like an excuse. She hadn't, she remembered suddenly, even told Yale at the time. He'd had no idea that she'd been getting therapy on it for weeks; she and Madame Sasanova had agreed that she didn't need the extra pressure of the media speculating whether she'd be able to skate or not. Other performances by athletes had been affected by such endless conjectures at times like that, and there had been enough tension at the time without adding to it.

"But you didn't compete after that," Mimi said. It was more a puzzled statement than a question, and Kira smiled sadly again.

"No," she agreed. "I didn't. By the time I had recovered enough to start training again, my father died. Money was tight, and I didn't feel it was fair to ask my sister and my mother to sacrifice any more than they already had."

Mimi was silent for a moment, gazing somberly out at the frozen pond. "I don't know what I'd do if I had to give up skiing," she said at last. "I think I'd die."

"No, you wouldn't," Kira said. "You'd find that life goes on—"

"Not without skiing, it wouldn't!" Mimi said fiercely.

Startled, Kira looked at her charge. Two bright spots of color had flared on Mimi's fair cheeks, and her eyes had darkened with emotion. "Of course it would—" she started to say.

Agitated, Mimi jumped up. Kira winced at the abrupt movement, but Mimi was apparently too swept away to notice any discomfort. "You don't understand, do you?" Mimi cried. "You don't understand! I *have* to ski, don't you see? I'm nothing without that!"

Alarmed at the sudden change in the girl, Kira jumped up, too. Mimi looked poised for flight, and she reached out quickly and grasped her arm. "Mimi—"

"Oh, never mind!" Mimi cried, and tried to jerk away. "Just leave me alone!"

Kira refused to let her go. "No, I'm not going to leave you alone," she said intensely. "And I want to understand, if you'll just give me the chance. Now tell me, what is it that you're really afraid of?"

"I'm not afraid of anything!" Mimi shouted.

Even more alarmed at the undercurrent of hysteria she heard in the girl's voice, Kira tried to get control of the situation. Deliberately lowering her own voice, she said, "All right, then, but I know something is bothering you. If you won't tell me what it is, how can I help?"

"I don't want your help!" Mimi's face was white now, the only color the blue of her wide, frightened eyes. "I know why you brought me out here today, why you told me all that about your accident!" she cried. "You don't think I'm going to get well, do you? It was your way of telling me I'm not going to ski again!"

Kira gasped. "That's not true!"

Mimi stared at her a moment longer, then her face crumpled. Sobbing, she put her hands over her eyes. "It is true," she wept. "I know it!"

Kira didn't think about it; she reached out and enfolded the weeping girl in her arms. Murmuring soothing sounds, she let Mimi cry until the last of her sobs faded away into shudders. She knew the storm had passed when Mimi disengaged herself and turned away, wiping her eyes with the backs of her hands.

"I'm sorry," she muttered. "I didn't mean to do that."

"That's all right," Kira said. "We all need a good cry now and then. And you've been through a lot these past few months. You deserve it."

"I hate to cry," Mimi said, embarrassed. She reached down to grab a handful of snow to rub over her face. "It makes my freckles show."

Kira smiled. This was more the girl she knew. But she couldn't ignore what Mimi had said about never skiing again, and she was about to say something when Mimi

looked up. "There's Hilda," Mimi said, in quick relief. "I guess I'd better go."

Dismayed, Kira followed the direction of her glance
and saw the housekeeper waving to them from the back
porch of the clinic. She acknowledged with a wave of
her own, but she didn't want to let Mimi go without
talking about this. She had the feeling that if they
didn't discuss it now, the opportunity would be lost.

"Mrs. Trent can wait a minute," she said. "I'd like
to talk to you about—"

Mimi looked even more embarrassed. "If you want
to talk about that stupid remark I made about not
skiing again, forget it," she said. "I was just spouting
off. You know I didn't mean it."

Kira wasn't going to let it go that easily. "I don't
believe you," she said evenly. "I think you did mean
it, and I'd like to know why."

"Aw, come on, Dr. Stanfield," Mimi said. "I was
just teasing, kidding around—you know? I do things
like that all the time, it doesn't mean anything. I'm
sorry, I guess I shouldn't have played a joke like that
on you."

Before Kira could reply, Mimi had turned around
and started up the snowy path toward the clinic. Kira
let her go; she knew that if she forced the girl to talk to
her now, she would only make the situation worse. But
as she watched Mimi hobble up to the housekeeper and
the two of them leave, Hilda's arms around the girl, her
mouth tightened. First the father, she thought, now the
daughter. It seemed that she was destined to be made
to feel incompetent by everyone in the Duncan family.
All she needed now was—what was her name? Ma-
rina? Marissa? Whoever Mimi's mother was—to show
up, and her day would be complete.

YALE WAS THANKFUL that only minutes remained until the end of the game. Because of some problem with one of the football players he represented, he'd had to fly to Dallas at the last minute instead of New York, as he'd planned, and he definitely wasn't in the mood for football today, not when he had so many other things on his mind. It didn't help that most of the sixty-five thousand people who packed the stadium were Dallas Cowboy fans; every time anyone on the field made a move, the resulting roar of approval could probably be heard in California. Yale just wished the damned game would end. He didn't even care who won.

Another roar went up, and at the same time, the sports writer in the booth next to him pounded him on the back. "Did you see that?" the man shouted. "Lord, I haven't seen anything like that since—"

Whatever he'd been about to say was interrupted by another roar from the crowd. As Yale craned to see the distant figures running down the field, the sports writer leaped up and began to speak excitedly into a recorder. "I don't believe it," he crowed. "My boy Willie took the snap from center, and when Dallas blitzed, he stepped right into the pocket. He had a second—two at the outside—to get rid of the ball. But good old Nelson Biddle was right there, twenty yards downfield. Willie rifled the ball, Nelson caught it and ran right by those Dallas safeties fifty yards to goal. I've never seen anything like it in my life!" He turned triumphantly to Yale. "Have you?"

"Yes," Yale said calmly. "Last year, when your boy Willie was responsible for taking his team to the National Football Conference Championship."

The sports writer looked deflated. "Oh," he said, and turned away. Yale reached down and grabbed his briefcase. The game was over, but it would be awhile before he could talk to his client, Willie Mott, the quarterback who had just saved the day. In the meantime, now that the press box was clearing, he might be able to get some work done.

A few minutes later, he sat back and rubbed his eyes. He'd brought some contracts with him, but when he realized he'd read the opening page of one of them three times and hadn't the faintest idea what it said, he put it aside.

Trust Kira to put ideas into his head. If she hadn't said anything last night about his being gone so much, he wouldn't have given it another thought. His mouth tightened. She'd always been able to do that to him; right from the beginning a word from her could nag at him for days. He'd thought things had changed, but now he realized that they hadn't, not even after all these years.

Restless, he stuffed the contracts into his briefcase and put it aside. He stood up and stretched, wandered over to the coffee urn, poured a cup of horrible-looking black syrup and distastefully put it down again. He had to get this thing with Kira straightened out, or he'd never be able to get anything accomplished. As it was, it seemed that the only thing he'd done was think about Kira from the time he'd left her last night. Remembering some of the things he'd said, he winced. The evening that had started out so well had ended badly, and it was all because of him. Now he couldn't get what she'd said out of his mind. The hell of it was that even though he'd talked to Mimi about it this morning, he still wasn't sure which one of them to believe, Kira or his daughter. Gloomily, he recalled the scene.

"Do you think I'm gone too much on business, Sprite?" he'd asked cautiously. She had been having breakfast—mercifully prepared by Hilda, who never served runny eggs or lumpy oatmeal, as they'd been suffering through these past weeks—but he hadn't been eating because he hadn't slept well. It was all because of that argument with Kira, and after tossing and turning all night, he'd finally decided that maybe the best thing was to ask Mimi outright what she thought.

Her blue eyes amused, his daughter had looked at him over the rim of her orange juice glass. "What would you say if I said yes?"

He'd looked at her in dismay. "I'm not sure. *Do* you feel that way?"

"Of course not," she said, and grinned as she attacked her favorite breakfast. He'd glanced away from the chocolate chips embedded in her pancakes, the whole stack topped with whipped cream, and tried not to shudder. Sometimes he felt that Hilda spoiled her abominably. But she was chewing in bliss when she looked up at him curiously. "Why do you ask, Dad?"

He didn't want to get involved in a lengthy explanation about Kira and why he had taken her to dinner; he already regretted letting slip the fact that he and Kira had known each other before. As soon as she'd found out, Mimi had pestered him endlessly about it, until finally—more out of self-defense than anything else—he'd told her about Kira's skating career. Then he'd made the mistake of showing her that picture of Kira at the World Championships. He didn't know why he had saved that photo all these years; maybe because the photographer had caught her in the perfect moment, her head dropped in that beautiful layback, her hair fanning out, that supple spine arched with her arms held gracefully overhead. Nothing could match the joyful, exultant look on her face at that instant—the supreme self-confidence she'd always had on the ice, the perfect mastery of her sport. Kira had been born to skate, and that picture showed exactly why she had won the Worlds. That's why he'd been so angry that she hadn't skated that final program. She would have won; he had never doubted it.

But he didn't want to think of that, and so he brought himself firmly back to the present. "I was just curious," he said evasively. "Since we've been together so much these past few weeks, I guess it made me realize how much I was gone before. I just wondered if you minded."

Mimi mopped up the last of her pancakes. "I know you've got your work to do," she said, sounding unconcerned. "And besides, just because I'm laid up doesn't mean you have to stay home." She looked at him again with another grin. "Besides, this way I won't feel so guilty going off on the World Cup circuit when I start skiing again."

He still wasn't convinced. "Are you sure?"

"Come on, Dad," she said, rolling her eyes. "Now, go on, or you'll miss your plane."

Remembering that conversation, Yale wondered why he was still bothered by it. He'd asked Mimi if she minded his being gone, and she'd told him what she thought. Instead of stewing about it, he should just accept what she'd said and forget it.

But it was still preying on his mind when he finally left the press box to meet Willie, and he thought that maybe he'd try to cut this trip short, after all. He'd planned to go to New York after leaving Dallas, but it could wait. His daughter was more important than a new hockey client, and if Mimi thought he was suddenly being overly solicitous, he could always say that he'd taken a fancy to Vermont.

CHAPTER SIX

KIRA WAS TESTING Mimi on the isokinetic machine when Miles came in to ask how they were doing. One eye on the computer screen, the other on her patient, Kira acknowledged his arrival with a lift of her head, but Mimi didn't stop. Her red hair plastered to her cheeks and forehead, beads of perspiration on her upper lip, she glanced up at Miles then back down to her leg again while she continued with the exercise. Her ankle was strapped to the arm of a machine that measured such things as torque on extension and flexion, and range of motion of the knee, and she had been working hard to show how much she had improved since her operation. Miles watched silently until Kira finally said, "All right, Mimi. That's enough."

Breathing hard, Mimi sat back with a heavy sigh. Kira was handing her a towel to wipe her streaming face when the printer attached to the machine's computer chattered. Ignoring the towel, Mimi craned eagerly forward. "What does it say? How'd I do?"

With a smile, Kira showed the printout to Miles, who nodded in approval. "Very well, Mimi," he said, scanning the report before he looked at her. "In most cases with an injury like yours, it takes six to seven months to work up to ninety percent strength. I think that you'll be there long before that."

"How long?" Mimi asked breathlessly.

Kira took the report. "I think another month or two, don't you, Miles?"

"A month!" Mimi cried. "But I thought I was doing so well!"

"You are," Kira assured her, and quickly handed her the report. "See for yourself."

Mimi glanced at the printout and looked ready to cry. She knew how to read it; she had persuaded Kira to teach her the first time she had tried the machine. In addition to the results, the computer charted graphs of the patient's progress, and one glance told the story. To Kira and Miles, the charts showed extremely promising improvement; Mimi obviously didn't agree. Her face working, she handed the report back to Kira and reached down to unstrap the heavy leather cuff that had been attached to her ankle. Helplessly, Kira looked at Miles.

"I think it's time to have a conference in my office," he said. "Why don't you get changed and we'll meet there? Will fifteen minutes give you enough time, Mimi?"

The girl straightened. Tears glittered in her eyes, but she blinked them away. "I guess so," she muttered, and jumped down from the chair. Kira noticed that she automatically favored her injured leg, and she silently handed her the brace. She knew how disappointed Mimi was, but she also knew that it would be futile to try to comfort her now, and she and Miles watched her walk dejectedly toward the shower room before they went to his office.

"I take it things aren't going well," Miles commented, seating himself behind his desk.

Kira sat opposite him and brushed back a lock of hair. "They never do when we have a session with the

Lido," she said. "I think I'm beginning to dread that more than she does. Despite her progress, she's always so disappointed."

Miles glanced again at the printout he'd placed in front of him. "Have you explained to her what this means?"

"I've tried," Kira said with a sigh. "But every time she gets on the machine, she expects to be a hundred percent. She just won't accept anything else."

"Well, in a way, you can't blame her," Miles commented. "She's young, and it's difficult for her."

"I know, but when I tried to show her how well she's doing compared to some of our other patients, she just said that she didn't care about anybody else. *They* weren't supposed to be training for the World Cup."

Miles sat back. "I see what you mean," he said, and was silent a moment. "Do you think it would help if we asked her to get involved in the winter carnival?"

"In what capacity?" Kira asked, concerned. "She certainly can't participate in any of the skiing or the races."

"No, but I could assign her to one of the committees."

Before she could reply, Mimi arrived. When she came in and sat disconsolately beside Kira in the other chair, Miles glanced at Kira before he said, "We were just discussing the upcoming winter carnival, Mimi."

"What about it?" she asked listlessly.

Miles shot Kira another look, but she just shrugged. She had seen these quicksilver changes of mood in Mimi before, and sometimes she felt just as helpless as Miles obviously did now.

He cleared his throat. "Well, as you may or may not know, I'm the chairman of the carnival, and I wondered if you would like to help out this year."

"How?" Mimi asked bitterly. "I can't participate in any of the sports. Am I supposed to stand at the finish line and congratulate the winner?"

Without waiting for an answer, she stood up sullenly and went to the window. She had changed into jeans and a sweater, and Kira noticed that someone—obviously Hilda Trent—had added a seam to Mimi's jeans so that she could wear the knee brace underneath and it wouldn't be noticeable. Making a mental note to say something to the woman the next time she saw her, Kira said, "There are other things you could do, Mimi."

The girl turned back from the window. "Such as?"

"You could help with the treasure hunt," Miles offered.

Mimi glanced at him. "What treasure hunt?"

Sensing a glimmer of interest despite her indifferent pose, Miles explained. "Every year we hide a treasure medallion somewhere in town, and the newspaper prints daily clues until someone finds it. A committee decides where to hide the medallion and writes the clues for the paper." He paused. "Do you think you'd like to join them? It wouldn't take too much of your time."

Mimi hesitated. "I don't know," she said slowly. "I've never done anything like that before."

"Then this might be just the thing," he said cheerfully, and took out his notebook. Reaching for a pen, he said, "Shall I add your name to committee, then?"

Mimi looked from Kira's encouraging smile back to Miles. "I want to ask you something first."

He looked up curiously. "What is it?"

"Do you have any skating at this winter carnival of yours?"

"Yes, we have a hockey tournament, and of course the speed skating. Is that what you mean?"

"No, I mean figure skating. Do you have any of that—like a demonstration or something?"

Miles looked surprised. "Well, er ... no. At least we hadn't planned on anything like that."

Kira didn't care for that look in Mimi's eyes. She suddenly knew what the girl intended, and she said warningly, "Mimi ..."

Mimi pretended not to hear. "If I'm going to participate in the carnival, I think it's only fair that my therapist does, too," she said, and looked triumphantly at Kira. "I'll work on the treasure hunt, but only if Dr. Stanfield gives a skating exhibition."

Kira was not going to be trapped. "I'm sorry, Mimi," she said evenly. "But that's absolutely out of the question."

"Wait a minute," Miles said thoughtfully. "I think that's a wonderful idea. I wonder why I didn't think of it before."

Kira looked at him in horror. "You can't be serious! I haven't skated in years!"

"That's all the more reason to try, isn't it?" Mimi asked. "Besides, it'll be more like an exhibition, not a competition. You won't have to worry about being scored or anything."

Kira could have cheerfully hustled her right out of the room. "You're right about that," she said. "I won't have to worry about anything, because I'm not going to do it."

Mimi was all innocence. "But why? Aren't you the one who's always saying not to worry when you're out of training for a while because it all comes back?"

Kira had said that; she couldn't deny it. She said that to all her patients to encourage them when they were depressed. But she had never expected Mimi to use her own words as an argument against her, and she sputtered, "Yes, but that's different. I'm not in competition anymore. I haven't been for years!"

Miles entered the discussion. "As Mimi pointed out, Kira, this isn't a competition. And even you have to admit the suggestion has merit. Who better to give an ice skating demonstration than a former world champion? You'll be the star attraction of the carnival!"

Kira glared at him. She and Miles had never discussed her skating career because she had deliberately fostered the idea that she didn't want to talk about it. He had respected her wishes until now, and she was annoyed with him for breaking their unspoken agreement. Further, she was irritated with Mimi for trying to blackmail her, and she pushed back her chair and stood.

"I'm sorry," she said flatly. "It's absolutely out of the question."

She didn't give them time to say anything, but left the office and went to her own, where she collapsed into her chair. How had this happened? she wondered with her head in her hands. Even if she wanted to take Mimi up on her suggestion—which she most emphatically did not—an exhibition was out of the question. For one thing, she hadn't skated in fifteen years; for another, if she went out on the ice, it wouldn't be an exhibition, it would be a performance. She didn't care what Mimi or Miles said; she knew that's what people would expect. After all, she wasn't someone who had strapped on a pair of skates one day and took a few lessons at the local ice rink; she *had* been a world champion. People expected more of someone who had risen to such heights, even if it had been a lifetime before. She couldn't blame them; she might expect it herself.

No, she couldn't do it; she wouldn't do it. And if that meant that Mimi wouldn't participate in the carnival, either, well . . . so be it. She and Miles would just have to find some other way to handle these depressions of Mimi's.

And if they couldn't handle the situation, she decided irritably, then Yale would just have to take his daughter to another clinic. She would not be blackmailed into doing something over which she would only make a fool of herself, and that was that.

What are you afraid of?

The haunting question rose at the back of her mind, and she exclaimed in frustration. She wasn't *afraid* of anything, she told that mocking little voice, and pulled a stack of paperwork toward her.

But a picture of that final practice flashed into her mind again, and she could see, as she had thousands of times before, that little figure clad in red. She pressed her hands over her eyes, but the image refused to go away, and the sequence inexorably unfolded: the lift, the turn, the descent, the blade slipping out from under her, the awkward sprawl on the ice.

Her face white, she lifted her head from her hands. A shudder passed through her, and she realized beads of perspiration had leaped out on her forehead. It was always the same whenever she relived that accident; she had never been able to control the panic that just the thought of skating again brought on.

Her hands shaking, she reached for the folder in front of her and opened it. But she still hadn't read a line when Trudy buzzed some time later to tell her that her next appointment had arrived. Stiffly, she got up from the desk and went to greet her patient.

TRYING TO HOLD ON to his temper, Yale leaned against the rail at the Sky Rink in Manhattan, the practice arena for the New York Rangers. He'd come to New York after all, because his superstar hockey client, Roger Clary, insisted he be on hand while he filmed a commercial for a national hamburger chain. The chain was giving away a Rangers decal as part of a promotional stunt for their hamburgers, but when Yale had walked in, he was surprised to see Harvey Windemere, as well. Harvey was a client from a rival team, and as soon as Yale saw his face, he knew there was trouble. Aware of technicians and sound men and a host of others about, he pulled him aside and asked him why he was there.

Harvey ran his hand through his cropped hair. He normally wore a bridge to replace the two front teeth knocked out long ago by an errant hockey puck, but he wasn't wearing it today, and the gap was distracting. "Can you do something, Yale?" he asked. "Listen, I know I should have called you before I agreed to do this commercial, but I knew the guy, and hell—they promised me it was going to be a favored-nations deal. Now I get here and find out that it isn't."

Yale sighed. A favored-nations deal meant that all the celebrities in a commercial or doing a TV guest shot would earn the same amount of money for doing the same amount of work. The concept had been designed to sooth egos and eliminate jealousy, and normally, it worked pretty well—as long as the celebrities consulted their agents first. Harvey had obviously decided to do this on his own, and now he was sorry.

"Why didn't you call me?" Yale asked.

Harvey looked embarrassed. "Well, Jeez, I didn't think it would matter. A friend of mine asked me to do it, and I said I would if they paid me the same as Roger."

"And what was that?"

"A thousand."

Yale was always suspicious of deals made by friends, especially where athletes were concerned. Sports figures, until they had adjusted to celebrity status—and sometimes not even then—had a tendency to be too trusting and naive. Suspecting in advance what the answer was going to be, he asked, "They told you Roger was getting a thousand?"

"Well, not exactly," Harvey admitted uncomfortably. "They said I'd get the same as him."

Yale sighed. "I take it you didn't check with Roger first."

"Well, no, man. I mean, this guy was my friend. Why shouldn't I believe him?"

Why indeed, Yale thought, and didn't say the obvious.

"Can you do something, Yale? I'll pay you."

"It's not the money, Harvey," Yale said, and meant it. He honestly doubted he could change things at this point. It was obvious that the agency responsible for doing the commercial had pulled a fast one by calling Harvey through a friend and offering him the thousand. He had accepted only because he thought that's what they were paying Roger. He didn't know that the agency had then called Yale, who had made a completely separate deal for his other client for a great deal more money.

"Come on, Yale, I really feel like I got the raw end of this."

Yale was tempted to tell him that since he'd made the agreement himself he had to abide by it. But then he looked into Harvey's square, boyish face with the missing teeth and relented. Harvey's job was to play hockey; Yale's job was to protect him from things like this. "All right," he said. "I'll see what I can do."

The agency wasn't very happy, but as Yale thought to himself when he hung up the phone, he wasn't the pushover Harvey was. A new deal agreed upon, he stood by the rail and watched the confusion for a while as the director tried to get everyone into place. But after a few minutes his thoughts began to wander, and suddenly, he wasn't seeing the hockey players in their uniforms or the confusion of cameras and wires and cables; he was seeing Kira, the first time they'd met.

She'd been national champion then, or so he had found out later. At the time he had run into her—literally, he recalled with a rueful smile—he hadn't known that she was already being compared to the American greats in women's singles: Tenley Albright, Carol Heiss, Janet Lynn, Peggy Fleming. She hadn't known who he was, either, he remembered. They had both been so involved with their individual sports at the time that it was as though they had tunnel vision.

He'd been coming down the street just as she emerged from a dance studio. They were both training in Aspen, and he'd been jogging—something he used to do a lot of in those days, trying to build strength and

endurance for those bone-crushing runs on the Downhill. At the end of his workout, he hadn't been watching where he was going, and he had run right into her.
Somehow, he managed to catch his balance, but she'd
gone sprawling. Chagrined, he had reached down to
help her up, but she had brushed away his hand and
leaped to her feet unaided, glaring at him with the
greenest eyes he'd ever seen.

"Why don't you watch where you're going?" she
snapped, and bent down to massage her knee.

"Are you hurt?"

She gave him another scathing look with those incredible eyes. "No thanks to you. Who do you think
you are, anyway?"

He was taken aback that she obviously didn't know.
He'd made quite a name for himself that year, and the
press was already touting him as the first American
with a chance to win an Olympic medal. His ego
wounded, he looked at her curiously. "My name is
Yale Duncan," he said, sure that would ring a bell.

"So?" she said coldly, and reached down to pick up
the duffel bag she'd dropped. The zipper had come
partly open, and when he saw a glimpse of leotard inside, he assumed she was a dancer.

"Look, I'm sorry," he said. Then, because he didn't
want her to go, he asked, "Are you a dancer?"

"No," she said icily. "I skate."

Zipping the pack shut, she started to walk off. He
couldn't let her leave before he found out who she was,
and he had called after her, "Wait! What's your
name?"

She didn't stop. "Kira Blair," she said over her
shoulder, and added frostily, "Not that it matters to
you."

He found out later from a buddy on the team that she was more than just a skater. When he learned that she was the current national champion and America's latest hope for a gold at the Olympics, he'd been intrigued enough to sneak into one of her practice sessions to watch. He'd been interested after that awkward encounter outside the dance studio, but once he saw her on the ice, he'd fallen completely under her spell. He had never seen anyone before or since who could match her breathtaking grace and fluid motion.

"Mr. Duncan! Can you do something with your client? He's...oh, damn. Now everything is ruined!"

Yale came back to the present with a jerk. He had been too preoccupied to pay attention to what was going on in front of him, and now he saw Roger heading in one direction, Harvey in the other, and the director throwing his clipboard down in a fury. He caught Roger as he went by.

"What happened?"

Roger turned furiously on him. He wasn't a big man, but he gave that impression because he was nearly as wide as he was tall. "I'm not going to do the commercial, that's what," he snarled. "I just found out that creep is getting the same amount of money as me."

"That creep" was obviously Harvey Windemere, and Yale's jaw tightened. He knew how volatile Roger was; if he hadn't been so preoccupied, he might have seen this coming. Angry with himself, he told Roger he would take care of it, and somehow persuaded him to wait. With one hockey player seething on the sidelines and the other casting murderous looks in every direction, he finally managed to talk everyone into finishing the commercial so they could all go home. But as

Roger was leaving, he stopped by the rail where Yale had been waiting.

"I don't like to be jerked around, Yale," he warned. "I did this because my name was on the paper, but don't expect me to do it again. I'll think about it, but maybe I need a new agent."

Yale didn't trust himself to answer. By the time he got back to his hotel, he was furious—with Harvey for putting him in that position, with Roger for threatening him, and most of all with himself for letting the situation get out of hand. What was the matter with him lately? He hadn't had this much trouble with clients since he'd first started in the business, and it was all because of Kira. Seeing her again had stirred up the past he'd wanted to leave buried, and he was exasperated that the least little thing could make him think of her. Now he couldn't get her out of his mind, and what was even worse, he was starting to feel guilty about leaving Mimi to go off on business. It had never bothered him before, but Kira's accusation was like a thorn in his side. Damn it, why had she said anything? Why had he listened? Now whenever he was gone, he felt as though he had abandoned his child. It was nonsense, ridiculous; Mimi was in good hands with Hilda, and he'd never worried before.

He wasn't worried now. Feeling as though he wanted to smash something, he wandered around the elegant hotel room, wondering what to do. Running a hand through his dark hair, he glanced at the phone. Maybe he needed a distraction, he thought, and wondered if Claudette was in town. She was a model he dated occasionally when he was here, and remembering that cool, exotic beauty of hers, he impulsively dialed her number.

"Why, darling," she said, when she found out who was calling. Her voice had a breathless quality that had intrigued him before, but which for some reason he found annoying now. "I'll be delighted to have dinner with you." She paused. "Are you free all night?"

The implied invitation would have pleased him at another time, but tonight he wasn't sure how he felt about it. Remembering suddenly that Mimi and Claudette weren't exactly fond of each other, he regretted giving her a call. But it was too late to back out now, so he said, "No, I have to catch a late flight."

"Oh..." she said, obviously disappointed. "That's too bad. Dinner it is, then. Shall we meet, or will you pick me up?"

He had a limousine at his disposal, so he arranged to collect her. She was waiting when he arrived, a tall, stunning dark-haired beauty who turned heads wherever she went. Usually he was proud to have her on his arm, but as they entered her favorite restaurant, the famous Windows on the World in the World Trade Center, he caught the envious glances cast his way and wanted to hand her off to the first man he saw. Why hadn't he ever noticed how totally self-involved she was?

With Claudette pretending to study the menu while she glanced covertly around to see if anyone important was there, Yale ordered her favorite Perrier-Jouët and admired the decor. At a hundred and seven floors up, the restaurant had a spectacular wraparound view of the city, and he had always been impressed by the stone-lined, mirrored reception area. The multi-tiered main dining room had touches of brass and wood and greenery, and when the waiter, dressed in a white uniform with gold epaulets, presented the champagne, he couldn't help wondering what Kira's reaction would be if he brought her here. He could see her lips parted in that breathless way she had when she was excited; he could see those beautiful eyes of hers aglow....

" . . . what do you think, darling? Should I take the cruise assignment, or hold out for the movie deal?"

Abruptly, Yale came out of his reverie. Claudette was gazing expectantly at him, and he hadn't the faintest idea what she'd been talking about.

"Well, the movie offer would give you more exposure," he said cautiously, and thankfully didn't have to say more. She immediately launched into a detailed description of her interview with the producer, and between the "And so I saids" and the "Then he saids," Yale could feel his eyes glazing. He couldn't help but contrast Claudette's self-involved commentary with the conversation he and Kira had had at the Stonebridge Inn that night, and by the time the dessert cart was brought around, he was glad the limousine was waiting. He hadn't realized it, but while Claudette had barely taken two sips of the champagne, he'd helped himself liberally. It was the only way he could get through the evening.

"Darling," Claudette said, when the driver stopped outside her brownstone, "you've hardly said a word all night. Aren't you feeling well—" she glanced at him archly "—or is it me?"

As he looked into those heavily made-up exotic eyes of hers, at the famous cheekbones that had graced countless magazine covers, at the perfectly outlined lips and the dark hair sleeked back into an elegant chignon at the nape of her swanlike neck, he thought how beautiful she was and wondered what he had ever seen in her. Kira's face flashed into his mind just then, the wide green eyes, the brilliant smile, the straight nose and uncompromising chin, and without realizing it, he sighed. The contrast between this exotic creature and the image in his mind had never been more apparent to him, and he couldn't help thinking what a fool he'd been all those years ago.

"No, it's me," he said. "I guess I've got a lot on my mind."

She smiled that brilliantly fake smile that had been emblazoned on all those magazine covers and leaned toward him. Brushing her lips against his cheek, she said, "I understand, darling. Call me the next time you're in town?"

Promising he would, knowing he wouldn't, he saw her up to her suite, and then ordered the driver to take him back to the Plaza. The next morning, he boarded the plane to Vermont in a foul mood. It seemed that nothing had gone right this trip, and the worst part about it was that he knew he had only himself to blame.

CHAPTER SEVEN

"BUT WHY won't you skate, Dr. Stanfield?" Mimi asked Kira for the third time that morning.

Kira hid her frustration. She'd been trying to keep Mimi's mind on her therapy today, but every time she thought she had successfully diverted her from the maddening topic of the winter carnival, Mimi would stop in the middle of what they were doing and give her a wounded look. She had refused to discuss it thus far, but now she said, "I don't want to talk about it, Mimi. I gave you my answer, and that's the end of the subject."

Mimi was silent, staring sullenly down at her leg, which Kira was treating at the moment with ultrasound. "All right, but I still don't understand," she said sulkily.

"You don't have to understand," Kira replied. "Your job right now is to sit still until we finish this."

Mimi obeyed, but reluctantly. After a few seconds of tense silence, she asked, "When can I start circuit training, then?"

Kira stifled a sigh. This was almost as sensitive an area as the Winter Carnival. She and Mimi had had a discussion about circuit training after Mimi had overheard one of the other patients mention it, and she had demanded to know when she could begin the program herself. She hadn't listened to Kira's explanation that circuit training was used only when someone was nearing full recovery and all muscle systems could be placed under maximal stress. She refused to believe that she wouldn't be ready for that for quite some time.

"We talked about that before, Mimi," Kira said now, a warning that she wouldn't be pushed much further in her voice.

Mimi was in one of her moods, determined to ignore Kira's tone. "But why?" she asked petulantly. "I'm ready, I know it."

Thinking that few of Mimi's admirers in the press would recognize this sullen, peevish girl as the darling of the sports world, Kira switched off the ultrasound machine and looked sternly at her rebellious patient. "What do you really know about circuit training?" she asked.

"Well, I...I know that it's got something to do with strengthening—"

Kira decided it was time to acquaint Mimi with a few of the facts. "There's more to it than that, Mimi. We start with thirty repetitions on the isotonic knee flexion-extension machine, followed immediately by high-speed knee work on the isokinetic machine. Then we follow that by a one-minute isometric contraction of the quadriceps."

Her mouth turned down, Mimi shifted on the table. "I could do it," she muttered. "I know I could."

"Over and over again, as many times as possible without a break?"

Mimi was silent, picking at the edge of the table she was sitting on. "Well, I could try," she said sullenly, and glanced up at Kira. "There's no harm in that, is there?"

Kira sighed. Trying to be patient, she said gently, "There's no harm if you're at eighty percent, Mimi. You've seen the isokinetic printouts on your workout. You know how far you've got to go before you reach that stage."

"But I'm so tired of just sitting around!" Mimi cried. "My tutor comes over to the house every day, and when she leaves I sit and study. Nobody will let me do anything else! Every time I want to go somewhere or do something, either you or Dad or Hilda tell me I can't. I feel like a prisoner here. When are you going to trust me?"

Alarmed by the return of that underlying hysteria she had heard before, Kira said quickly, "We do trust you, Mimi. But you've got to trust us—"

"I don't want to trust you!" Mimi cried. "If I listened to all of you, I'd be an invalid the rest of my life!"

Kira was horrified. "That's not true!"

"Then why won't you let me do anything?" Mimi wailed, and before Kira could stop her, she jumped down off the table. She was too agitated to adjust for her injured leg, and when she winced upon landing, Kira reached out hastily and tried to steady her. Ignoring her helping hand, Mimi grabbed on to the table instead.

Kira bit her lip. She wanted to put her arms around the girl, but she knew that Mimi was too upset to accept her offer of comfort, so she said, "I know how you feel, Mimi."

Mimi's head snapped up. Her eyes were a stormy blue. "Do you? How?"

Taken aback, Kira said, "What do you mean, how?"

"*You* never skated after *your* injury. *You* never went back at all. Well, I'm not going to be like you, Dr. Stanfield, I am going to ski again! In fact, I'm going to go out on a few practice runs with Jack and Alison. So there!"

Kira wasn't sure she had heard right. "You're going to what?"

Mimi's chin lifted defiantly. "I said I was going to go skiing with my friends, that's what!"

For a moment, Kira didn't know what to say. Finally, her voice steely, she warned, "You'd be making a big mistake if you did that, Mimi."

The girl flushed, but she still looked defiant. "I might have known you wouldn't understand," she said bitterly. "How could you, if you gave up skating so easily? It's obvious that it didn't mean to you what skiing means to me."

"What does skiing mean to you, Mimi?" Kira asked sharply. She decided to have this out right now. Mimi had been spoiling for a fight for days, and it might do her some good to vent her frustration. "Go ahead, tell me. Just what does skiing mean to you?"

Mimi turned away from Kira's penetrating look. "You wouldn't understand," she muttered.

"Try me."

"Look, what difference does it make? Why do you even care?"

"I care because you're my patient," Kira said evenly. "I'm not going to let you ruin weeks of therapy by trying to ski before you're ready."

"A few practice runs isn't skiing! You're acting like I'm going to compete in the Downhill or something!"

"You're not going skiing at all!"

"Oh, yeah? And how are you going to stop me?"

Kira paled at the contempt in Mimi's voice. For a moment she didn't trust herself to answer, but finally she managed a taut, "I think we've worked enough today, Mimi. Perhaps it would be best if you dressed and went home."

Kira was almost at the door when Mimi cried out. "Dr. Stanfield, wait!"

Kira looked over her shoulder. As soon as she did, Mimi's face crumpled and she burst into tears. "I'm sorry," she sobbed. "I didn't mean it...."

Instantly, Kira forgave the outburst. Despite Mimi's accusation, she did know how it felt to be injured, how frustrating it was to remain idle for the necessary time it took to heal. Her expression sympathetic, she went back to Mimi and put her arms around her. "It's all right," she murmured. "I understand."

Mimi sobbed against her white coat. "I'm sorry," she wept again. "I'm never this mean and horrible, usually. I don't know what gets into me sometimes!"

"I do," Kira soothed. "You're just impatient. I know it's not easy to be prevented from doing the things you want to do. I know how anxious you are."

"It's just that it's so hard to wait!" Mimi wailed. "I sit around and keep thinking of everybody at practice, of how much I'm missing, and I get so frustrated I want to scream!"

"I know," Kira said again, and tried to be encouraging. "But you're getting stronger every day, Mimi. You're already far ahead of other patients who've had the same injury."

"I don't care about them," Mimi sobbed. "All I want to do is ski!"

Kira decided this wasn't the time to press Mimi about her reasons for wanting to ski, and on sudden inspiration, held the girl away from her. "I think you need a diversion."

Mimi wiped her eyes with the back of her hand. "What?"

"How about that sleigh ride?"

"But that's been canceled," Mimi said, and looked ready to cry again. The sleigh ride she'd heard about when she first came to Stonebridge had been postponed because Elmer Tomlinson, who owned the sleigh, was also the town's only carpenter. Miles had commandeered Elmer's services to build the speaker's platform for the carnival. He'd been working on it ever since, and along with the others, Kira had endured the banging and pounding outside for days now. Following tradition, the rostrum was being constructed near the pond. Sure she could persuade Miles to release Elmer from duty one night, she smiled at Mimi.

"If I could talk Elmer into bringing the sleigh around, would you go?" she asked.

Mimi's face brightened. "Do you mean it?"

"Of course I do. I think we all need a break, don't you? We'll invite Miles and Betsy and Noreen and all the patients who want to come, and maybe we could have an old-fashioned marshmallow roast before we come home again. What do you think?"

Mimi smiled for the first time that morning. "I think it'd be great. Could we have s'mores, and everything?"

Kira hadn't thought of the marshmallow and chocolate-filled graham cracker treats in years. Wincing at the thought of what nutritionists would say, she laughed. "If you like."

"All right!" Mimi exclaimed, and gave her a hug. "Dr. Stanfield, you're the best!"

Kira smiled. "You're not so bad yourself. And while we're at it, why don't you call me Kira? I think we know each other well enough by now, don't you?"

Suddenly shy, Mimi nodded. "I'd like that."

"So would I," Kira said, and gave her a gentle push. "Do you want to call your friends and tell them, or should I?"

"I'll do it," Mimi said enthusiastically, and paused at the door. "Kira . . . is it all right if I invite my dad?"

Kira hesitated for the barest instant. "Oh, is Yale home?" she said, as casually as she could. "I thought he was away on business."

"He was, but he came home the other night," Mimi said, and rolled her eyes. "And boy, has he been in a bad mood since!"

He's not the only one, Kira thought. "Then maybe you shouldn't bother him with a sleigh ride. He probably has other things on his mind."

"Oh, no," Mimi said earnestly. "I think it would do him good." She hesitated. "But if you don't want him to come . . ."

Somehow, Kira forced a smile. "Nonsense. The more the merrier."

Grinning, Mimi opened the door. "Thanks, Kira," she said softly, and sped away.

As soon as she was gone, Kira slumped against the therapy table. She hadn't anticipated Yale being in town, and now she regretted her impulsive suggestion. She had resolved after what had happened the last time they had seen each other that she would do her best to avoid him, and now she felt trapped.

Maybe he won't be able to come, she thought hopefully, and recognized the irony with a grimace. She had resented the time Yale was away from home on business because of Mimi, but now all she could think of was that he wouldn't be in town the night of the sleigh ride. Shaking her head, she went in search of Miles to tell him what she had proposed.

"I think that's a wonderful idea!" Miles exclaimed when she explained. "Did you say that you had promised Mimi a marshmallow roast? Maybe I can go on ahead that night and get the fire ready. I used to be a Boy Scout, you know."

Kira looked dubious. "Are you sure you remember how to start a campfire?"

"Of course I'm sure," he said indignantly, and gave her a broad smile. "Don't you rub two rocks together, or something?"

"Or something," Kira said dryly. "Maybe I'd better ride ahead with you and help."

"Nonsense. You just get together with Elmer and decide on the night, and I'll be there. If you're lucky, I might even bring some chocolate bars and graham crackers, and we'll have a real feast."

Kira was amused. "Oh, so you know about those, too."

"Doesn't everybody?" he asked, and waved her out of his office so he could get some work done.

It didn't take long for Kira to make the arrangements. Elmer was enthusiastic about the venture when she approached him, but when she told him that Trudy already had a list of about fifteen youngsters who might come, he decided the hay wagon would be better than the sleigh.

"Just as long as you got someone to help you chaperone," he drawled with a wink. "I'm not so old as I don't recollect those hay rides on cold nights me-self."

"Come to think of it, I remember something like that, too," Kira answered with a laugh.

"I'll have Ben and Dave and the wagon out front of the clinic at seven that night," Elmer said, and shook an admonitory finger playfully at her. "But remember, I ain't gonna be responsible for no shenanigans."

"Don't worry about that," she assured him. "Miles and I will be keeping an eagle eye out."

But in the end, it wasn't Miles who arrived to help her chaperone the eager group of teenagers that night, it was Yale. When she saw him pull up in the car with Mimi at his side, she tried to tell herself there was no reason to feel tense. After all, she had known he was coming. But for some reason, the knowledge didn't help, and when he got out of the car wearing a thick parka and heavy boots and carrying an armload of stadium blankets, the last hope she'd had that he wouldn't come with them vanished. Without realizing it, she muttered under her breath, and Noreen, who was standing nearby, glanced at her. "What did you say?"

Embarrassed that she'd been overheard, Kira improvised quickly, "I was just hoping Miles remembered to take the cider and the hot chocolate with him."

"He did," Noreen assured her with a grin. Her face under the streetlights was happy and rosy, her eyes sparkling with the excitement that everyone, no matter what their age, somehow seems to feel at the prospect of a hay ride. "In fact, he was so loaded down with goodies I'm surprised he had room for himself in the car."

Yale was helping Mimi cross the street now, and Kira had to jerk her eyes away from the sight. Smiling at

Noreen, she said, "I guess this little sleigh ride of ours got out of hand."

The other therapist glanced amusedly at the milling teenagers, some clustered around the wagon, some already engaged in snowball fights. All of them were shouting at the top of their lungs from excitement, and she leaned closer to Kira and said, "Yes, but it's going to be fun, don't you think?"

Kira had thought so when she impulsively conceived the idea, but now she wasn't sure. Before she had a chance to reply, Mimi came rushing up to her and excitedly grabbed her arm. "Boy, this is great! I'm sorry we're late, but I couldn't get Dad out of the house. We brought some extra blankets, is that okay?"

"Sure, that's —" Kira started to say, but Mimi had already gone off, instantly surrounded by the jostling teenage crowd, the center of attention wherever she went. There was nothing Kira could do but turn reluctantly to face Yale.

His eyes were sparkling like everyone else's, but whether from the cold or because he was secretly amused at something, she couldn't tell. "Hello, Yale," she said cautiously. "It was nice of you to bring the blankets."

"I thought we might need them," he said easily, and glanced toward the big wagon.

It was a flat-bedded, three-sided affair, and Elmer had half filled it with piles of loose hay. Kira had learned earlier that the big horses, Ben and Dave, were Belgian draft horses, and she had received a lecture from their proud owner that Belgians were the widest, deepest, most compact and most massive of any of the draft breed. A quick look at these two representatives confirmed that, Kira thought, for her head barely reached the top of their broad backs. They looked strong enough to pull this big wagon with ease, and she'd been relieved when Elmer had gone on to say that Belgians were also extremely docile and patient. She believed it now, for both horses simply stood there, shifting from foot to massive foot, while curious teenagers swarmed around them. The animals' breath spewed out in great plumes from their nostrils, and every movement they made jingled the bells Elmer had affixed to their harness. The cheerful sound rang out in the cold night, mingling with the joyous shouts of the youngsters, and as Kira glanced up at the scattered snowflakes falling from a black sky still resplendent with glittering stars, she had to smile. It was a perfect night for a hay ride.

Elmer seemed to agree, for just then he climbed up onto the wagon seat. Cupping his hands around his mouth, he shouted, "All right, ever'body in. Let's get this show on the road!"

Yale glanced at Kira. "You sure you want to do this?" he asked, indicating the wagon with a jerk of his head.

Kira's expression was wry as she saw the rowdy group of teenagers elbowing and pushing and maneuvering to be first to climb into the hay. She looked heavenward again, but this time for strength. "As ready as I'll ever be," she said, and suddenly felt herself lifted into the air and deposited on the wagon bed. As she glanced back in surprise, she met Yale's laughing eyes and couldn't be upset with him. This wasn't a night to air their differences, and on impulse, she held out a hand to him, grinning when she saw *his* surprise.

"I thought we'd try it again," she said.

"What?"

"That truce we talked about the other night."

"Think we can manage it this time?"

"We can try."

He smiled the smile that had always been able to make her feel weak, and still did. It was an effort, but she kept her hand out, and after a moment, he grasped her fingers. Vaulting easily up to the wagon bed, he looked around at the teenagers, poking and prodding at each other amid squeals from the girls and loud laughter from the boys, and murmured, "I think we'll be safer in front, don't you?"

Kira wasn't sure at the moment if she would be safe anywhere with him. He hadn't released her hand, and even through her glove she could feel the warmth of his fingers. Embarrassed by the answering tingle of her body, she simply nodded, grabbed a blanket and started to climb over the bodies sprawled on the hay.

She was trying her best to ignore the knowing smiles and sly laughter she heard from the group when Yale spoke up. She stopped to listen. "All right, you guys," he said solemnly as he stood in the center of the wagon. "I know you're going to find this hard to believe, but I was young once myself. You're not going to get away with anything I haven't already tried, and Dr. Stanfield and I are going to make sure of that. You got the message?"

There was an answering chorus of mock groans and catcalls and good-natured ribbing, and Kira had to smile. She was just starting forward again when Elmer whistled to the horses and the wagon lurched ahead. She wasn't expecting the sudden movement, and she exclaimed as she lost her balance. Yale was right behind her, and as his strong hands came around her waist to steady her, she felt such a jolt at the contact that she stiffened. It was a moment before she could turn her head to look at him, and when she did, she was surprised to see the startlement in his eyes.

"Thanks," she managed. Her voice was breathless, the word almost a gasp. She was still shaken by that instant response to such a simple contact, and she didn't even feel the wagon moving under her as the horses settled into a steady walk. Neither noticed that Elmer guided the animals off the road and down a country lane that looked as though it had come off a postcard; they were too caught up in this unexpected moment.

Yale's eyes appeared almost black in the night, and his expression was one she couldn't interpret. They gazed at each other, caught in that breathless time, until the wagon went over a bump. She hadn't realized that Yale was still holding on to her until, from somewhere in the wagon, a young voice said dryly, "Yeah, we got that, Mr. Duncan, but do you?"

There was an answering laugh, and Kira was so embarrassed that she jerked away from his grasp. Bending down, she quickly retrieved the blanket she had dropped and hastily climbed over the sprawled bodies until she reached the front of the wagon. Mortified, she slid down against the backboard into the hay, resisting the urge to cover her face. After a moment, she felt someone sit beside her, and knew it was Yale even before she heard his rueful laugh.

"Well, I guess we showed them, didn't we?"

She looked over, right into his eyes. She could have played it either way at that point, and decided to ignore the alarm bells shrilling at the back of her mind. With Yale looking at her like that, his face ruddy from the cold, his eyes sparkling, his smile alone enough to banish the chill, she ignored the clamoring danger signals and laughed softly, too. *One night won't hurt,* she told herself, and said, "Yes, I guess we did."

She didn't object when Yale's hand sought hers under the blanket, and as she glanced at him again, her breath caught. There was no mistaking the look in his eyes, and as his hand left hers and went around her shoulders, drawing her close, she was powerless to resist. Slowly, ever so slowly, his head dipped to hers. It seemed forever before their lips touched, but when she felt that light-as-a-feather contact, the sensation was so exquisite that she forgot everything else. The joking and jostling and jockeying of the teenagers around them in the wagon faded into silence as the pressure of his mouth increased on hers, and as she gave herself up to the bliss of being kissed by Yale again, the thought flashed through her mind that nothing had changed, after all. He still had the power to ignite her instant response, and it was all she could do not to cling to him and demand more. Some last shred of sense reared its ugly head just as she was about to drown in the tumult of emotions Yale had aroused in her, and even though it took every ounce of will she had, she managed to pull back. Gasping, she looked away from him.

"Kira..."

"Don't say it," she muttered thickly. She still couldn't look at him; she was afraid of what she might do if she did. Every sense she possessed seemed aware of Yale: her nostrils were filled with his scent, she could taste him on her lips. Her body throbbed with unfulfilled desire for him, and so strong was her longing that she crushed a handful of straw in her hand.

In an effort to distract herself, she took a deep breath and looked around. The kids had settled into groups, and Mimi caught her eye. She was sitting slightly apart from the rest of the crowd, deep in conversation with a good-looking boy. Achingly aware that Yale was watching her, Kira gestured with a movement of her head. Striving to resume some degree of normalcy, she said lightly, "It looks like Mimi is having a good time, don't you think? Isn't that Tad McAlister she's with?"

She knew very well it was Tad; the sixteen-year-old high school basketball all-star had been coming to the clinic for an elbow injury, and though he was Betsy's patient, she had checked on his progress herself several times. She had introduced him to Mimi some time ago, and knew Tad had been instantly smitten.

Yale sensed her unease. Taking the cue, he glanced at his daughter and said, "Yes, that's Tad. Or at least I think it is. It seems there's always a boy or two underfoot at the house these days. Mimi has a way of attracting attention."

As though she sensed them talking about her, Mimi looked up just then. She grinned and mugged and winked at them before returning to her conversation with Tad, and Kira smiled despite herself. That tense moment with Yale had passed. "Mimi has a way, all right. Tad looks a little in awe, if you ask me."

It was a few seconds before Yale answered. "I know how he feels," he said finally. "I used to feel the same way about you."

Used to feel? The words stabbed like a knife, and Kira stiffened. It seemed clear now that Yale's kiss had been an impulse, a gesture brought on by the laughter and the bells and the starry night. It hadn't meant anything at all to him, and she felt mortified that she had wanted it to mean so much more than it had.

Somehow, she forced a laugh. "I used to feel the same way about you, too," she said lightly. "But we were so young then, what did we know?"

She was so tense she barely felt his withdrawal. "Yes," he said in a strange voice. "We were so...young."

She didn't have a chance to reply, for just then Elmer called to the horses, and the wagon rocked to a halt. Miles was waiting in the clearing, tending a huge bonfire, and he called out cheerfully at their arrival, one hand holding a charred marshmallow on a stick, the other clutching a chocolate bar. Kira was so relieved to see him that she jumped down and gave him a hug. He smiled back at her, pleased despite himself, and joked, "I don't care what you do, you're not going to steal my marshmallow. I've worked hard to get it to just the right degree of doneness."

Because she was so unnerved, she laughed more shrilly than she intended, pretending the sight of the blackened lump at the end of the stick was the most amusing thing she had ever seen, trying at the same time not to notice Yale staring at her from across the fire. When she finally mustered the courage to look directly at him, he had already moved away, and she couldn't prevent herself from following him longingly with her eyes. Miles seemed not to notice her tension. Munching contentedly on his chocolate bar, he said, "So how was the ride? Did you have any problems?"

Kira forced a smile as she turned to him. "None at all. But I think it's only fair if I take the car and you ride back on the wagon."

"Not on your life," he said with a shudder. "These old bones are too fragile to be bounced around on a hay ride."

She had to laugh. "You just say that because you don't want to chaperone all these inexhaustible kids."

"You're right," he said with a wink. "Besides, I think you and Yale are doing a splendid job. I wouldn't dream of breaking up the team at this point."

Without realizing how his worlds stabbed through her, he winked again and went to talk to Yale, who was standing by the fire, surrounded by Mimi and some of her friends. They were asking him about his skiing exploits, and because the last thing Kira wanted to be reminded of was that time in their lives, she went to relieve Noreen with the hot chocolate.

"No, you go ahead," Noreen protested, when Kira said she'd take over. "I'm fine here."

"Nonsense. You look like you're frozen. Why don't you go over by the fire?"

The therapist cast a longing look in that direction, and when Kira glanced up and realized that Noreen wasn't looking at the bonfire, but at Yale, she was surprised at the sharp stab of jealousy she felt. Humiliated that she could react that way even now, she hurriedly poured a cup of hot chocolate to take to Elmer.

"You okay, Dr. Stanfield?" Elmer asked, after he'd taken an appreciative sip of the liquid.

Kira stood beside him at the wagon, absently stroking one of the horses. The big animal radiated heat, and she was tempted to lean against him. She felt cold from the inside out, but she knew that it wasn't because of the night chill. Resolutely keeping her eyes away from the happy group around the bonfire, she gave the horse a final pat. "Of course. Why do you ask?"

He was silent a moment, puffing on his pipe. The cherry-scented tobacco smoke drifted to her nostrils, a pleasant odor that mingled with the wood smoke from the fire. "Oh . . . you just seem a little off stride, that's all," he said finally.

She looked away. "No, I'm just tired, I guess."

"Well, you can sleep on the way back."

But she didn't sleep on the way back. By the time they had doused the bonfire and collected everything they'd brought, she was keyed up again. She couldn't face the thought of being with Yale in the wagon, so on impulse she asked Elmer if she could sit up front with him. If he was surprised, he didn't show it.

"Sure," he said, and gave her a hand up. She was so busy tucking the rug he handed her over her legs that she didn't see Yale standing by the side of the wagon, a look of pain on his face as he watched her.

"Come on, Dad!" Mimi called just then from the bed of the wagon. "We're going to sing the ant song on the way back, and we want you to start."

The last thing Yale felt like doing was singing, but he couldn't disappoint his daughter, so he climbed in and sat beside her. Tad was looking at her adoringly from the other side, and under other circumstances, Yale would have smiled at the sight of his love-struck expression. He didn't feel like smiling tonight, not after what had happened. He remembered too clearly now how it felt to be love-struck himself.

His glance strayed to Kira again, her back to him as she sat on the wagon seat. Sighing, he knew he never should have kissed her, and was angry with himself. He should have known it would ruin everything between them, but damn it—he hadn't been able to stop himself. Just sitting next to her had set his blood to racing, and it didn't have anything to do with memories of the past. In all these years, he hadn't allowed himself to think of the woman she might have become; because of that she had remained a girl in his mind. Now he realized she was no girl, and he was not that lovestruck twenty-year-old any longer. What he felt for Kira now was what a man felt for a woman, and yet for all the good it was going to do him, he might as well be in Tad's shoes. It was painfully obvious from what Kira had said that she regarded what had happened between them all those years ago as a youthful romance; she wasn't interested in trying to recapture the past.

Was he?

He still wasn't sure what the answer was when Mimi nudged him. He came out of his reverie to realize that his impatient daughter had started the song without him, and that they were into the fourth verse. Wincing, he wondered how he could have been so oblivious; everyone seemed to be singing at the top of his lungs.

Except Kira, he thought, his eyes straying to her again. Like him, she was silent while the nonsense song rang out around them, coloring the night.

"The ants go marching four by four, hurrah...hurrah. The ants go marching four by four, hurrah...hurrah...."

Mimi poked him with her elbow again. "It's your turn, Dad," she hissed.

Yale's mind was a complete blank. "You take it, honey."

Mimi rolled her eyes, but she picked up the tune, her strong young voice ringing out with laughter into the night.

"The ants go marching four by four, THE LITTLE ONE STOPS TO SLAM THE DOOR, and they all go marching down . . . to the earth . . . to get out . . . of the rain, boom, boom, boom . . ."

Yale glanced at Kira once more. His heart heavy, he thought somehow the verse seemed symbolic.

CHAPTER EIGHT

"KIRA," MILES SAID, at the end of one of their early-morning conferences, "I hate to bring up the subject, but I really do need to know if you plan to skate at the winter carnival."

Kira nearly choked on the bite of croissant she had just taken. Miles jumped up to clap her on the back, but she waved him away and grabbed her coffee instead. Swallowing hard, she sat back with a gasp. "What did you say?"

He looked taken aback. "If I'd known it was going to cause that reaction, I wouldn't have asked."

Now that she'd caught her breath, she pushed the plate away. She'd lost her appetite again—or maybe she just hadn't found it after the hay ride last week. She'd been depressed ever since that night, and she knew why. After Yale had made that comment, nothing had been the same, not even that breathless moment when they kissed. Oh, she'd been over it again and again in her mind, but no matter how she tried to put it together, there was only one conclusion. Like a fool, she had allowed the past to take hold of her, and now she was paying for it. Returning to reality was a painful process, and as ridiculous as it was, she hadn't eaten or slept properly since. She knew she looked a wreck.

And now Miles wanted to know if she planned to give a skating exhibition at the winter carnival. If she hadn't been so afraid that she might burst into tears, she would have laughed at the thought. That's all she needed. She already made a fool of herself with Yale; now Miles wanted her to to the same thing in front of the entire town.

"I can't imagine why you did ask," she said. "I thought we had decided that."

"Well, not really. I mean, we never did discuss it."

"There's nothing to discuss!"

"Now, don't get excited—"

"I'm not excited!" she said sharply. She hated being told that. It was almost as bad as someone telling her to calm down. "I'm not excited," she repeated, more calmly. "I just don't understand why we're talking about this again. I thought I made my feelings perfectly clear when Mimi suggested the idea."

Miles held up a hand in surrender. "All right. I just thought I'd ask. There's no harm in that, is there? After all, we never have talked about your skating career...."

"No," she said evenly. "We haven't."

He got the message. Glancing down at his plate with the chocolate-covered doughnut on it, he grimaced and put it on the desk. It was obvious that he'd lost his appetite, too, and when Kira saw how unhappy he looked, she relented.

"Look, Miles," she said gently. "I'll be glad to do anything else to help with the carnival, you know that. But I just don't want to skate."

Obviously still embarrassed, he quickly gathered the things he'd brought in with him and stood. "I understand," he said, and gestured vaguely, anxious to leave. "Well, I guess I can't procrastinate any longer—if I don't fill out those equipment vouchers, we're not going to have anything to work with. I'll see you later, all right?''

She nodded, but her expression was as unhappy as his. As soon as the door closed behind him, she sprang up, too restless to sit. She wished Mimi had never brought up the subject of her skating. Now her refusal was making things awkward between her and Miles, and they'd always had such a good working relationship. Why did things have to get so complicated?

Muttering to herself, she went to the window. As always when she stood here, her eyes automatically went to the house Yale had rented, and as much as she despised herself, she couldn't help wondering if he had come home today. Mimi had mentioned that he'd gone to Houston on business, and she tried to convince herself that she was glad. After making a fool of herself last week, she hoped to avoid him from now on while he was here.

Sighing, she leaned against the windowsill and absently traced a pattern on the frosty glass with a finger. She couldn't avoid him; she had to talk to him about Mimi. The hay ride had smoothed things over for a while, but now that the excitement was over, Mimi had reverted again to the sullen, difficult patient she'd been right before Kira suggested the outing. She didn't really believe Mimi would keep her defiant threat to go skiing with her friends, but she couldn't completely dismiss the possibility. The girl seemed so frustrated and restless; sometimes Kira wasn't sure what she would do.

Frowning, she knew that meant she had to talk to Yale. She and Miles had discussed it this morning before the unfortunate remark about her skating in the winter carnival, and Miles had been as alarmed as she had been.

"I think Yale should be told about this as soon as possible, Kira," Miles had said when she told him about that conversation with Mimi. "I don't even want to think about what she could do to herself if she tried to ski before she was ready."

"I agree," Kira had said. "Especially since we both know that if she gets near a ski run, it won't be the bunny slopes."

He nodded, his face creased with concern. "I'm afraid we don't have that much influence over her. You'd better talk to Yale."

"Me!" She looked at him in dismay. "But I thought you'd talk to him!"

He seemed surprised. "But you're her therapist."

"Yes, but—" She stopped, unable to finish the protest because she knew he was right. Shuffling the papers on her desk, she avoided his eyes. "All right," she had muttered finally. "I'll talk to him. Assuming—" she had added tersely "—that he's ever home long enough for me to make an appointment."

Turning away from the window now, she glanced at the phone. Maybe she should get it over with. Before she could change her mind, she reached for the receiver and dialed Yale's number.

"Duncan residence."

"Mrs. Trent?" she said, recognizing the housekeeper's voice. "This is Kira Stanfield, from the clinic. I'd like to talk to Ya—to Mr. Duncan, if he's available."

"I'm sorry, Dr. Stanfield, but Mr. Duncan is away on business," Hilda said, as Kira's grip tightened on the phone. "Is there a message, or shall I have him call you when he returns?"

It was an effort, but Kira held on to her impatience. It wasn't the housekeeper's fault that Yale was never home, she reminded herself irritably, and was further annoyed that she couldn't talk to him after she had geared herself up to do it. "I would like to talk to him as soon as possible," she said.

It was the wrong thing to say. Instantly, Hilda became concerned. "Is something the matter with Mimi?"

Kira heard the anxiety in her voice and quickly reassured her. "No, no, please don't be alarmed. I just...I just wanted to give him a progress report so that we can decide where to go from here," she said, and told herself it wasn't exactly a lie. "Can you tell me when he'll be back?"

Sounding relieved, Hilda said, "Yes, he should be back tomorrow, Dr. Stanfield. I'll tell him to give you a call the instant he comes in."

Kira thanked her and returned to her desk, not sure whether she was relieved or not. Now she had until tomorrow to decide what she was going to say to Yale, how she would act, and from the way her heart was pounding, it was obvious that she needed to prepare herself before she saw him, even if all she wanted to do was discuss Mimi.

Was that really all she wanted to discuss?

Disturbed at the idea, she was just checking her calendar when someone knocked. Relieved not to be alone with her thoughts, she smiled when Betsy, one of the other therapists, poked her head around the door. "Got a minute?"

"Sure. What's the problem?"

Betsy came and sat down. In contrast to Noreen, who was tall and thin and dark, Betsy was round and blond, with big blue eyes and an ever-present smile. She looked as though she had come right off a farm—and had, in Ohio. Her sturdy arms and strong hands were perfect for massages, and she often joked that living on a dairy farm had prepared her for the work she did now. Unfailingly cheerful, she smiled at Kira across the desk.

"No problem," she said, and added with a grin, "unless you want to count Rodney Geiger, who *won't* come in for his massage at the time he's scheduled."

Kira grinned back. Betsy always had been able to make her feel better, if just by her cheerful presence. "I can't say as I blame him," she said, remembering the massage Betsy had given her once for a stiff neck. The therapist's strong fingers worked magic, but the process could be a painful one, and Betsy, despite her winning smile, was merciless when she was working. "Do you want me to give him a call?"

"No, I can manage him," Betsy said. "I just came in to ask you if the rumor was true."

Kira sat back. "What rumor?"

"About you giving a skating exhibition during winter carnival."

Kira bolted upright again. "What! Who told you that?"

Betsy looked disappointed. "Then it's not true?"

"No! Where did you hear such a thing?"

Startled by Kira's tone, Betsy said, "I don't know...around, I guess. I told you it was just a rumor."

"And it's going to stay that way," Kira said firmly. "I've no intention of skating at the carnival, and that's that."

"Hey, don't bite my head off, I just asked," Betsy said, and hesitated. But then, because they had become friends, she added, "You can't blame people for asking, Kira. After all, you were a world-class skater."

Kira didn't want to discuss it. "That was a long time ago."

Betsy got the hint and stood. She went to the door, but she paused there and glanced back. "No offense, okay?"

Already regretting her abrupt tone, Kira sighed and said, "None taken. I'm sorry, Betsy. It's just a...a sore subject, all right?"

Betsy studied her a moment longer, then she nodded. "All right. I understand—I guess. And if anyone asks, I'll set the record straight."

"Thanks, I'll owe you one."

"In that case, maybe you can take Elaine Myers when she comes in," Betsy said with another grin. Elaine was twelve years old, the current Junior National Gymnastics champion. She would have been a sweet kid if she'd ever let anyone forget her achievements.

"You drive a hard bargain," Kira said with a mock frown.

"Hey, you offered," Betsy said blithely, and shut the door before the smiling Kira could protest.

Kira wasn't smiling by the time she left the office that night. The day had started out badly with Miles and had gone downhill after that, and she was tired and out of sorts. She was halfway home before she remembered that she was out of cat food, and she knew Purr would never forgive her if she arrived empty-handed, so with a sigh, she made a detour and stopped at Stonebridge's market. Because the townspeople did most of their shopping in nearby Manchester, the prices were outrageous, but it was close and convenient tonight, and besides, she loved the small-town ambience of the little grocery. There was even a pot-bellied stove in the corner, and the floors were of shining black-and-white ceramic tile. Most of the shelves were made out of wood, and she'd been fascinated when she first shopped there to see the genuine pickle barrel. It was like stepping back in time, and the store's owner, Roscoe Hepplewhite, confirmed the impression with his round, wire-rimmed glasses and white apron.

"Good evening, Dr. Stanfield," he said with genuine pleasure as she pushed open the door. A little bell chimed melodiously above the sash as she did, announcing her arrival. "What can I do for you?"

"Just cat food, Mr. Hepplewhite," she said, returning his smile. She had asked him to call her Kira, but he persisted on using her title, and she had finally given up the attempt to be less formal. Returning with several cans for Purr, she set them on the counter. "It's cold out tonight, don't you think?"

"I do believe we're in for another cold snap," he agreed. "But that's all the better for the winter carnival. We can't have those ice sculptures melting before they're judged, can we?"

Kira glanced at the frosted windows of the little store. They were rimmed with ice even though the stove radiated heat. "I don't think there's much chance of that," she said wryly.

He chuckled comfortably and began to ring up her purchases on the old-fashioned cash register. "Are you going to skate at the carnival?" he asked.

She looked at him in dismay. "Not you, too!" she exclaimed, before she thought. "Where did you hear that?"

He glanced curiously at her over the top of the register. "Why, I don't believe I *heard* it anywhere," he said slowly. "I suppose I just assumed..." His voice trailed away, and he looked as embarrassed as she felt. "I'm sorry," he said, swallowing so hard that his Adam's apple bobbed up and down in his thin neck. "I didn't mean... It's just that I used to watch you on the television. You were so beautiful on the ice, so breathtaking—"

He stopped abruptly, color flooding his pale face up to his balding pate. "That'll be three dollars and thirty cents, Dr. Stanfield," he said, and bent to get a sack from under the counter.

Kira was uncomfortable, too. She tried to think of something to say to relieve the awkwardness of the situation, but her mind was a complete blank. It was inevitably the same: she was always embarrassed when someone remembered her and spoke of it, because she had always felt so guilty that she had let so many people down. It was bad enough to have gone so far and not been able to complete the final program, but the fact that she had never returned to skating afterward weighed on her. Now she didn't know what to say to the store owner, and because she was so unnerved, she quickly counted out the change, thanked him, and grabbed the sack. At this point, she thought it might be better for both of them if she just left.

But she could feel his curious eyes on her as she hurried out of the store, and her cheeks burned all the way home. Because she was uncomfortable, she became angrily defensive. Was it a conspiracy? she wondered. It seemed that everyone she'd talked to today had mentioned something about her skating during the Carnival. Maybe she should wear a sign around her neck, she told herself as she ran up the cottage's front steps. Would NO, I AM NOT GOING TO SKATE do it? Fitting the key into the lock, she opened the door, and then slammed it behind her. Leaning against it, she clutched the sack tightly in her arms and realized with horror that she was near tears.

Blinking rapidly, she switched on the living room lights and went into the kitchen. She wouldn't cry, she told herself fiercely, because there was nothing to cry about. Setting the sack on the counter, she began removing the cans of cat food from it, but after a few, her hand slowed, and then stopped. Without volition, her glance went to the pond beyond her kitchen window.

The moon had come up, and as the moonlight touched the frozen surface, it became a magical sight. The banks were puffed with snowdrifts, the tall pines stood sentinel, and over all was that soft silver light. The ice glittered, the crystals glinting like thousands of tiny stars.

An owl swooped over the ice as she watched, as white as the snow, wings silent in the night. As it disappeared into the trees, she knew that if she could stop being so emotional about the subject, she might realize that the interest expressed in her skating was normal. After all, she had won the national title three times and the World title twice; it was natural for the townspeople to want her to skate, natural for them to assume that she would. She was a champion, and champions loved to perform. It was their reward for all the long hours of practice, the sacrifice, the hard work.

Purr jumped up on the counter with a soft meow just then, and began rubbing against her arm, looking for his dinner. Absently, she opened a can and fed him, but her thoughts were far away as she looked out the window again. She hadn't meant to relive it, but now that she thought of it, she remembered back to the time she had loved to perform.

Dreamily, she leaned against the counter. Nothing could compare to the applause of the crowd at the conclusion of a successful program, she thought. It was a heady feeling, because it meant that she had somehow touched her audience, given them something that only she could give. Oh, she had felt that way so many times.

Her smile faded. It hadn't lasted, that feeling, for after winning those National and World titles, it was time for the Olympics and the pressure was on. She had loved skating from the time she laced up her first pair at age five, but suddenly it wasn't fun anymore. The hours and hours of practice ceased to be pleasurable and became drudgery instead, and yet she couldn't tell anyone how she felt because so many people were depending on her. Her skating had dominated her family for as long as she could remember. Parties and celebrations and occasions were planned around what competition she might enter and where she would compete next, and after her mother and father and sister had sacrificed so many years, she couldn't suddenly say she didn't want to compete anymore because it had stopped being fun. She'd felt so ungrateful because she knew of so many others who had been forced to struggle, who hadn't been blessed with the advantages she'd had, who hadn't been born to parents who could afford the expensive lessons and the travel and the costumes and everything else that went with creating an Olympic champion.

Like Yale, for instance, she thought suddenly, and cringed. She hadn't meant to think of Yale, but now that she had, the hurtful words they'd hurled at each other during that last terrible argument rose in her mind, and she closed her eyes.

"You can't just give up!" he'd shouted at her, when he found out she wasn't going to skate her final performance. He'd just won his silver in the Downhill, and he should have been on top of the world. But that's what the quarrel had been about, too. "You've come too far!"

She'd already felt so guilty at letting so many people down, so embarrassed and humiliated and angry at the situation—and at Yale—that she hardly knew what she was saying. "I'm not giving up!" she'd shouted back. "But how can I skate when my ankle won't even hold me?"

"How do you know it won't?" he yelled. "Have you tried?"

Furiously, she gestured toward the thick bandage. "And just how do you think I'm going to do that?"

He wouldn't let her off so easily. "You'd find a way if you wanted to, if it meant something to you!"

"How dare you say that to me! You know how hard I've practiced, how much I've sacrificed . . ."

He'd laughed derisively. "And how much is that, Kira?" he asked with scorn. "No, you'd get out there and try your damnedest if you'd ever had to worry

about money, or how you were going to afford training, or who's going to finance your next trip, believe
me! You wouldn't let something stupid like this stop
you, not after you'd come all this way!''

"You don't understand!''

"No? I understand that you're a spoiled little brat
who's never had to work hard for what she gets. If you
had, you'd never give up so easily. You'd compete tomorrow, or die trying, like the rest of us would who
haven't been so lucky!''

"Like you, I suppose!'' she flung at him bitterly.

"Yes, like me!'' he'd shouted, too swept up to watch
what he was saying. "How do you think I get the
money to ski? Do you think my old man foots the bill?
Hell, my mother's too busy trying to keep him from
drinking the rent money every month!''

She remembered now how, even in her anger, she'd
been appalled at his admission. She and Yale had never
talked about finances; she had always just assumed
that his parents paid for everything as hers did. Then
she was furious, too angry to believe him. "You're just
saying that!'' she'd cried. "If you didn't get any help
you couldn't even be on the circuit!''

"Oh, I had help!'' he'd flung at her. "I went out and
got it! Why do you think I use the brand of skis I do,
why do you think I wear those particular boots? Do
you think it's all an accident? No—the manufacturer
is paying me! I wear their equipment, and they finance my skiing. It's as simple as that!''

She couldn't have been more shocked if he'd said
he'd robbed a bank. "You're getting money under the
table? But Yale, that's against the rules!''

She could tell by his expression that he realized he'd
gone too far, but that it was too late to back out now.

His handsome face reddening, he spat, "Don't tell me about rules! Rules are for innocents like you, who have daddies with open checkbooks!"

She felt as though he'd slapped her. "But there must have been another way!"

"There was no other way, not if I wanted to ski!" His expression became even more bitterly angry. "And I'll tell you something else," he sneered. "That silver medal you're so proud of? Well, I would have gotten a hell of a lot more money if it had been the gold!"

She looked at him in horror. "What...what are you saying?" she whispered. She'd heard of other athletes, from other countries, being rewarded for top honors and gold medals, but to hear it coming from Yale...

"You know damned well what I'm saying!" he shouted, and told her about the company who would have rewarded him with a fat endorsement contract if he'd crossed the finish line first instead of second. If he'd been just one hundredth of a second faster, he wouldn't ever have had to worry about training fees again. "The World Cup would have been a cinch," he finished angrily, "but now if I want to continue, I'll have to turn pro."

She couldn't believe this was happening, that Yale of all people, whom she trusted and loved and admired more than practically anyone in the world, could have done something like this. In one instant all her respect for him vanished, along with her dreams of a future with him. Now she was the one who had contempt in her eyes.

"I don't know why," she'd said furiously. "You should be able to continue on just the way you are—as long as you can find a company who's willing to pay for a silver instead of the gold.''

"At least I'll be competing," he'd flung angrily back at her. "I won't be a quitter like you!"

The voices faded from her mind, and Kira opened her eyes with a shudder. Afraid that she had somehow been transported back to that terrible time, she was relieved to find that she was standing in her own kitchen, with Purr contentedly finishing his supper. She stared blankly at him as he gave his whiskers the swipe that passed for cleaning his face, then, unwillingly her eyes went to the pond again. When she saw it, gleaming in the moonlight, she made up her mind. Her mouth tight, she whipped around and headed toward the bedroom.

Her skates were buried in their carrying case at the back of her closet. Burrowing behind suitcases and extra blankets and pillows and heaven knew what all, she finally succeeded in hauling the heavy container out into the bedroom, but it was a few minutes before she could open it. Kneeling on the floor, she could feel her pulse begin to pound, and her palms were suddenly so clammy that she had to wipe them against the slacks she'd worn to work. Finally, tentatively, she reached out, unsnapped the locks and opened the lid.

They were just as she'd left them, nestled in protective foam, the blades glinting silver in the light. Just seeing them brought back so many memories that she closed her eyes and didn't open them until she felt the cat brush by her to investigate.

"What do you think, Purr?" she whispered. "Shall I try it or not?"

He looked up at the sound of her voice, his amber eyes round and curious, and once again she heard scraps of conversation in her head.

"Are you going to give an exhibition, Kira?"

"I think you should skate."

"I remember when you won."

"I thought you were the most beautiful thing on ice."

And then, a final voice raised in anger.

"At least I won't be a quitter like you!"

Her head jerked, and she pulled the skates out of the case. *A quitter, Yale?* she thought. *We'll see about that!*

YALE GOT OFF THE PLANE at Rutland in a foul mood. He'd intended to return to Vermont the day before, as he'd promised Mimi, but once again things hadn't gone according to plan. He'd met a new client in Houston, a tennis player by the name of Carey Davis, who had just won the U.S. Pro Indoor Championships in Philadelphia, and he was on his way home when his secretary in California tracked him down to tell him that Wesley Rider wanted to see him. Wesley was a race-car driver who had won Daytona last year, and it seemed he was being besieged by product endorsement offers and didn't know what to do. In need of an agent, he was home in Indianapolis at the moment, and because the opportunity was too good to pass up, Yale agreed to see him. Then, feeling guilty, he'd called Mimi.

"I'm going to be a day late getting home," he'd told her when she answered the phone. "Is that okay with you?"

She hadn't hesitated. "Sure, what's up?"

He'd explained about Wesley, and then cautiously asked how things were going there.

"Oh, fine," she said, sounding bored. "School-work, therapy, same old thing, I guess."

"Then you don't mind if I stop to see Wesley first?"

"Is that the guy who looks like Tom Selleck?"

He smiled. "Does it make a difference?"

"Well, I thought that if it was, I wouldn't mind at all," she said, and giggled. "As long as I could meet him sometime, that is."

Only partially convinced, he'd hung up the phone. Ever since Kira had accused him of being gone so much when his daughter needed him, he'd felt guilty about leaving Mimi, and for some reason the fact that she didn't seem to mind at all hadn't taken away the sting of the accusation. Now, in spite of her reassurances, he wondered if she was telling the truth.

Damn it, he thought angrily. If Kira hadn't said anything, he wouldn't feel this way. He and Mimi and Hilda would have gone on just as they'd been doing before, in a routine that suited them all, and he wouldn't be questioning his performance as a parent.

The situation nagged at him all the way through his meeting with Wesley, who had indeed been besieged. The driver had met him in the VIP lounge at the airport, as agreed, and he'd brought with him an envelope containing hundreds of offers. There were deals for T-shirts, jackets with his name on them, postcards showing him with his car, running-shoe deals, offers for TV and movie appearances, an offer to do a shaving cream ad—even one for lingerie.

"All I want to do is drive, Mr. Duncan," Wesley said with some bewilderment. "What do I need with all that?"

What indeed? Yale had asked himself, sorting through the piles. "Most of these are just promises," he'd explained, pulling out one at random. "You see this one? Like all the others, it's a contract stating that you'll get five percent of the gross profit on whatever carries your name. But if you read the fine print, *gross* is defined as whatever's left after expenses. You'd get very little money, if any, if it didn't come up front."

Wesley had looked at him helplessly. Yale poured more coffee and made a mental note to tell Mimi that the driver did resemble that television star. Or maybe he wouldn't tell her, he thought with a smile. Knowing Mimi, she'd make a pest of herself until he brought her along one time to meet him.

"What should I do, Mr. Duncan?" Wesley asked.

Yale considered. "Well, a few of these are legitimate offers, Wesley," he said finally. "Why don't you let me take these back with me and look through them? Then I can tell you which ones I think you might endorse."

"Would you?" Rider looked so relieved that Yale had to laugh.

"That's my job."

"Thanks, Mr. Duncan."

"If we're going to be working together, why don't you call me Yale?"

His flight to Vermont had been called just then, and he'd said goodbye to Wesley and boarded the plane. He'd intended to use the flying time to catch up on some contract work, but once in the air, he found he couldn't concentrate. He kept seeing Kira the night of the hay ride, and he thought that even in jeans and sweater and bulky parka, with a scarf around her throat, she'd been more beautiful than Claudette when he'd taken her to the World Trade Center. *It shouldn't be that way,* he thought, and cursed the day he'd heard of the Stonebridge Clinic. He wished he'd never come to Vermont, because now all those memories of Kira had been revived and he knew nothing would come of it.

The flight attendant came by just then to offer him something, and he absently accepted a cup of coffee before he turned to continue staring blindly out the window. The jet droned into the night, and he knew he should get to work. But every time he started to reach for his briefcase, all he could think of was that he seemed to be in limbo since he and Mimi had come to Stonebridge. He couldn't return to the past, as part of him longed to do, but he couldn't make plans for a future that didn't include Kira.

Dismayed and surprised by the thought, he rejected it at once. Just because he and Kira had been... involved... once was no reason to think they could be again. After all, as she'd said, what they'd had before had been a youthful romance, an adolescent fling, brought on in part by circumstances. And when he thought about it, he remembered that they had never really agreed on anything important. Their last quarrel was a perfect example of that. He might have been wrong for bending the rules a little, but if she hadn't been so stubborn and narrow-minded about it, he would have explained.

With a sigh, he closed his eyes and rested his head against the back of the seat. It didn't matter now anyway, he told himself. She had made it clear that she had no regrets for what might have been, and if he looked at the situation dispassionately, he knew she was right. The past was just that... for both of them.

Was it? Despite himself, he recalled with longing the feel of her small waist under his hands the night of the

DREAMS TO MEND 165

hay ride; the softness of her lips when they had kissed. She had responded; he knew she had. Why wouldn't she admit it?

For the same reason he couldn't, he told himself despondently: too much had happened in the years since they'd known each other. They were no longer the skating queen and the skiing star, and the romance of that magical time had long since faded. He should put her out of his mind, forget her. What they'd had was gone, as it should have been.

But for some reason the knowledge didn't comfort him, and when the plane landed at Rutland he was totally depressed. Finding his car covered with snow in the parking lot didn't help matters, and by the time he finally pulled onto the highway and was heading toward Stonebridge, his bleak mood had turned black.

CHAPTER NINE

Kira stood poised on the edge of the pond, her arms wrapped tightly around her body, staring out over the frozen expanse of ice. She was wearing a cable-knit sweater and leg warmers over her jeans, and she shivered, but not from cold. Her skate blades rasped against the ice as she shifted from one foot to the other, and the sound seemed both familiar and alien at the same time. It had been so long since she'd heard that particular noise.

Could she do it? Now that she was here, she wasn't sure. The impetus that had brought her out to the pond seemed to have vanished, and she couldn't even really remember why she had come. The frightened pounding of her heart in her ears was the only thing she could hear, and she clutched her arms more tightly around her waist. Forcing herself, she glanced down and took another experimental swipe with one of her skates. The surface of the pond seemed rough to her, completely foreign after all those years in an ice rink. Wouldn't it be humiliating to get out there and fall!

She couldn't think about it all night; she'd freeze if she stood here any longer. The air was still and cold, the silvery moonlight her only company. There wasn't a sound except for the thumping of her heart, and before she could change her mind, she stepped off the bank and glided out. The ice wasn't as uneven as she'd thought, and before she knew it, she was at the center of the pond, and the shore seemed an impossible distance away.

What was she doing, out here, all by herself? Proving something to Yale or anybody else seemed the farthest thing from her mind right now, and for a horrible instant she felt paralyzed. What if she fell and hurt herself, as she had the last time she'd been on skates? She could lie here for hours and no one would know. She'd freeze to death and wouldn't be found until morning. She'd cry for help and no one would hear.

Stop it! she commanded herself, and clapped her gloved hands over her ears as though that would halt her panicked thoughts. She wouldn't fall, and even if she did, she'd manage to get back to the cottage...somehow. She was scaring herself for no reason; all she had to do was turn her head to see the comforting light streaming out her kitchen window. All she had to do was put one foot in front of the other....

It was easier than she'd thought. Once she overcame her panic, all those years of training took over, and before she knew it, she was skimming easily over the ice. Even the occasional bumpy spot didn't bother her; it was as though her body instinctively knew how to adjust. She found herself bending her knees slightly, holding her shoulders back, her arms out to either side. She'd always been known for her straight and supple back, that graceful carriage that made her appear to float over the ice, and she felt herself assuming that posture now. Without consciously thinking about it, some of the gestures she had practiced for hours—the arm bent just so, the fingers gracefully positioned—came back to her. That effortless balance took over and freed her for other things, and she dared to try a three turn, and then another—turning from front to back to front again on one skate. Delighted at her success, she tried it with the other foot, and with every passing second, every movement on the ice, she gained confidence. Soon she was skating backward, legs scissoring as she built up speed, and without thinking about it, she turned and stepped up into a single turn, landing as light as a feather on the other side, skimming backward again as though she had never left the ice. She tried it again and laughed aloud. She hadn't felt this...this free...in years. It was as though something had been sleeping inside her and was only now coming to life. It was such a glorious feeling that she wondered why she hadn't tried it before.

She wouldn't think about that, not just yet. She didn't want to think about anything except how wonderful it was to be skating again, and soon she was gliding over the ice almost as elegantly as she ever had, so caught up in the magic of the moment that she closed her eyes and surrendered to the bliss of doing something she had trained so hard and so long to do. From somewhere at the back of her mind a sound was growing, and then she realized what it was, she laughed again. The sound was the roar of applause, the shouting and whistling and stamping of the crowd, and even though it was only a memory, she responded to it, urging her body to more complicated moves, to spins she wouldn't have tried before, to flips and turns that seemed impossibly difficult only moments ago.

She skated until she was exhausted, until her legs were trembling from the unaccustomed exercise, until her breath was coming in gasps and, as cold as the night was, until she was drenched in perspiration. But she was elated when she moved automatically into a last layback, her head dropped and her spine curved in that incredibly graceful arch that no one at the time could duplicate, and which had been named for her: the Blair Layback. Straightening, faster and faster she whirled until she was a blur on the ice, and when she came out of the final spin, the imaginary applause had become a roar. Without thinking about it, she dropped to one knee in the bow Madame Sasanova had drilled into her. She had done it! she thought triumphantly. She had actually done it!

She was so ecstatic that it was a moment before she realized that the clapping she heard was real. Startled, she looked up. When she saw Yale standing on the bank, she leaped to her feet. They were about fifteen feet away from each other, and if she hadn't left her blade guards where he was standing, she would have fled.

"What—" She had to stop to catch her breath. Still gasping, she tried again. "What are you doing here?"

"Watching you," he said softly, and thought that if ever there was a cure for depression, it was seeing Kira skate. He'd been in such a terrible mood by the time he got home that as tired as he was, he knew he'd never sleep. Quietly, so as not to awaken Hilda or his daughter, he'd tiptoed into the kitchen, and had been pouring a brandy when he happened to glance out the window. He'd been so surprised when he saw Kira skating on the moonlit pond that he'd just stood there for a moment, staring, unable to believe his eyes. Then, brandy forgotten, he'd gone out. It was as though some powerful force had drawn him to her, and he'd been entranced, oblivious of the cold, until she came out of that final spin. It had been so long since he'd seen her skate that he'd almost forgotten how glorious she was on the ice. Nothing in his memory could compare to seeing her perform, and without realizing it, he'd walked halfway around the pond just to watch.

"That was..." he began, and had to clear his throat. But his voice was still hoarse with emotion when he started again, and without taking his eyes off her, he said, "That was beautiful, Kira. You look like you never left the ice."

She relaxed a little at that, breaking out of that frozen position she had assumed when she saw him there. Pushing off with one skate, she glided over to where he stood. When he saw her blade protectors and discarded boots on the nearby bench, he reached to get them for her. Feeling more awkward by the second, he held them out.

"Thanks," she muttered, and sat down to take off her skates.

He sat down with her. "I thought you said you didn't skate anymore."

She glanced up at him. "I don't," she said curtly.

He looked toward the pond. The patterns her blades had made on the ice were clearly visible in the moonlight, and when she followed the direction of his glance, her mouth tightened.

"It was an impulse," she said, despising herself for feeling as though she had to explain. "A stupid one, it turns out."

He looked surprised. "Why do you say that?"

She stood. "Never mind. I don't want to talk about it."

He stood with her. "Kira—"

"It's late, Yale," she interrupted. "And I really don't think we have anything to talk about."

She shuddered just then, and Yale realized she was cold. Without thinking about it, he took off his coat and started to put it around her shoulders. "Here, take this."

She stiffened and removed the coat. "No," she said, sounding angry. "I don't need—"

"Yes, you do," he said firmly, when she shivered again.

She seemed about to say something else, but then her mouth tightened and she turned away. Reaching down, she grabbed her skates and muttered, "Thanks. I'll give it to Mimi in the morning."

He didn't want her to go. "Kira—"

Impatiently, she turned back. "What?"

Now that he had her attention, he didn't know what to say. Then he knew by her expression that it wouldn't matter what he said. Maybe she was right, he thought. He should just leave it.

"Nothing," he said. "Good night."

"Good night," she said shortly, and turned away.

Yale watched her for a second before he resignedly started back the way he had come. He hadn't gone two steps when he heard her muffled cry. Startled, he looked over his shoulder and was horrified to see that she'd fallen to one knee in the snow. Her head was bowed, and she was clutching her leg. He reached her in three strides. "What is it?"

Her face was contorted with pain. "Cramp," she gasped. "I can't straighten my leg."

He didn't stop to think. Sweeping her up into his arms, he took her swiftly toward the cottage, some part of his mind wondering what he would do if the door was locked. It wasn't, and he carried her through the kitchen into the living room. He had a fleeting impres-

sion of warmth and noticed a streak of orange running toward the stairs, but that was all. He was more
concerned with Kira, and as he deposited her on the
couch, he asked tersely, "Where does it hurt?"

She was grabbing her thigh by this time with both
hands, tears running silently down her cheeks, and because he'd never seen her cry with pain before, he panicked. Not sure whether this had something to do with
her old injury or not, he decided quickly that he hadn't
time to find out. "What can I do?" he asked, running
a hand through his hair. He was afraid to touch her for
fear he'd do the wrong thing.

Her teeth clenched, she shook her head. "No...
nothing..." she panted. "It'll go away."

He was feeling more distraught by the second.
Maybe she had strained something he thought, and
then was galvanized by the notion that she'd fractured
her leg. He'd seen things like that happen before.
Greenstick fractures, they were called, or something
like that; he couldn't remember now. Glancing around
wildly for the phone, he said, "I'll call a doctor."

"No. It'll be all right...." She rocked forward again,
still clutching the leg. "I feel a knot..."

He didn't stop to think about it; didn't even remember that she was a physical therapist and trained to deal
with such things. Anxious to help, unable as always to
bear the sight of her in pain, he bent down quickly and
took hold of her jeans. Fortunately they were old, silvery from frequent use, and the material wasn't as
strong as it once was. With one movement, he ripped
up the leg.

"Yale!" she cried in dismay, the pain forgotten for
a second. "What are you—"

He didn't hear her; he could see muscle bunched in her slender thigh, and he began kneading with his strong fingers. It seemed to take forever, but eventually the knotted muscle relaxed under his massage, and finally, Kira leaned back and took a shuddering breath.

"That'll teach me," she said, and gave a shaky laugh. "Lord, I'd forgotten how much those things can hurt. I thought for a minute I'd fractured a bone."

Yale sat back on his heels. Now that the crisis was over, he felt he could breathe again, too. "I thought you had, too," he said. "Are you all right now?"

Tentatively, she straightened her leg. Then, her expression rueful as she looked down, she said, "I am, but I can't say the same for these jeans."

He glanced at the ragged edges of her pants leg. Embarrassed, he said, "I'm sorry. I guess I got carried away."

She looked at him in amusement. "I guess so."

They smiled at each other, and then she giggled. The sound was infectious, and he found himself laughing at the absurdity of the situation. She started to laugh, too, and before they knew it, they were doubling over, consumed with mirth.

"You should have seen your face," she said with a gasp, her eyes streaming.

"You should have seen yours when I ripped open your jeans," he returned, collapsing against the couch.

"I thought—"

"I was sure—"

They laughed until they couldn't laugh any more, holding on to their sides, bursting into renewed gales every time they looked at each other.

"Oh, stop!" she cried at last. "I can't stand it!"

Gradually, their hysteria subsided, and they sat quietly beside each other on the couch. Still trying to catch her breath, Kira glanced across at Yale, and when their eyes met, she was swept with a new emotion that had nothing to do with laughter. For a breathless moment they stared at each other, and then Yale brought his hand up and touched her face.

"Kira..." he whispered.

She knew it was wrong, that she would regret it, that she should just get up and tell him to go while she could. But his hand was warm against her face, and when his fingers gently traced the curve of her jaw, she couldn't help herself: she reached up and put her hands over his. Slowly, his eyes never leaving her face, he took her hand and brought it up to his mouth. Turning her palm up, he pressed his lips there, and a shudder raced through her body.

"Yale..."

He moved closer to her on the couch. "Don't say it," he pleaded, and took her in his arms. Gazing down into her upturned face, he whispered, "If you knew how long I've waited for this moment..."

She had waited a long time, too—a lifetime, it seemed—for this to happen. But she was no longer the seventeen-year-old girl she'd been so long ago with him; she was a woman, with a woman's wants and needs. Gently, she disengaged herself and stood. She held her hand out to him, and when he took it, she led the way upstairs.

Her bedroom was a loft, walled on three sides, open on one end to the living room below. A railing ran along that length, and the roof sloped to a dormer window over the bed. Moonlight splashed from the window onto the quilt that covered her double bed, and

. . . be tempted!

See inside for special
4 FREE BOOKS offer

 Harlequin Superromance™

✓ Clip and mail this postpaid card today!?

BUSINESS REPLY CARD

First Class   Permit No. 717   Buffalo, NY

Postage will be paid by addressee

Harlequin Reader Service
901 Fuhrmann Blvd.
P.O. Box 1394
Buffalo, NY 14240-9963

NO POSTAGE
NECESSARY
IF MAILED
IN THE
UNITED STATES

because they'd neglected to turn off the living room lamps, the diffuse light found its way to the loft and gently illuminated Yale's face. His eyes were in shadow when she turned to him, but she could see the gleam in those deep blue depths as he stared at her, and she caught her breath when he reached out and pulled her into him. He was already aroused, and when she felt the bulge of him against her, she pressed even closer. She wanted to be as near him as possible; she wanted to melt into his flesh, to become one... Urgently, she raised her face to his.

Their kiss this time wasn't tentative and gentle, as it had been before, but a swift coming together, hard and demanding and filled with long-awaited desire. She uttered a helpless sound when his mouth covered hers, and when his tongue caressed her lips, she opened her mouth and took it, as she would take him later. He ran his tongue over the roof of her mouth, and she shuddered and fell against him.

He held her upright, his hands sliding beneath her sweater to caress the tingling flesh of her back. When he pulled upward and the sweater slipped over her head, she reached blindly for him, but he held her back.

"No," he whispered. "Let me...."

She was helpless to resist, and when he stared at her with burning eyes before he dropped his head and kissed the pulsing beat at her throat, she groaned again and arched back, wanting him to touch her more than she wanted anything.

Slowly, he pushed the slender straps of her bra off her shoulders. His lips left a burning trail from her throat to the curve of one breast as he found the catch behind her back, and the wispy material fell away, ex-

posing her. He raised his head, then, to look into her
eyes for a moment before his eyes were drawn down
again.

"You're so beautiful," he breathed, and gently
cupped a breast in each hand, bending to kiss the
swelling flesh before dropping to her swollen nipples.

She couldn't bear it any longer. He was wearing a
dress shirt, as though he'd just come home from a
meeting and had only taken off his tie, and she reached
with trembling fingers for the buttons down the front.
Her breath caught as the shirt dropped to the floor, for
he was just as lean and muscular and fit as she remembered. She had never cared for hirsute men, and his
chest was as broad and smooth as a young man's.

But it was no young man who put his hand under her
chin and tipped her head up to look at him, and when
he bent down to kiss her again, she wrapped her arms
around him and held him close. The sensation of flesh
against flesh was exquisite. Her breasts crushed against
his wide chest, she surrendered to the emotions well-
ing up inside her and kissed him fiercely. She could feel
him reaching for the top button of her jeans, and she
helped him, wanting to be free of the restricting cloth-
ing. Tugging jeans and bikini panties over her hips, she
let them fall to the floor and reached for his trousers.
Then, together, they half fell onto the bed, and he
rolled over on top of her. Raising his head, he stared
down into her eyes and said hoarsely, "I don't believe
this is happening. I've thought about it, dreamed about
it for so long, and now..."

She'd dreamed about it, too, but nothing she had
ever fantasized could compare to the reality of his
weight pressing her into the bed, or of his arms around
her, holding her close. Her hands trembling, she

reached down to stroke the muscular legs, the firm buttocks, the strong back and trim waist. She closed her eyes, letting her fingers explore him, almost drugged with sensation. She could feel the ripple of muscles as she traced them lightly with a fingertip; she could feel his hard body contracting as she touched him in sensitive areas, moving at last to hold him in her hand, cupping and stroking in such a way that he dropped his head to the curve of her neck and groaned.

"God, you're wonderful," he murmured, and found with his lips again the beat of her heart in the hollow of her throat. His hands roamed over her body, touching her as she had touched him, exploring those sensitive areas until she wanted to cry out that she couldn't wait any longer, that she had to have him now.

Twisting under him so that they were face-to-face, she looked into eyes that were black with desire, but before she could pull his head to hers, he had dropped his mouth to her breast again. Pushing her gently back, he circled first one nipple, then the other, teasing her until she grabbed fistfuls of his hair and brought his gaze up to hers. Moonlight struck his face, and his eyes gleamed. Just for an instant, his glance dropped to her open mouth, and then his lips descended hungrily on hers, his tongue thrusting inside, his entire body beginning to shake with suppressed desire. Reaching down again, she found him and cupped him in her hand, stroking slowly back and forth at first, then with increasing rhythm until he moaned.

"Kira..." he panted, and raised his head to look down at her. His face was distorted with desire, and he reached up with one hand. His fingers in her hair, he pulled her head back and kissed her hungrily.

She couldn't bear it any longer. When he moved on top of her, she was ready, opening herself to take him, clinging to him with mindless desire. He straightened, holding her easily with both arms wrapped around her. The sensation was so exquisite that a shock wave of passion flashed through her, and suddenly her body was no longer her own. Yale had taken it over, filling her with every thrust, torturing her with every caress, every frantic kiss. Without even knowing, she drew him deeper and deeper inside, her muscles contracting convulsively, squeezing and kneading and demanding more. She could feel the climax building, and when it rushed over her, she stiffened, clutching him to her. When it came again, seconds later, building to an even greater crescendo, she cried out and arched her back. He put his hands under her and pulled her to him with every thrust, and when that indescribable pleasure built to fever pitch a third time, he cried out, as well. Frenziedly, they clung to each other, both of them straining to hold that blissful sensation that carried them higher and higher until Kira was sure she couldn't stand it any longer. A hoarse cry was torn from her throat again, and when Yale arched over her and laughed in triumph, she was too weak to do anything but collapse. Seconds later, he fell to one side of her, and they lay in each other's arms, gasping.

Some time later, Kira awoke with a start. Disoriented at first, she lay under the heavy weight of Yale's arm and wondered what had happened. Slowly, it all came back to her, and she turned her head. Yale was sleeping beside her, and perched on the pillow above his head was her cat. His rumbling purr was what had awakened her, and when she saw him there, she giggled. Yale muttered something in his sleep and turned over. The movement dislodged the cat, who rolled in-dolently down the pillow, and the sight was so comical that Kira laughed again.

Yale opened his eyes. "What's the matter?"

She didn't have to tell him, for just then Purr started making himself comfortable again behind Yale's back, and he frowned. "What's that?" he asked.

She smiled. "My cat."

"Your what?"

"My cat."

Yale bolted upright. The sudden movement startled Purr, who gave an indignant meow before he vaulted off the bed, and Kira dissolved in laughter at the sight of Yale's face.

"For Pete's sake!" he exclaimed and clutched the sheet.

"Don't worry," Kira said, trying to smother her laughter. "I'll protect you."

Yale gave her a dirty look. "Very funny." He leaned back against the headboard and grumbled, "I bet you trained him to do that."

Levering herself to a sitting position, too, Kira tried not to smile. "No, he learned it all by himself."

He still wasn't ready to forgive her. "He could have given me a heart attack."

She looked at him mischievously. "You—the fear-less downhiller?"

Reaching out, he grabbed her and hauled her to his side. "That was a long time ago," he said, dropping a kiss on her head before he ruffled her hair. "As you well know."

Still sated and languorous from their cataclysmic bout of lovemaking, Kira snuggled against him. "Not to hear Mimi tell it," she murmured.

"What do you mean?"

She began tracing a pattern on his chest with her fingertip. Amused at the thought, she said, "Well, according to your daughter, you could still take on all comers and beat everyone with a margin of two seconds to spare."

Yale laughed. In a sport where sometimes milliseconds determined as many as the top five finishers, they both knew the statement was absurd. "Yes, well, my daughter always has known the right thing to say," he said, and grabbed her hand. "If you keep doing that, I won't be responsible," he added with a grin.

"Is that so?" Kira murmured, and was tempted to put him to the test. Unfortunately, now that she'd brought up the subject of Mimi, she knew she should pursue it. They might not get another chance like this, and as much as she wanted this moment to last, she couldn't pretend she wasn't worried about Mimi. Taking a breath, she began, "Yale, did you ever talk to Mimi?"

"About what?"

She could feel his subtle withdrawal, and almost regretted asking. But in the weeks Mimi had been at the clinic, she had become more than a patient; now she was someone of whom Kira was very fond. The thought occurred to her that if circumstances had been different, Mimi could have been her daughter, and she was so startled at the thought that she blurted, "About her skiing."

He sighed. "What about it?"

She sat up, clutching the sheet to her. "About why she feels this . . . this *compulsion* to start training again before she's ready."

Yale sat up, too. "I thought we discussed that," he said with a frown. "I thought we agreed that desire was normal."

"No. You said that, not I. And now I'm even more worried."

"Why?"

"Because the other day she said she was thinking about going skiing with some friends."

"Is that all?" he said with a laugh, and relaxed against the headboard again. "You know Mimi. She was just kidding around."

Kira shook her head. "No, she wasn't, Yale. I'm really concerned."

He looked at her thoughtfully. "You are, aren't you?"

"Yes. If she tried a stunt like that before she was ready, she could ruin weeks of therapy."

"So I take it you want me to talk to her."

She was so relieved she let out the breath she hadn't even realized she was holding. "Would you?"

He reached for her and pulled her close again. "If that's all that's bothering you, of course I will. But I guarantee you, Mimi might fool around, but she'd never do something stupid like that."

Kira wasn't so sure. Remembering that underlying note of hysteria in Mimi's voice the day she threatened to go skiing with her friends, she wondered if she should tell him about that conversation. Then she decided against it. Yale had already said he'd talk to his daughter, and she couldn't ask more than that.

Or could she?

"Yale," she began hesitantly. "Could I ask you something?"

His hand was on her bare shoulder, his fingers absently stroking her, making it difficult for her to think. "What?" he murmured, his lips in her hair.

Wondering if she was doing the right thing, she said, "Why do you think Mimi is so obsessed with returning to skiing? Do you suppose it has something to do with you?"

"I'm her father. Of course it has something to do with me," he said, nibbling at her ear. "She wants me to be proud of her, and I am."

"Does she know that?"

He drew back to look at her disbelievingly. "Of course she knows it," he said, an edge creeping into his voice. "What are you getting at?"

She'd started this; she had to finish it. "Well, it just seems to me that she might not be so anxious about all this if you weren't gone so much."

"Oh, so we're back to that again," he said, and shifted away. "Well, for your information, I talked to Mimi about that, and she accepts the fact that sometimes I have to be away on business."

"How do you know she accepts it?"

"Because she told me so, that's how," he answered impatiently. "Why, did she tell you something different?"

"Well, not exactly...."

"Then what are we talking about?" he demanded.

She didn't care for that tone. "We're talking about a young girl who might do herself irreparable harm if she won't listen to reason!" she said, more sharply than she intended.

"I told you I'd talk to her. What more do you want?"

"I want—" she started to say, and stopped. What did she want? She wasn't sure at this point. She just knew that if one of them—she or Miles or Yale—didn't reach Mimi soon, she might do something that would affect her the rest of her life.

"Look, Kira," Yale said, obviously trying to control himself, "I know you're concerned, and I appreciate that. But don't you think I know my own daughter?"

"But Mimi is so obsessed—"

"Weren't you at that age?" he shot back. "As I recall, there was a time when all you could think about, or eat or breathe or sleep, was skating. Is Mimi so different?"

"No, Yale, but—"

"Then what's the problem? I thought you, of all people, would understand her need to compete!"

"I do understand," she said sharply. "And I know all about a need to compete! But I don't think that's what's bothering Mimi."

"And just what do you think is bothering her?"

Stung by the sarcasm, she couldn't hide her annoyance. When Yale threw back the covers and got out of bed to grab his trousers, she didn't try to stop him. Grabbing a robe, she climbed out the other side and faced him.

"What I think," Kira said slowly, "is that Mimi is skiing for all the wrong reasons."

Yale snatched up his shirt and threw it on. "Oh, so now you're a psychic, on top of your other talents!"

"I don't need psychic abilities to see what's happening with Mimi!" she snapped. "She's so anxious to please you—to keep you home for five minutes—that she's willing to try anything to accomplish it."

"That's absurd!"

"Is it? Well, maybe if you weren't gone so much, you'd see it, too."

"Damn it, Kira, I have a business to run!"

"And is that more important than your daughter?"

He looked as though she'd slapped him. "Nothing is more important than Mimi to me," he said. "Nothing."

He had finished dressing; now he turned and started down the stairs. She was after him in an instant. "Yale—wait!"

He turned briefly to look up at her. "What?"

He looked so thunderous that she didn't know what to say. "I...I..." she stammered, and tried to get hold of herself. "Yale, I'm sorry," she finished weakly.

He looked at her a moment longer. Then, very quietly, he said, "I am, too."

Seconds later, she was alone, and wondering desperately what had happened. Sinking down onto the stairs, she put her head in her hands and tried not to cry. It seemed impossible to believe that they'd ever laughed or made love, and when she bleakly raised her head, she knew the chill in the air wasn't because the fire had died, but because of the finality in Yale's voice before he walked out the front door.

CHAPTER TEN

KIRA DRAGGED HERSELF to work the next morning, uncertain whether she felt more emotionally bruised or physically unfit. Muscles she hadn't used in years were protesting violently from her impromptu skating session the night before, and she hadn't slept well again after that argument with Yale. Grimacing as she limped along, she marveled how it was possible to go from the heights of ecstasy to the depths of despair within the space of a single night, and when she let herself in the clinic's back door, she wondered dismally how she was going to get through the day.

Longingly, she glanced inside the whirlpool room as she passed. She was tempted to change into a swim suit and sink her stiff body in that swirling, hot water, but she couldn't afford the luxury. She still had to decide what to do about Mimi, and as she trudged along to her office and shut the door behind her, she hoped she would have a few minutes to herself before any interruptions. With a heavy sigh, she gingerly lowered herself into the desk chair.

Unfortunately, now that she was here, she still didn't know how to handle the situation. She had deliberately come in early so she could decide what to do, but when she realized she wasn't any closer to a decision now than she had been during that long, restless night, she uttered an impatient exclamation. It should have been so simple: all she had to do was make it clear to Yale that last night had been a mistake, one she intended not to repeat. After all, their only concern should be Mimi, and it was obvious after their argument that they didn't see eye to eye about her and never would. Now, because he was being his usual stubborn, narrow-minded self, she was torn. If Yale didn't agree with her, if he didn't even see there was a problem, it seemed pointless for her to continue supervising Mimi's therapy. Plagued by the thought that because of her involvement with him, she might be doing Mimi more harm than good, she wondered if it was time for someone else to take over the case.

Then she sighed. She knew how Miles would react to that idea. He'd been adamant when Mimi first came that she be the one to work with the girl, and she'd eventually had to admit he was right. But the situation had changed now, and the more she thought about it, the more convinced she became that it was time for someone else to take over. One of the other therapists might have more success getting through to Mimi, and that was more important than any possible publicity. If she assured Miles that she'd be supervising Mimi's therapy personally, he couldn't object, and on that thought, she approached him with the idea as soon as he came in that morning.

"Let me get this straight," he said, over their usual coffee and doughnut meeting in her office. She'd been waiting anxiously for his arrival, with a fresh pot on the coffee maker and the jelly-filled pastries he loved in a prominent place on her desk. She'd made a special trip to the bakery because she felt she needed all the help she could get, but unfortunately the bribe hadn't worked. When she explained what she had in mind, he carefully put down the unfinished doughnut and glowered at her.

"You want to assign Betsy or Noreen to Mimi's therapy?" he repeated. "I thought we had settled all that. We agreed you would handle Mimi's case personally."

"We did, Miles," she said, "but that was before. The situation has changed now."

"It has? How?"

She'd tried to marshall all her arguments ahead of time, knowing that she had to be precise and logical about this or he would never agree to the change. The only problem was that she couldn't tell him the complete truth, and she knew she'd never been a convincing liar, so she'd had to improvise. He'd never accept the excuse that she was becoming too involved with Mimi to be objective about her therapy, but she couldn't say that her involvement with Mimi's father was the real reason she had stopped being effective. He'd want to know why, and she'd have to think of some explanation, and then the whole awful truth would probably come out. That was when she decided to keep it simple.

The fact that they were in the process of admitting a new patient helped. Birgitta Bauer was a speed skater in strong contention for both World and Olympic titles, and she had pulled a groin muscle in training a short time ago. She was coming to the clinic for therapy soon, and Kira planned to use that as leverage if she had to. Given her background, Miles would certainly understand her interest in the skater, especially if she reassured him that Mimi was far enough along in her therapy now that she didn't need her direct supervision.

At least that's the way she had planned it. It had seemed so logical and straightforward when she thought of it, but as she sat across the desk from Miles now, she wondered what had happened to the beautiful simplicity of her argument. Right now it seemed like a lame excuse, and she glanced away from that speculative look in Miles's eyes.

"You were saying that the situation with Mimi had changed," Miles prodded. "In what way?"

Kira handed him the latest printout on Mimi's progress with the isokinetic machine. "You can see that she's nearly eighty percent in the involved leg now, Miles. She's doing so well that I just feel my time could be better spent working with some of our patients who have more serious problems."

Miles studied the results she had given him. "Yes," he said, almost to himself. "I see what you mean. She's made remarkable progress, hasn't she?"

"Yes," Kira agreed, but she sounded so hesitant that he looked up.

"You don't sound entirely convinced of that."

She started to say that she was, but then she sighed. She should have known this wasn't going to work, she thought, and said instead, "I'm sorry, Miles, but I'm not. Mimi and I seem to have reached an impasse."

He looked immediately concerned. "In what way?"

She sighed again. "Well, ever since I told her I wasn't going to skate for the carnival, things seemed to have taken a turn for the worse. Oh, not physically," she said, gesturing toward the printout he held. "You can see that for yourself. No, it's more her attitude. I really think that at this point one of the other therapists might have more success with her."

Miles still looked doubtful. "Well, I trust your judgment. I suppose we could give it a try. Just as long as you continue to supervise her therapy—from afar, so to speak."

Relieved, Kira nodded. "Don't worry about that. I'll keep my eye on her every step of the way."

"Who did you want to assign to her?"

She had considered that carefully, too. "I think Betsy might be the better choice," she said slowly. "Noreen is very good, of course, but Betsy's attitude is more easygoing, even though she gets the job done just as well. I think if we relieve some of the pressure to perform that Mimi feels, she might relax on herself a little. Betsy is the better one to accomplish that, I think."

"I think you're right," Miles agreed, and took his coffee and the rest of the jelly doughnuts back to his office to finish in peace.

As the door closed behind him, Kira sat back, exhausted. She hadn't expected to win so easily, and she tried not to feel guilty about not telling him the whole truth. Arguing that her point wouldn't have been served any better if she'd dragged in her involvement with Yale as the reason for switching therapists, she told herself just to be thankful that things had gone so well. Finishing her coffee, she went out to take the first of her appointments that day.

It wasn't until later that afternoon, when she was supervising a hydrocollator treatment for Miss Elvira Jones, the Stonebridge librarian, that she heard from the Duncan family again. Elvira had pulled a muscle in her neck while attending, of all things, a boxing match. The clinic specialized in the treatment of athletic injuries, but Miss Jones was eighty-one, and a fixture in the town. Besides, she was a peppery little old lady, and Kira had thought with a smile that her injury could conceivably be considered sports related. She was about to place the hot pack carefully on Miss Jones's frail neck when Mimi burst unannounced into the room.

"I want to talk to you," Mimi said, her expression ugly.

Kira had looked up in surprise at the interruption. Frowning at that peremptory tone, she said, "I'm busy right now, Mimi. It will have to wait until later."

"No," Mimi said stubbornly. "Now."

Raising an eyebrow, Kira's own tone was perceptibly cooler when she said, "I don't think you heard me, Mimi. I'm with a patient now. You'll have to wait."

Mimi's voice rose. "I can't wait! I have to talk to you now!"

"It's all right, Dr. Stanfield," Miss Jones said gently, placing a papery little hand on her arm. "I understand how impatient the young can be. I'll wait."

Indecisive, Kira glanced down at the librarian. She didn't want to give in to Mimi when she'd been so rude, but she had heard that hysterical undertone in the girl's voice, and she wasn't sure what Mimi might do if she refused. The last thing she wanted was a scene, and so she carefully placed the hyrdocollator back in its steaming vat and said, "Thank you, Miss Jones. I won't be a moment."

Elvira waved. She had brought a boxing magazine with her, and she was already absorbed. "Take your time, dear," she murmured. "I'm not going anywhere."

Kira barely waited until she had closed the door of her office behind them before she turned to Mimi.

"Just what is so important that you had to interrupt a therapy session with another patient?" she demanded angrily. "Your rudeness was inexcusable!"

Mimi didn't even flinch. "And what about you?" she cried. "You could have at least told me that you weren't going to be my therapist anymore! Why did I have to find it out from somebody myself?"

Ah, so that was it, Kira thought. But because she was still irked at Mimi's spoiled behavior, she said, "Are you angry because I assigned you another therapist, or because I didn't consult you first?"

"Neither!" Mimi cried. "No...both! Oh, I don't know. I just don't think it was fair for you to do something like that without telling me!"

Feeling anything but calm, Kira leaned against the edge of the desk, and said quietly, "I'm sorry you feel that way, Mimi. I thought it was best."

"For who?" the girl flung at her bitterly. "Me, or you?"

"For you, of course!" Kira said sharply. Mimi's blue eyes had a wild look that she definitely didn't like, and she debated about calling for Miles. Then she decided she'd handle this herself. After all, she told herself grimly, it had been her decision.

"I'd be glad to explain," she said carefully, "if you're prepared to listen—"

"I don't want to listen!" Mimi cried. "I don't want any other therapist but you!"

"Now, Mimi..."

"No, I don't want to hear it. You promised you'd work with me, I heard you tell my father!"

"Let's leave your father out of this for the moment," Kira said curtly. "I think this is between you and me."

Mimi glared at her, but when Kira held her gaze, she finally threw herself into a chair. Her mouth a sullen line, she muttered, ''All right, I'll listen. But it had better be good.''

Stifling the urge to shake the girl, Kira said, ''I don't know why you're so upset. I thought you'd be pleased.''

Mimi shot her a look. ''Pleased! How can you say that?''

''Because in a way, this is a step up,'' Kira said. ''You're doing so well that you don't need my direct supervision any longer.''

The sullen expression became bitter again. ''But you still won't let me ski!''

''No, not yet,'' Kira agreed calmly. ''But if you continue to improve, it won't be long.''

Mimi wasn't going to be appeased by that. ''I've heard that before,'' she said sulkily.

Kira tried another approach. ''I thought you liked Betsy.''

Picking at the arm of the chair, Mimi said, ''I do. But it's not the same as having you.''

''Betsy is as good a therapist as I am.''

''If that's true, why are you the head of the department and not her?''

Kira lost patience. ''I can see that despite your promise, you're not in the mood to listen to anything I have to say, so I'm afraid you'll just have to accept my decision. Now, if you'll excuse me, I have a patient who is waiting.''

She ushered Mimi out of her office before there could be any more objections, and though she hated herself for doing it, she left Mimi standing in the hall as she went back to the therapy room where Miss Jones was waiting so patiently.

"Did you get everything settled?" the librarian asked, glancing up from her magazine.

"Yes, I think so," Kira replied, starting the hot-pack treatment all over again. But as she drained the hydro-collator, she knew it wasn't true. Feeling guilty about leaving Mimi standing in the hall, she left Miss Jones blissfully reading about Sugar Ray Leonard and went back to look for her. But Mimi was gone, and she sighed. *She'll get over it,* she told herself, *she has to.* She had made her decision, and now she and Mimi would just have to live with it.

That evening before she went home, she wasn't so sure. The phone rang for her just as she was leaving, and she picked it up with a weary hello.

"What's this about you assigning another therapist to treat Mimi?"

Of course she recognized the voice immediately, and she stiffened at Yale's abrupt tone. Like daughter, like father, she thought acidly, and said, "Good evening to you, too."

He wasn't put off by the sarcasm. "Well?"

"Obviously you have an objection to my decision," she said, and despised herself for feeling so off balance. If she'd been thinking, she would have expected this call hours ago, and she forced herself to relax her death grip on the phone. Calmly, she sat in her chair.

"I certainly do have an objection to it," Yale said. "If this is some childish retaliation for what happened last night—"

She shot to her feet. "How dare you imply—"

"I'm not implying anything," he interrupted. "But I find it more than coincidental that when we quarreled last night after—" He broke off, and hastily amended, "That the morning after our quarrel, you decide to assign another therapist to my daughter's case."

"You can find it however you like!" Kira replied hotly. "You obviously don't believe it, but I do have Mimi's best interests at heart. I've felt for some time that she would progress more quickly with another therapist."

"Then why didn't you say so?"

Even though she took another grip on her temper, she couldn't prevent the sarcasm. "You might recall that I did try to talk to you last night about Mimi, Yale. But it seems that no one in the Duncan family listens to anyone but themselves. Mimi wouldn't listen when I tried to explain this morning, either."

Boxed in on that, Yale tried another tack. "Did you talk to Miles about this?"

Irate at the implication that she was incapable of making the decision herself, she said coldly, "As a matter of fact, I did—but only as a courtesy. In case you weren't aware of it, *I'm* the head of the physical therapy department here, and responsible for all decisions affecting therapy of our patients."

His voice was just as cold. "Then if it's not too much trouble, perhaps you could explain to me why you broke our contract. As I recall, when we first came to the clinic you agreed to supervise Mimi personally."

"As *I* recall, I agreed to supervise the case," she snapped back.

"Oh, I see," he said caustically. "Obviously you don't feel it's the same thing."

"As a matter of fact, I don't. However, if it will set your mind at ease, Mimi will still receive my personal attention," she said, and couldn't help adding pointedly, "just as all the patients at the Stonebridge Clinic do."

He obviously wasn't impressed by that statement. "And how will you manage that, if someone else is working with Mimi?"

She'd had enough. It was difficult enough talking to him like this after what had happened between them, but to make matters worse, she kept recalling fragments of that glorious lovemaking scene last night. She knew it was just her imagination, but her lips still burned from his kisses, and her body tingled with the memory of his hands and mouth and tongue . . .

Almost violently, she thrust the memories away. If she'd ever had any yearnings about getting involved with him again, they were dispelled now. She'd known last night was a mistake, but like a fool she had ignored all the alarm bells and warnings sounding off in her mind because she'd been so physically swept away by him.

No more, she thought, and said curtly, "If you're questioning my competence, we should discuss this matter with Miles. Or perhaps you would prefer taking Mimi to another clinic."

Yale was silent at that, and Kira was just thinking in satisfaction that she had won when he said, "That won't be necessary. I have no intention of uprooting my daughter again . . . yet. But if she doesn't make the same or better progress with this new therapist—"

Kira wasn't going to be threatened. "Then of course we will make other arrangements," she said crisply, and couldn't prevent herself from adding, "Despite what you may believe, Yale, the welfare of the clinic's patients is my primary concern."

"Just as my daughter's is mine," he replied, and broke the connection.

Kira hung up the phone, thinking that despite the points she had scored, she still felt in some indefinable way that Yale had bested her with that last remark. Irritated, she grabbed her coat and went home.

YALE SAT looking at the phone for a long time after his conversation with Kira. He wanted to call her back and apologize for his abruptness, but every time he reached for the receiver, he changed his mind. She'd been angry, and now that he'd had time to review what they had both said, he couldn't blame her. He hadn't meant to sound as though he was questioning her competence, only her decision. No wonder she'd been annoyed.

His mouth tight, he got up from the desk and went to the window. The frozen pond was there before him, serene and empty; he couldn't even see the marks Kira's skates had made. A light snowfall and then a slight thaw this morning had obliterated them all, and it was as if it had never happened.

His frown deepened. It was as if that euphoric bout of lovemaking had never happened, either. It hadn't escaped him that they'd both avoided any mention of what had taken place at Kira's cottage last night, and as he thought about it, he muttered a curse. It seemed that he was doomed to repeat the same mistakes with Kira this time as he had the last. He remembered too well how he always seemed to be on the wrong foot with her before, and it seemed that things hadn't changed now. Maybe her decision to assign another therapist to Mimi was for the best, after all. If he wanted to talk about his daughter's progress he'd be conferring with Beth or Beverly or Betsy or whatever the hell her name was, instead of Kira. It seemed that all they had done so far was argue about Mimi, anyway. It would be a relief not to be constantly agitating about his personal life when what he was really concerned about was his daughter's welfare.

Then why did he feel so depressed? He should be glad he wasn't going to see Kira anymore; he hadn't wanted to get involved in the first place. He'd never intended for last night to happen. It had been—

Just one of those things?

He winced. Even he couldn't convince himself that it had been that; his attraction to Kira had been growing from the first moment he saw her at the clinic. Or maybe it had never really died—he didn't know. He didn't seem to know anything at this point, and that was the most depressing thing of all. What had happened to the man who had known for years exactly where he was going and just how he was going to get there? He had planned his future far in advance; he had mapped out every step of the way. And until he'd come to Stonebridge, everything had been going according to schedule.

And now things couldn't have gotten further off track. He'd thought he had a handle on things, that he could manage anything that came his way. But Kira had changed all that, and the most frustrating part of it all was that she didn't seem to give a damn that his entire life was one giant turmoil, and all because of her. That was why he'd been so abrupt on the phone; she'd been so much cooler and in control that it had irked the hell out of him. His glance focused on the pristine pond again and he grimaced.

"Dad?"

Startled at the sound of Mimi's voice, he turned sharply as his daughter poked her head around the door to the study. "Did you call her?"

Yale groaned inwardly. He'd been so deep in thought that he'd forgotten the reason he'd phoned Kira in the first place. Mimi had been so upset about the change in therapists that he'd promised to call on her behalf and persuade Kira to change her mind. Knowing his daughter, they were in for a storm when he told her he'd failed, and he tried not to sigh as he moved back to the desk and sat down. "Yes, I called," he said.

Mimi came into the room and eagerly took a seat across from him. "Well?" she demanded. "What did she say?"

Because he didn't want to give a direct answer, he tried the oblique approach first. He knew his daughter, and he doubted that it would work, but it was worth a try. "Let me ask you something first, all right?"

Mimi looked at him suspiciously. "What?"

He despised himself for this blatant effort at placating her in advance. His only excuse was that she'd been through so much these past few months that he couldn't bear to see her hurt or disappointed even more. Assuring himself that there would be time for a return to discipline later, he said cautiously, "Would it be so bad if you had another therapist, Sprite? I mean—"

He didn't get a chance to finish the sentence. Bolting upright in the chair, Mimi said accusingly, "You didn't get her to change her mind, did you?"

"I tried, Mimi."

She shot to her feet. "It's not fair that I'm caught in the middle, just because you and Kira had a fight!"

He was horrified. "How do you know...?" he blurted before he realized what he was saying. Changing tactics swiftly, he said sharply, "You're not in the middle of anything. When Ki—when Dr. Stanfield explained her reasons for assigning you to another therapist, I had to agree—"

"You don't have to call her Dr. Stanfield in front of me, Dad," Mimi said scornfully. "I know all about you two."

"What do you mean? There's nothing to know!"

"Oh, come on, Dad," she said. "I wasn't born yesterday. I *am* nearly sixteen, after all. I know what's going on."

Yale couldn't believe they were having this conversation. "There's nothing going on," he said. But his voice sounded weak in his own ears, and to make matters worse, he knew he looked as guilty as hell. He went on, more forcefully, "I don't know what you think you know, Mimi—"

"I know that you and Kira used to go together," she said smugly.

"That was a long time ago," he said curtly.

"Oh, sure."

"What does that mean?"

Obviously enjoying herself now, Mimi threw herself back down in the chair. Casually draping one leg over the arm, she looked at him and said, "I've seen the way you two look at each other. And remember the hay ride? I bet you thought nobody noticed you two snuggling at the front of the wagon, kissing each other."

"We weren't *kissing* each other! Where did you get—"

"Well, if you weren't *kissing* each other," she said mockingly, "you sure looked like it. I'm not the only one who noticed, either. Everybody in the wagon did."

Feeling as though he was having a bad dream, Yale sat back and stared at her. Now that his shock had worn off, the first thing he thought of was what Kira would say if she knew about this. He winced. She'd be even more appalled than he was to know that the kids were gossiping about them. When she found out what they were saying, heaven alone knew what she'd do. His mouth turned grim. She'd blame him, that's what she'd do, he thought, so he'd better put a stop to this right now.

"I really don't think Kira would appreciate everyone gossiping about her," he said severely.

She looked innocently up at the ceiling. "It's not gossip if it's true, is it?"

"You know very well what I mean, young lady," he said sternly. "And I'm sure you wouldn't want to be responsible for helping to ruin Dr. Stanfield's reputation. I thought you liked her."

Mimi looked sullen again. "I did like her," she said. "Until she decided she didn't want to be my therapist anymore."

"Is that what all this is about?" he asked, his voice sharp. "Are you just angry because Kira has assigned you another therapist, and you're trying to get back at her?"

Mimi shifted in the chair. Avoiding his eyes, she muttered, "I'm not trying to get back at her at all. Besides, if anyone should worry about ruining her reputation, shouldn't it be you? After all, you were the one who was kissing her."

Yale didn't know what to say. He never had learned to deal with these exasperating changes of mood Mimi had indulged in since her accident; it wasn't like her to be spiteful and sullen and mean. He was used to her sunny disposition, her unfailing cheerfulness, her mischievous jokes. Sometimes he thought he didn't even know this person sitting in front of him; there were times when he couldn't believe this was even his daughter. The doctor had tried to warn him that mood swings and depression were normal after surgeries like Mimi's; he had indicated that things might get worse because her therapy and rehabilitation were going to be long and painful. But he hadn't believed it…or maybe he just hadn't wanted to believe. He would have given anything to have his little girl back, and sometimes he wished to hell he'd never taught her to ski.

Then he brought himself up short. Hadn't he been the one to assure Kira that Mimi was born to ski? He didn't know if it was inherited or not, but it was obvious from the first that she was a natural, and because he knew his strong-willed daughter, he knew that she would have learned with or without his help. He'd figured then that the least he could do was give her the benefit of his knowledge and teach her properly. The accident hadn't been his fault, and he wasn't going to start thinking it was.

But maybe he was responsible for other things, he reflected, and remembered again the argument he and Kira had had just last night. Wincing at the memory, he looked thoughtfully at his daughter. He could decide what to do about this rumor business where he and Kira were concerned another time; right now, Mimi was more important. So instead of giving her the sharp reply he'd intended, he said carefully, "I know you're upset about Kira's decision to change therapists, but can't you at least give it a try? After all, we came to the clinic because it had such a good reputation, and I think we should assume they know what they're doing.''

Her mouth still that sullen line that sometimes drove him to distraction, Mimi wouldn't look at him. ''I never said they didn't,'' she muttered.

Encouraged, though he wondered why, Yale thought again about what Kira had said. Wishing he could just quit while he was ahead, he said, ''This really isn't about Kira or me or the new therapist, is it, Mimi?''

She glanced quickly at him. ''I don't know what you mean.''

''I think you do,'' he said, and came around the desk to squat in front of her chair. Reaching out, he put a hand under her chin and gently forced her to look at him. His voice quiet, he said, ''I think it's about your wanting to ski again, don't you?''

Mimi looked at him for a long moment. Then, tears springing to her eyes and her face crumpling, she threw herself into his arms. ''Oh, Dad!'' She sobbed against his shoulder. ''Sometimes I think I'm never going to ski again!''

Holding his weeping daughter in his arms, Yale looked over her head and closed his eyes. But he had to ask, and so after a moment, he held her slightly away so he could see her face. ''Would that be so bad, Sprite?''

She looked at him disbelievingly through her tears. ''How can you ask me that? You know it would be the worst thing in the world!''

She started wiping her tears away with the back of her hand. Silently, Yale handed her his handkerchief, and then took a deep breath. "Why?"

"Why! Because...because...well, it just would be, that's why!"

Once again, he just wanted to leave it alone. But Kira's accusations haunted him, and he had to find out. "Why is it so important to you, Mimi?" he asked. "Is it because of you—" he took a deep breath "—or me?"

She stiffened. "What do you mean?"

He wasn't sure what he meant. Cursing Kira for planting all these doubts in his mind, he stood up, gently bringing Mimi to her feet, too. Gazing down into his daughter's face, he thought how much he loved her, and how all he ever wanted was for her to have the best.

To have the best, or to be the best?

The question flashed into his head, and he considered it honestly before he rejected it. In his mind, Mimi already was the best. She didn't need skiing trophies or gold medals or world titles to prove herself to him; she didn't have to do anything except be herself. He was glad she was so good at her sport, but only because it gave her a sense of pride and satisfaction and achievement. But if she'd been the biggest klutz on the block, the most uncoordinated kid he'd ever seen, he couldn't have loved her more. She was his daughter; she was everything to him, the best *he'd* ever done.

But before he could tell her that, Mimi uttered a shaky laugh and squirmed out of his arms. "Jeez," she said, "we're getting serious all of a sudden, aren't we? If I'd known this was going to cause such a problem, I wouldn't have made a big deal about it."

Yale was caught off guard by this sudden change of mood. "But I thought—"

Mimi laughed again. Reaching up on tiptoe, she gave him a brief kiss on the cheek. "Hey, look...no problem. I'll give it a try, okay?" She grinned, the old Mimi. "And who knows—maybe I will like Betsy better than Kira. After all, Kira said that the reason I had to change was because I was doing so well, so that's a good sign, isn't it? Maybe with Betsy, I'll be able to start training that much faster."

Alarmed, Yale said, "I think—"

Mimi gave him that fond, exasperated look. "Don't *worry*. I'll be a good little girl, I promise."

He gave up. "Somehow, I doubt that," he said resignedly.

She went to the door and pulled it open, but she hesitated before going out, turning to look back at him. "And about that other thing...you know, what you asked me about skiing?"

"Yes," he said warily.

She grinned again. "I hate to disappoint you, Dad, but I don't really do it for you."

"You don't?" He didn't know whether to be relieved or not.

"Of course not," she said with a laugh. "Don't you know that I've always thought it would be neat to beat my old man? It's as simple as that. Nothing Frundian about that, is there?"

"Freudian," he corrected with a smile.

Mimi airily waved her hand. "Whatever. Just as long as you understand."

"It takes me awhile," he said, smiling in return. This was the Mimi he knew; the mischievous girl he loved. "But I think I've got it now."

"Good," she said, and blew him a kiss before she shut the door behind her.

Feeling as though he'd just survived a storm, Yale sank into his desk chair. So much for *that*, Dr. Stanfield, he thought, and wondered why he still felt a nagging doubt as he pulled his neglected work toward him.

CHAPTER ELEVEN

KIRA WAS JUST LEAVING for work when the phone rang. Glancing at the clock, she debated about answering, for it was almost ten, and she was already late. Miles had asked for a new equipment list, and though he told her she could do it at home, it had taken her longer than she had anticipated. The phone rang again as she stood there indecisively, and with a sigh, she reached for the receiver.

"Kira?"

"Jilly!" she exclaimed, pleased to hear her sister's voice. She was in the kitchen, and she sank down onto the edge of one of the bar stools by the counter. "What a nice surprise!" And then, quickly, "Is anything wrong?"

Jilly laughed. "Why is that the first thing we always ask each other?"

Kira laughed, too. "I don't know. Maybe it's because we want to get it out of the way."

Her sister laughed again, and Kira could picture her at the other end of the phone, brown-haired and blue-eyed, the same height, but with the heavier build she had inherited from their father's side of the family. Jilly was a year older, and they had always been close. She would never forget her help and support during Gil's illness and that terrible lost time she'd endured after his death. Sometimes she wondered what she would have done if it hadn't been for her sister.

Completely forgetting about the time and the office, she slid into a more comfortable position on the stool. "Aren't you supposed to be teaching today, or is there a holiday I don't know about?"

"No holiday," Jilly said happily. "At least, not an official one. I just got word that the school basement is flooded, so we don't have to go in. What are you doing home at ten, anyway? I just called the office and they said you hadn't come in."

"I had some work to do. I've been meaning to call, it's just that I've been so busy...."

"Haven't we all," Jilly said. Then, she asked directly, "Does all this busyness have anything to do with Yale, perchance?"

Kira felt her cheeks redden. She should have known it was a mistake to mention in one of her letters that Mimi and Yale were at the clinic; Jilly wasn't one to let things like that go. "I think you've been correcting too many papers," she said evasively. "You're beginning to sound a little Elizabethan yourself."

"Don't change the subject," Jilly said briskly. "What's going on?"

"What makes you think anything is?"

"Oh, I don't know," Jilly said dryly. "I suppose it's because you mentioned Yale once, and I haven't heard one word since. Knowing you, that can mean one of two things—either things are going really well, or they couldn't be worse."

"You always did exaggerate," Kira said. "Things are going fine. In fact—" She stopped. She couldn't lie; she and Jilly had always been too close. Besides, her sister was sensible and to the point, and maybe that's what she needed right now to help her straighten out her confused feelings about Yale.

"No, that's not true," she said unhappily. "Things aren't fine at all."

As always, Jilly homed in right to the heart of the matter. "I thought you said you could handle Yale being at the clinic with his daughter."

"I thought I could."

"Oh, boy. Something's happened, hasn't it?"

"Well..."

"Oh, boy," Jilly said again, this time with a sigh. "That does complicate things, doesn't it?"

"Not in the way you think," Kira said glumly.

"What do you mean?"

"We got into a fight about his daughter," Kira said, her mouth tightening at the memory. "I was concerned about her attitude, and he told me to mind my own business."

"What did you say?"

"What could I say?"

"No, I mean about his daughter?"

"Just that I was concerned about her reasons for wanting to return so quickly to competition, and that if he was home more instead of away all the time on business, he might see that something was wrong, too. That's all."

"That's all?" Jilly asked wryly. "No wonder you got into a fight."

"You sound like you think I was wrong."

"No..." Jilly said slowly. "But I think you might have come on a little too strong."

"I was worried about my patient!"

"And he's concerned about his daughter," Jilly pointed out reasonably. "I think that's obvious, don't you? Otherwise, he wouldn't have brought her all the way across the country to your clinic.''

Perversely annoyed because she had wanted Jilly's advice, and now didn't like it once she had received it, she refused to concede the point. ''Well, if he's so concerned,'' she said sullenly, ''why didn't he listen to me when I said I thought Mimi's obsession with skiing was unhealthy?''

Jilly was silent a moment. ''You know, I remember someone who was that way about skating.''

''If you're talking about me, that was entirely different!''

''Was it?'' Jilly asked calmly. ''As I recall, you used to get a little hysterical yourself if you thought you weren't going to be able to skate. Remember the time you sprained your ankle before the...which was it? The Junior Nationals, I think. We all thought we were going to have to put you in a straitjacket when the doctor said it would be better if you didn't compete.''

Kira hadn't forgotten, but she had deliberately pushed it to the back of her mind. She had always suspected that that incident had contributed to the disaster at the Olympics; she never had felt strong on that ankle after she'd sprained it, and she probably shouldn't have competed. But it hadn't stopped her from winning the Junior National title, even if she had paid for her stubbornness later. She remembered that the ankle had swollen to three times its normal size after the competition, and she couldn't even get a shoe on for a week, much less her skates. She had fretted and fumed and had made life miserable for everyone, and they'd all been glad when she could finally return to practice.

"That was different," she repeated. "I loved skating."

"And you think Mimi doesn't love skiing?"

"I didn't say that," Kira said uncomfortably. "It's just that I think she's skiing to please her father."

"Didn't you want to please Mom and Dad?"

"Whose side are you on, anyway?" she asked indignantly. "Of course I wanted to please Mom and Dad. That's only natural, isn't it? But I think Mimi's obsession about skiing goes deeper than that. I'm beginning to believe she thinks that's the only way she's going to get her father's attention."

Jilly was silent at that, and while Kira waited, she realized how glad she was that she had finally said what had been on her mind these past weeks. If Jilly thought she was off base, then she would have to accept that she was overreacting. She had always trusted her sister's judgment, and if Jilly disagreed with her, at least she had brought it out into the open where it wouldn't fester inside her anymore.

"Well?" she asked, when Jilly didn't answer. "I suppose you think I'm nuts."

"No, I think you might have a point," Jilly conceded. "But let me ask you something, Kira. Have you considered the possibility that your concern about this is because you're more involved with Mimi's father than you want to admit?"

Kira hadn't expected that. "Are you saying that I can't keep my personal feelings separate from my professional judgments?"

"Can you?"

"Of course I can! Honestly, Jilly!"

"Okay, okay," Jilly said hastily. "I just asked. But maybe you should think about your involvement with

Yale. After all, you two were pretty hot and heavy once."

Kira didn't want to talk about Yale; in fact, she didn't want to pursue the subject any further. For some reason, she was feeling guilty and defensive, and she didn't like the feelings at all.

"That was a long time ago," she said finally. "And if I didn't believe it before, I know how much things have changed now. It was stupid to think we could re-capture the past."

"Is that what you thought you were doing?" Jilly asked quietly. "Or was it that you wanted to see if you had a future together?"

Kira hesitated. The question had made her feel even more uncomfortable, and what was worse, she wasn't sure what the answer was. "Whatever I thought, it doesn't matter now," she said. "Yale and I have so many differences that we could never reconcile them all. Not that I want to," she added hastily. "In fact, I'll be glad when we can release his daughter from the clinic so that we can all go our separate ways."

"Well, if that's what you want...."

"It's what I want," Kira reassured her. Then, be-cause they'd been on the phone so long, she said, "Give my love to Brad, will you? And thanks for call-ing, Jilly. The next one is on me."

"Let me know what happens, will you?"

"Nothing's going to," Kira said, but her expression was doubtful when she hung up. As she went to collect her coat and gloves, she couldn't help wondering if she was only fooling herself about wanting Mimi to leave the clinic. Did she really want them all to go their sep-arate ways? Wouldn't her life feel...empty...now, without Yale and his daughter?

Angrily, she shook her head. The thought was absurd. She'd been doing just fine before the Duncans arrived at the clinic; she'd do equally well when they were gone. She had made a new life for herself here; she was finally leaving behind all the sad memories in Seattle. The last thing she wanted was someone to disrupt her newfound security, and she didn't need anyone at the moment to make her life more complete. She loved the clinic and what she was doing there; she felt fulfilled and productive and satisfied, and she couldn't ask for more than that. Bending down to pat Purr goodbye, she shut the cottage door firmly behind her and went to work.

Later that afternoon when she was finally getting around to the neglected paperwork she'd planned to handle that morning, Betsy knocked on the door and asked, "Can I talk to you a minute?"

Kira looked up from the list of equipment she was marking. "Not if it's about the winter carnival," she said, only half teasing. "Anything other than that... come in."

Betsy didn't respond with a smile as Kira had intended. "It's not about the carnival," she said as she sat down. "I thought I'd tell you that Mimi has canceled her last two appointments, and it looks like she's going to miss the one she had today."

Disturbed, Kira sat back in her chair. "Do you know why?"

"The first time she said she had to meet her father's plane, and the second time it was because she wasn't feeling well. I don't know what the excuse is today because I can't get in touch with her. Every time I call, the line is busy."

"What time was her appointment?"

"Three."

Kira glanced at the clock. It was thirty minutes past that now, and she frowned. "That's interesting," she said, more to herself than to Betsy. "Somebody should have called if she wasn't going to be here."

"I know. I thought it was funny, too. That's why I came to tell you. I would have told you about the other two appointments before, but I really didn't think anything about it. After all, patients cancel all the time—"

"Don't worry about it," Kira said, and reached for the phone herself. "We'll try again."

But a busy signal buzzed in her ear, too, and she replaced the receiver with a shrug. "Maybe something came up," she said, and looked at Betsy. "You haven't heard anything about Yale—about Mr. Duncan being out of town again, have you?"

"How could I? Mimi hasn't kept one of her appointments since I took over her case."

Kira's mouth tightened. "Oh, great."

"I'm sorry, Kira."

"It's not your fault," Kira said. "But I think it's time I had another talk with Mimi's father. If she's going to keep canceling appointments, or worse, not ever showing up for ones she's scheduled, she'll have to find another clinic. We can't put up with that. We have too many other patients to think about."

Betsy put a hand on either arm of the chair and stood. "I agree," she said. "That's why I wanted to talk to you. I hope nothing's wrong."

Kira assured her that she would find out, but as Betsy left, she sat back in the chair again, her expression grim. Maybe the only thing wrong was that Mimi was still angry about being transferred to another therapist and was showing it by skipping all her appointments.

The thought made her shake her head in exasperation, and she reached for the phone a second time, only to be frustrated by the same busy signal. Deciding that she'd try again later, she went to check on Miss Jones, who was receiving another hydrocollator treatment, this time from Noreen. After chatting with the librarian a few minutes and learning more than she wanted to about the upcoming heavyweight match, she went on to her next patient, a young basketball player who had fallen on his shoulder trying a slam-dunk.

"What's this?" he asked, eyeing the machine she brought out with suspicion.

"It's called a Transcutaneous Electrical Nerve Stimulator," she said with a smile. When he looked blank, she added, "TENS, for short."

"It looks like a torture machine," he complained, and shuddered when she began to attach the electrodes.

"Come on, it's not so bad," she said calmly, and set the dials. "Besides, a few applications of this, and you'll be back on the court in no time. We use it in cases like yours because it allows earlier muscle and joint function."

"Go ahead, then," he said bravely. "I'm ready."

Trying not to smile when he closed his eyes and gritted his teeth in anticipation, Kira switched on the machine. It was a few seconds before he realized there was no pain, and when he cautiously opened his eyes and looked at her sheepishly, she had to hide her amusement. "See?" she said.

He blushed furiously, but salvaged his pride by saying, "Aw, I knew it all the time. I just wanted to see if you were paying attention."

"I see," she said solemnly, and didn't press it. He was embarrassed enough at his reaction to the machine; she wasn't going to tease him about it...this time.

It was four o'clock before she had time to try Yale's number again. When she got a busy signal a third time, she hung up with a frown. Now what to do? Wondering if she should let it go, and find out what had happened when Mimi called for another appointment, she checked her schedule and decided to go home. She was just taking her coat down from the rack when she stopped with a sigh. She couldn't let it go. It wasn't like Yale not to call, or ask Hilda to do it, and she wondered now if something really was wrong. Now that she thought about it, it did seem strange that the line had been busy all day; even if Yale had called every client he'd ever known, either she or Betsy should have gotten through once on all the tries they had made. Maybe the only thing to do was stop by on the way home and find out directly. It would only take her a few minutes out of her way, and it would set her mind at ease.

It would also give you an excuse to see Yale, wouldn't it? a little voice asked mockingly from the back of her mind.

She shook her head impatiently. She wasn't doing this on the chance that she'd see Yale, she assured herself. After all, Mimi had missed three appointments; there had to be a reason. She'd never forgive herself if something was wrong and she'd been too proud to pursue it, and on that thought, she resolutely started out.

Mrs. Trent opened the door when she knocked, a look of surprise on her face when she saw who was standing there. "Dr. Stanfield!" she exclaimed. "What a nice surprise! Do come in, please!"

Feeling somewhat foolish, Kira stamped the snow from her boots and entered the house. It seemed obvious from the housekeeper's reaction that nothing was seriously wrong, and she wished she hadn't come. But now that she was here, she might as well pursue her errand. She hadn't been inside the house before, and she couldn't stop herself from glancing around curiously. It was charming.

Because this was snow country, the entry was tiled, and an oak rack with hooks for snow gear was affixed to the wall beyond the door. The front door itself was a beautiful piece of work, with etched glass panels and an old-fashioned doorknob, and Kira remembered a melodious chime sounding through the house when she rang the bell. A Queen Anne chair and an antique telephone table stood to one side, the telephone itself looking incongruously modern and stark in contrast. Beyond, she caught a glimpse of the living room before she realized that Mrs. Trent had closed the front door behind her.

"May I take your coat?"

Embarrassed that she'd been staring so openly at the furnishings, Kira quickly shook her head. "No, I'm sorry, but I can't stay. I just stopped by to ask why Mimi didn't keep her appointment today. I hope she's not ill."

The smile faded from Hilda's face, and a puzzled look came into her eyes. "I'm sorry, but I don't know what you mean. Didn't Mimi come to the clinic today?"

It was Kira's turn to be puzzled. "Well, no," she said hesitantly. "That's why I came, to find out why. We expected her at three, but when we tried to call, the line was busy."

Hilda looked even more startled at that. "But...but I've been the only one here since this morning, and I haven't used the phone all day."

They looked at each other, and then at the telephone on the table in the hall. "Is there another phone?" Kira asked.

"Yes, one in the kitchen, and of course the one Mr. Duncan uses in his office. But he's away on business, and I— Oh, dear. I hope it hasn't been off the hook all this time!"

Hilda looked genuinely distressed at the thought, and Kira suggested that they check. As she followed the little woman down a hallway toward the den, she asked curiously, "Where is Mimi, then? Are you sure she knew about her appointment?"

The housekeeper glanced over her shoulder. "Oh, yes, I reminded her of it this morning when she wanted to go visit those new friends of hers, Jack and Alison. I told her I would pick her up in time to go to the clinic, but she said she'd feel like a baby if I had to come and get her, and she had already arranged for Jack to drop her off at three."

Kira was about to comment when Hilda opened the door of the study. They both saw the receiver lying on the desk at the same time. "Well, at least now we know why the line was busy all day," Kira said.

Hilda frowned as she went to put the receiver back in its cradle. Staring down at the instrument, she murmured, "I don't understand. I can't imagine Mr. Duncan leaving the phone off like that."

"Maybe it was an accident," Kira suggested. She really didn't want to talk about the mystery of the telephone; she was more interested in why Mimi hadn't kept her appointment. "About Mimi..."

The housekeeper was just turning to her when the phone shrilled to life. Both of them jumped at the unexpected sound, and Hilda hastily reached out to answer.

"Duncan residence."

Kira had started to turn tactfully away when the housekeeper gasped. She looked back in time to see the color drain from Hilda's face as she choked, "Is she... is she going to be all right?"

The first thing Kira thought of was that Mimi had been in an accident. The horrified look on Hilda's face as she listened to whatever the caller was telling her seemed to confirm her suspicions, and she thought Hilda was going to faint. Leaping forward, she grasped the woman's arm, and was completely taken aback when Hilda shoved the phone at her.

"You take it. I can't make any sense..."

Kira automatically grabbed the receiver. "This is Dr. Stanfield of the Stonebridge Clinic," she said. "Who's this?"

The voice at the other end let out an explosive breath. "Is that really you, Dr. Stanfield? Oh, thank God! This is Jack—Jack Riley."

Kira had already recognized the voice. She had also heard the panic in it, and she said sharply, "Calm down, Jack. Can you tell me what happened?"

"Oh, it was awful. I've been trying to call for hours and hours and the phone's been busy and I didn't know what else to do—"

Kira's voice was shrill in her own ears. "Yes, yes. Is Mimi hurt?"

To her horror, his voice broke. "We didn't think anything would happen, honest we didn't, Dr. Stanfield. It was just a little skiing trip, we weren't even going to take any big runs. Just enough to stretch out a little. Mimi said it was all right, that you had told her she could, and we believed her. Why wouldn't we?"

Kira closed her eyes. The thought flashed through her mind that Mimi had done exactly as she had threatened, but it was too late for recriminations now; there were more important things to find out. "We'll talk about that later," she said. "Now, tell me where you are."

"We're at the hospital!" he cried. "And it's all my fault!"

She couldn't take time to comfort him. "What hospital? Where?"

"In Rutland. Oh, Dr. Stanfield, can you come? I don't know what to do!"

Kira didn't hesitate. "We'll be there as soon as we can," she said, and slammed down the phone.

Her face white, Hilda gasped, "Did you . . ."

Kira shook her head. "I couldn't get much information out of him, he was too upset. But they're at the Rutland Hospital."

Hilda placed a hand over her heart. "The hospital! Oh, dear Lord! Is she going to be all right? Oh, what is Mr. Duncan going to say?"

Because she was so worried and anxious and upset herself, Kira suddenly became enraged with Yale for being gone at a time like this. Part of her realized that he couldn't possibly have known this would happen, but she angrily refused to accept it. This was just what she had tried to warn against all along, she thought furiously. If he had been home, this wouldn't have happened.

She was so angry that she didn't even ask where he was. Grasping the housekeeper by the arm, she said urgently, "I think we'd better leave right now, Mrs. Trent. Do you have the keys to the car?"

Hilda looked at her, eyes stricken. "I don't even know where the hospital is!"

"I do," Kira said quickly. She had been there before, with Miles, to look at some new equipment.

Hilda grasped her arm. "Oh, I'm...I'm so afraid."

They were both afraid, Kira thought; she didn't dare imagine what Mimi had done during this little skiing jaunt; she didn't even want to think about it. "I'll drive if you like. Now, go get your things. I'll meet you at the front door."

They were speeding away from the house in seconds, but it was a silent ride to the hospital. Kira drove grimly, her eyes glued to the road. It had recently been cleared so that they didn't need chains, but she didn't want to take the chance of an accident at this point, and she clung to the steering wheel with both hands. Once or twice she glanced across at Hilda, and didn't say anything when she saw the housekeeper's lips moving in silent prayer. Returning her eyes to the road, she drove on in tense silence until they pulled up at the emergency entrance.

Jack and his girlfriend Alison were waiting by the big glass doors, both almost in tears. Kira didn't give them a chance to say anything, but said curtly as soon as she was inside, "I'll talk to you two later. Right now we want to see the doctor. Where is he?"

His face white, Jack pointed to one of the rooms. "He's in there...with Mimi. She just got back from X-ray."

"Fine," Kira said. "You two stay here."

She didn't wait for an answer, but hurried after Hilda, who had already started in the direction Jack indicated. Kira knocked briskly, and when the doctor opened the door, quickly introduced herself and Mrs. Trent. When Hilda saw the abject and tear-stained Mimi huddled on the examining table, she uttered a cry and rushed to enfold her charge in her ample arms. That left Kira with the doctor.

The man gestured her outside the door. "She was lucky this time," he said quietly in answer to her urgent questions. "We just got the X rays, and there's no new damage."

Kira was so relieved she let out an explosive sigh. "Thank God. I thought she was going to be in surgery again."

"Not that I can foresee." It was obvious that he not only knew who Mimi was, but what her previous injury and treatment had been, and he added solemnly, "It would have been much worse if she hadn't been wearing her brace. As it was, she twisted the ankle, not the knee, but it did have some effect on that medial ligament. I'm afraid you're going to have your work cut out for you in therapy because of this."

Kira had already guessed that much, but that was the least of her worries at the moment. She was so grateful that the damage hadn't been worse that she didn't care about anything else. The fact that Mimi had done such a foolish thing would have to be dealt with, but later. Right now, all she wanted to do was take her errant patient back to Stonebridge.

"Are you keeping her for observation?" she asked.

The doctor considered it, then shook his head. "No, I think she can go home." He glanced around. "Is there any way to get in touch with the parents? Someone has to sign her release papers."

"I can do that, doctor," Hilda said. She had listened to part of the conversation after assuring herself that Mimi was all right. "I'm the Duncan housekeeper."

The doctor looked disconcerted for a moment, but then he nodded. "Well, we haven't admitted her yet, so I guess it will be all right," he said kindly, and smiled. "And I imagine our patient is anxious to get home."

The drive back to Stonebridge was almost as silent as the drive in had been. A subdued Jack and Alison had gone ahead in Jack's car, and as Kira followed at a slower pace, Mimi sat silently in the back seat. The seemingly endless trip finally halted when Kira parked in front of the house again. And as Hilda hurried inside to get things ready, Kira was left alone with Mimi.

"I'm sorry," Mimi said, speaking for the first time since they had left the hospital. "It was a stupid thing to do."

Kira couldn't have agreed more. But she didn't feel that this was the time for a lecture or that she was the person to give it. Without answering, she got out of the car and came around to assist the girl up the steps and into the house. Hilda had already turned down the bed in Mimi's room, and the housekeeper waited long enough to see them safely inside before she rushed off to call Yale's office again. They had left a message before, and she wanted to make sure he had received it. As soon as she had gone, Mimi turned to Kira and clutched her arm.

"I know I did a dumb thing," Mimi whispered, her eyes huge in her pale face, "but please don't hate me, Kira."

"I don't hate you, Mimi," Kira said. She reached out and touched the girl's soft cloud of red hair. "I'm just glad it wasn't serious. Now you get into bed and—"

"Are you going to leave me?"

Kira was startled. "You won't be alone. Mrs. Trent is here."

"Please don't leave!" Mimi cried. "If you leave now, I'll know that you hate me."

"You're being silly, Mimi. I already told you—"

"I promise I'll do everything you want," Mimi rushed on, still holding tightly to her arm. "I'll do all my therapy, and I'll never miss an appointment, and I'll work with anyone you say, just as long as you promise not to leave. Oh, please, Kira. I feel so scared!"

Kira saw that pleading look in Mimi's eyes and knew she couldn't refuse her now. She suspected that there was something more to this than she was aware of, and on impulse, she gave the girl a hug. "All right," she said. "I'll stay. But only until your father gets home."

Mimi buried her face in Kira's shoulder. "Thanks, Kira," she whispered. "I won't forget it."

Wondering if she would regret it, Kira helped Hilda settle their exhausted and penitent patient. The doctor had given them some medication for Mimi to take, and when she had drifted off to sleep, they sat in the kitchen over cups of tea.

"I'm getting too old for this," Hilda said, fanning herself. "When I think what could have happened—" She broke off with a shudder.

Kira felt like shuddering herself. "We were lucky this time. I hope Mimi realizes it."

"I think she does. Mimi is a good girl. It's just that this has been so hard on her...."

They were silent for a few moments, and then Kira glanced at the clock. To her surprise, it was almost eleven, and when she realized that she had forgotten all about Yale, she asked, "Did you ever track down Mimi's father?"

"I tried. I called the hotel where he was staying in Dallas, but he'd already gone. The only thing I could do was leave a message with his California office and hope that he checked with them before he caught another flight. He was supposed to be home tonight, but—"

She was interrupted by the crash of the front door. Startled, they both leaped up and rushed to the living room. Looking like a wild man, Yale was standing there with his coat open and his tie askew, and when he saw them he dropped his briefcase to the floor. "Where is she?" he demanded, tight-lipped. "What happened?"

Kira took one look at his white face and straining eyes and said quickly, "She's all right, Yale. She's home, upstairs in her—"

He didn't wait for her to finish the sentence, but whirled around and took the stairs three at a time. At a gesture from Hilda, Kira hesitantly followed, and came up to the landing just as Yale emerged from Mimi's room. When she saw him put his hand over his eyes and sag against the wall outside the door, she didn't know what to do. She was about to go quietly back downstairs when Yale dropped his hand. He saw her standing there and pushed himself away from the wall. He reached her in two strides, and his fingers clamped like a vise on her shoulders.

"You said..." His voice was a croak and he had to start over again. "You said she's all right?"

His eyes seemed to burn into hers, and she knew this wasn't the time to go into details about renewed therapy. "She's going to be fine."

"What happened?" His face was still white, his expression tense and strained.

"She went skiing with some friends—"

"Skiing!" He looked horrified.

"I know," she said. "I thought the same thing."

His hands tightened even more on her shoulders as he fought to get himself under control. "I don't understand...."

Kira wasn't sure she did, either. Mimi had been too upset and too exhausted to talk about her little expedition, and she hadn't pressed her for details. Surprised, she heard herself say, "Don't be too hard on her, Yale. As Hilda said, this has been very difficult for her."

Sighing heavily, he tilted his head back. "I know," he muttered. "It's just that when I got that message, I thought..." He stopped and brought his head down to look at her again. "Thank you for being here," he said simply.

She didn't know what to say. "Hilda would have done just fine without me."

"I know." His eyes seemed to burn into hers again. "But you were here, and I'm grateful." He paused. Then, his voice hoarse again, he asked, "Why did you stay?"

She knew that if she stayed any longer, she wouldn't want to leave. Aware of his hands beginning to tremble on her shoulders, she tried to turn away. But he held her fast, forcing an answer.

"Why did you stay?" he repeated, his eyes searching her face.

She looked up at him, lost in that deep blue gaze. Something had changed between them again. It was as if, united in their worry and concern about Mimi, all other considerations had been brushed away.

"Because I had to," she whispered, and knew when he drew her slowly toward him that she couldn't leave now if she wanted to. As if it had been planned, she had delayed too long.

CHAPTER TWELVE

"I THINK WE'D BETTER talk about what happened," Yale said, when he and Kira had joined Hilda in the kitchen.

They were sitting around the kitchen table, Kira and the housekeeper with fresh cups of tea; Yale with the strong coffee Hilda had made during their few minutes upstairs. Still bemused at the way he had held her tightly to him only moments ago, Kira stared somberly into her cup. She had seen Yale in many moods, but she hadn't realized until now that he could be so...tender. When he had put his arms around her and drawn her close, it hadn't been a sexual thing at all. It had been an expression of need...of comfort. His arms had trembled slightly, and she had heard the ghost of a sigh before he buried his face in her hair. Surrendering to the warmth she felt at being so close, she hadn't moved until he had eased her away from him. His eyes still dark with worry and concern, he'd murmured, "I think we'd better go talk to Hilda, don't you?"

So they had gone down to the kitchen. Hilda was at the stove, and she turned immediately at their entrance. "I'm sorry, Mr. Duncan," she said, wringing her hands. "I know you trusted me to watch Mimi, and I let you down."

"That's not true!" Kira exclaimed, and because the woman looked near tears, rushed over to where she stood. Placing her arm around the housekeeper's shoulders, she said, "It wasn't your fault, Hilda. Don't you remember what Mimi said?"

"Yes, but I feel so responsible."

As Hilda pulled a handkerchief from the pocket of her print dress to wipe her eyes, Kira glanced at Yale, signaling him to say something. Looking a little helpless, he said, "Don't cry, Hilda. I'm sure there's an explanation for all this. Maybe you'd better tell me what Mimi did say."

With Kira's encouragement, Hilda sat down at the table. She started several times to tell what had happened, but when it became apparent that she was too upset to talk about it, Kira took over. Carefully keeping any shade of blame from her voice, she said, "It was a lark, Yale—or so Mimi says. Apparently she had gone over to Jack's house with Alison to listen to records, and somebody suggested that they go skiing."

"Who?"

Kira had wondered that herself when Mimi was sleepily telling the story awhile ago, but she wasn't about to admit it. Yale could draw his own conclusions; she wouldn't accuse Mimi of instigating the incident, not when she had already expressed her fears to him before.

Avoiding his eyes, she said, "I don't know. It seems to have been one of those ideas that spring to life—you know how kids are. Anyway, before she knew it, they had piled into the car and were on their way."

Yale's jaw tightened. "I don't understand it," he said harshly. "Mimi's not easily led. She would never just blindly follow along. She *knows* she's not supposed to be anywhere near skis until she has permission—"

He stopped abruptly, and when Kira saw his expression, she knew he had followed his own argument to its logical conclusion. Now it was his turn to avoid her eyes, and as though he was too upset to sit still, he sprang up and went to pour himself more coffee.

"I'm sorry, Mr. Duncan," Hilda said, her voice breaking. "If I'd thought this would happen, I never would have given her permission to visit her friends."

Yale glanced at her over his shoulder, and when he saw her face crumple as though she was about to cry, he came back to the table and briefly pressed a hand on her shoulder. "I'm not blaming you, Hilda," he said, sounding bleak himself. His eyes met Kira's briefly, and he glanced away again. "No one could have predicted that she'd do something this foolish. It isn't like her at all."

Kira wisely said nothing to that, though she couldn't help thinking that she *had* predicted it. In fact, she had warned Yale that Mimi might try something exactly like this. If he hadn't been so preoccupied with business, he might have seen it, too, she thought resentfully, and then told herself to be honest. Remembering the conversation she'd had with Jilly this morning, she knew there was a time when she might have done the same thing herself. So would Yale. So would any young elite athlete who was bored and frustrated and kept from participating in his or her sport by well-meaning adults who were afraid of further injury. At that age, every minute counted, and after training so long and so hard, athletes like Mimi developed tunnel vision. There was only the next race, the next competition. The future was something to be worried about later, as were any physical disabilities participation might cause. Kids always thought they were indestructible, even when the evidence that they were not was right before their eyes.

Kira knew that she couldn't really blame Mimi for putting on skis today. It had been a dangerous stunt to pull, but now the important thing was not that she had done it, but why. *Why* did she feel this compulsion to ski before she was ready? Was it because of some drive in her to compete, or was it something deeper, something even she might not understand?

Troubled by her thoughts, Kira glanced at Yale. When she saw his worried expression, she realized this wasn't the time to raise the issue of why Mimi had done this foolish thing. She knew she would have to say something later, if only because Mimi's reasons might have some effect on her therapy, but she was relieved that she could postpone the confrontation. They all had enough on their minds tonight.

Yale took a shuddering breath. "All right," he said. "I guess there's no point in debating why this happened until I can talk to Mimi." He glanced at the silent women, and added grimly, "And believe me, I intend to talk to her about this."

"Don't be too hard on her, Mr. Duncan," Hilda pleaded, unknowingly repeating what Kira had said earlier. "You know how difficult all this has been for her."

"It's been difficult for all of us, Hilda," he said flatly, and looked at Kira again. "I intend to call the hospital myself, but can you tell me what they said tonight?"

He looked so anxious and concerned and bewildered that Kira's heart went out to him. But she didn't want to betray herself now, so she retreated into professionalism and related what the doctor had told them. Yale listened without interruption until she finished with, "He wants you to bring Mimi in tomorrow for a checkup, but he doesn't think there's new damage."

Yale closed his eyes briefly and let out a sigh of relief. When he looked at her again, his voice had regained its steadiness. "What does this mean in terms of therapy?"

"I don't know yet. I'll have to test her on the isokinetic machine before I can tell you that. It will give us a comparison study on both legs, before and after this . . . incident."

He smiled wearily at her hesitation. "I'd prefer to use another word, but we'll leave it at that," he said, and glanced at the clock. He looked startled when he saw what time it was, and said, "I hadn't realized it was so late. Kira, I'd better take you home."

"Oh, that's not necessary," Kira protested. "I can walk."

"You can, but you won't," he said firmly. "I'm not going to have you wandering around by yourself at midnight. God knows what could happen."

Kira smiled. "In Stonebridge? Probably the worst thing that could happen is that our one constable might stop to give me a ride home. Really, Yale, I can manage."

He wouldn't take no for an answer. "After all you did for us tonight? No. Get your coat. I'll take you home right now."

Realizing it was useless to argue further with him, Kira said goodbye to Hilda. "Don't worry," she whispered. "It wasn't your fault."

Hilda offered her a shaky smile. "Well, whether it was or it wasn't, from now on I'm going to keep my eye on that young lady every second," she declared.

Kira laughed. "I don't blame you one bit. Good night, Hilda."

"Good night," the housekeeper said, and then took Kira's hand in both of hers. "And thank you," she added softly. "I don't know what I would have done without you tonight."

On impulse, Kira bent and kissed the woman's cheek. "Oh, you would have managed, I'm sure." she said lightly, and went out to the car with Yale.

He handed her inside, and then went around to the driver's side and got in himself, but it was a moment before he started the engine. She looked at him curiously as he sat there, staring out the windshield, and she was about to say something when he shook his head.

"I just don't understand it," he muttered. "I talked to her before I left for Dallas, and she seemed just fine." He glanced helplessly across the seat at Kira. "What more could I do?"

Kira had no real answer for that. She felt handicapped because she wasn't a parent, and she didn't know what advice to give. She was feeling confused herself; it seemed that Mimi told one of them one thing, and the other something else. Had she ever been that way? A brief smile touched her lips. She couldn't remember. It had been a long time since she'd been fifteen.

"What are you smiling about?"

Yale sounded annoyed and Kira said quickly, "I was just wondering whether fifteen is more difficult on the teenager or the parent."

He grimaced and started the car. "On the parent, most definitely," he said, and shook his head again. "Sometimes I wonder what I'm doing," he added with a sigh. "If I'd realized how hard it was to be a father, I might not have volunteered for the job."

Kira smiled again. "Maybe that's why it's such a well-kept secret."

"Maybe," he murmured, and sounded so woebegone that Kira touched his arm.

"Jilly says that we were the same way at that age," she said, trying to comfort him as they drove along. "So maybe you shouldn't be too hard on Mimi."

"I'm not so sure about that," Yale said, and looked relieved at the change of subject. "How is Jilly? Lord, I haven't seen her in years."

"She's a high school teacher now, living in Seattle, married to a wonderful man named Brad."

"No children?"

Kira shook her head. "Not so far. But she's thinking about it."

"When she gets ready, tell her I can send her a teenager ready-made."

Kira laughed at his half-serious tone. "I'll tell her, but with thirty high schoolers to teach, I think she might want someone a little younger."

He pulled up in front of her house just then, and because she suddenly felt awkward, she didn't know whether to invite him in or not. Before she could decide, he had climbed out of the car and come around to open her door. He didn't release her hand as she stood, and for a moment, they simply stared at each other. Finally, she asked, "Would you like to come in for a nightcap, Yale?"

"I'd like that very much," he said solemnly, and put his hand under her elbow as they went up the icy walk. She felt the thrill of that simple contact through her heavy coat and wondered if she was making a mistake. Remembering her conversation with her sister this morning, she wondered how she could be so adamant one minute, so indecisive the next. But then, she thought, as she dug the keys out of her purse, Yale hadn't been standing right next to her this morning when she talked to Jilly. For some reason, his presence made a powerful difference.

"Do you always keep it this cold in here?" Yale asked, when they were finally inside. A hungry Purr had met them at the door, and Yale stepped gingerly around the cat, who eyed him balefully, as if he was the cause of his delayed dinner.

She'd gone ahead into the living room to take off her coat and toss her purse on the couch, and when she turned and saw Yale rubbing his hands and blowing on them for emphasis, she smiled and pointed at the wood-burning stove. "Be my guest," she said. "I've got to do something about this cat."

"You could always put him out and let him fend for himself," Yale commented. "He might lose a little of that bulk."

She looked at him indignantly, enjoying the byplay after all the tension-filled hours tonight. "He'll be the first to tell you that he's built for comfort, not for speed," she said haughtily, and followed the impatient Purr into the kitchen.

Yale came in just as she was wondering whether to make cappuccino or just offer a warm brandy. When she asked, he said, "Brandy, I think. If I have any more coffee tonight, I'm going to wash away."

"Good. We'll have two."

As she found the snifters and got the brandy out, Yale stood at the sink, staring out the kitchen window. She hadn't realized how quiet he'd been until she stopped bustling around, and when she looked at him and saw the faraway expression on his face, she didn't know whether to intrude on his thoughts or not. After a moment, as though he sensed her staring at him, he turned to look at her.

"I was just thinking about that night I saw you skating on the pond," he said.

She didn't want to talk about that. She still wasn't sure why she had done such a thing, and when she thought of it in those terms, she suddenly understood a little more about Mimi's behavior. If she couldn't explain why she had put on her skates after all this time, how could she expect Mimi to know exactly why she had strapped on a pair of skis this afternoon?

"Yes, well, that was an impulse I regretted the next day," she said, trying to make light of it.

Yale didn't smile as she intended. Instead, he turned and looked out at the pond again. "You know," he murmured, almost as though he was talking to himself, "Mimi is poetry on skis, but I always thought you were the most beautiful thing I'd ever seen on ice."

Despite herself, Kira flushed. "That was a long time ago, Yale."

He turned to look at her again. "Maybe so," he said quietly. "But the other night when I saw you out there, it was as though the past fifteen years had never happened."

She looked away. "We can't recapture the past, Yale," she said.

"No, we can't," he agreed softly, and came to where she was standing. She was powerless to protest when his arms went around her, and his eyes never left her face as he pulled her gently into him. "But we could find a future together...."

She wanted to say that they couldn't, that too much had happened, that they were no longer suited for each other, if they ever had been. But the words refused to come. She was trembling as he lowered his head, and when his lips touched hers, she forgot all her doubts. All the things they had left unresolved fled her mind, and there was only the pressure of his mouth against hers. She gave herself fully to the pleasure of it, leaning into him, winding her arms around his neck. When he finally raised his head to look into her eyes, she felt dazed and breathless and everything seemed right when he took her hand and led her out of the kitchen.

He hadn't set the fire in the stove as she had expected, but in the fireplace, and the leaping flames sent shadows dancing on the pine-paneled walls of the living room. "I'll get the brandy," he said gruffly, and was gone before she could reply.

Still feeling bemused, she sat on the hearth and stared at the flickering light until he returned. Her eyes uncertain again, she accepted the glass from him and then watched as he sat down opposite her. He held up his glass.

He had never looked more handsome to her than he did tonight, in the firelight, and she smiled tremulously as she whispered, "What are we drinking to?"

"To you," he said.

Touched and embarrassed at the same time, she tried to protest. "Oh, surely, we can think of something else."

"I can't," he said hoarsely, and kept his eyes on her face as he touched the rim of his glass to hers and then drank.

After a moment, she followed suit, and the warmed brandy felt like molten gold in her mouth. All her senses seemed heightened: she could hear the crackling of the wood in the fire; she could see the images of the flames dancing in Yale's eyes; she could smell the scent he wore, an irresistible combination of lime and spice. She breathed in deeply, appreciatively, and closed her eyes. She heard the faint clink the glass made when Yale set it down, and she felt him move closer to her. She opened her eyes just as he reached out to touch her face. Tracing her jaw with a fingertip, he moved to her eyebrows, and then, ever so lightly, touched her long eyelashes.

"You have the most beautiful eyes I've ever seen," he murmured. His fingertip moved to her mouth. "And the most expressive mouth. No wonder they called you the Faerie Queen. With that smile, you enchant . . ."

Very gently, so softly that she only felt it as a whisper, he bent to caress her lips with his. When he drew back, his own eyes were dark with suppressed longing, and she could feel the unsteadiness in his hand as he placed it on her shoulder.

"Kira . . ." he said with a sigh, and slid his hand gently up the curve of her neck, cupping her face. Lowering his head, he kissed her again.

This time his kiss was more than a whisper. She felt the tremble in his lips as they pressed against hers, and when he moved closer to her on the hearth and pulled her into him, she felt a tremor in his body. She was quivering herself with all the feelings she had repressed, and when she reached up to twine her arms around his neck, she heard him utter a groan. Her knees felt weak when he pulled her to her feet, but that was all right; his strong arms were around her, holding her up, holding her to him as though he would never let her go.

In the firelight, his eyes looked black, dilated with emotion. "You don't know what you do to me," he groaned, and buried his face in her hair. Together they sank to the rug before the hearth.

"Yale..." she breathed, when his weight pressed her down. Clothes were a barrier that separated them, and they flung them away. When they moved together again, skin to skin, flesh to flesh, it was Kira who sighed.

Yale instantly raised his head. "Am I too heavy?" he asked anxiously.

Kira laughed. "Never," she said. Smiling away his worry, she put one hand against the back of his neck and brought his head down to hers. She kissed him so deeply that he made a moaning sound low in his throat and grabbed her, rolling over and bringing her with him. His hands were all over her body, in her hair, grasping either side of her face as he returned her kiss, then he kissed her again and again, until she was breathless. When his mouth left hers, and he raised her up a little to run a tingling trail of kisses down to her breast, she gasped and arched against him, thrilled at the caress, her body on fire. She had never felt like this; it was as though they both needed this affirmation that they were alive, that everything was all right, that somehow, miraculously, disaster had been averted tonight, and they were celebrating the victory.

"Oh, Yale," she moaned, and wound her fingers through his hair, guiding his mouth to the other breast, gasping with pleasure as his tongue found the already erect nipple there.

The warmth that had begun deep in her belly had spread to her thighs, through her entire body. Holding her tightly with one hand, he brought the other lower, to the most sensitive part of her, finding that tiny peak that seemed to burst into flame as he caressed her. Her body began to undulate of its own accord, her hips moving against him, arousing him even more. Reaching down, she stroked him in turn until they were both panting, ready for each other, longing for the final consummation. Fastening her mouth on his, she guided him into her then moved so that he was on top. Wrapping her legs around him, she pulled him deeper inside her.

The position inflamed both of them even more. Now their movements were almost frenzied. It was as though they were running out of control, lost in a time where nothing mattered except the blissful sensation of making love. Each caress, each kiss and stroke and touch sent them closer to a peak of arousal that had been building since that first gentle kiss. From some distant part of her, Kira heard Yale moaning her name over and over as he kissed her breasts. She couldn't bear the fiery sensation; she knew if she let him continue, she wouldn't be able to stop the tumultuous climax that was throbbing for release now. Her hands in his hair again, she lifted his head from her breast and kissed him passionately as his hips ground against her.

"Don't stop," she pleaded through clenched teeth, her breath coming in ragged gasps as that glorious sensation built. "Don't stop!"

Yale groaned at her increasingly frenzied movements, and his own thrusting became faster, harder, driving them both on. Kira could hold back no longer. With a cry, she arched upward again, digging her nails into his back, gripping him tightly with her legs.

"Oh, Yale!" His name was torn from her. "Come with me...come with me!"

She was already spiraling away, lifted higher and higher by that exquisite sensation, when she heard his own cry of pure pleasure. The moment had caught him, too.

They held each other for a long time after the last spasm drifted away, until the fire died to embers.

Incredibly, she must have fallen asleep, because the next thing she knew, Yale was lifting her from the rug and depositing her gently on the couch. A quilt hung over the back of it, and he tenderly covered her before he started searching for his scattered clothes. Bemused, Kira watched him moving around the dim room, admired the power of his body, the almost-perfect musculature, before she realized what he was doing. She bolted upright, clutching the quilt around her.

"Are you leaving?" she asked, and didn't even care about the plaintive note she heard in her voice.

He had finished dressing by that time, and he came to sit on the couch beside her. Touching her face, he bent and kissed her gently. "I don't want to," he said. "I'd much rather stay here with you. But I think I'd better be there when Mimi gets up this morning."

Ashamed that she'd been so involved with herself and her own feelings that she had forgotten his daughter, Kira clutched the quilt more tightly to her. Glad that there was little light in the room for him to see her embarrassment, she said quickly, "Of course. I'm sorry. I should have realized—"

He stopped her with another kiss. "I'll be back," he said, and was gone.

When the door opened then closed behind him, letting in a tinglingly cold draft of air, Kira lay back against the couch pillows with a smile. She supposed she should get up and go upstairs to bed, but it hardly seemed worth the effort. She hadn't drawn the drapes, and she could see the stars twinkling in the black sky. Though she didn't have the faintest idea what time it was, she knew it was late.

Or early, she thought drowsily, and felt a thump as Purr jumped up on the couch with her. His fur was soft as he burrowed under the quilt and curled up by her side, and she thought to herself, *five minutes. I'll just lie here five minutes. . . .*

It was nearly eight o'clock when she woke again. She took one look at the clock and groaned. If she remembered correctly, she had an early appointment scheduled, and if she wanted to make it in time, she had to hurry. With a quick apology to Purr, she unceremoniously dumped him off the couch and scrambled up the stairs. She knew she didn't have time for a shower, but she took one anyway, racing in and out so fast she barely had time to get wet. Throwing on some clothes, she ran downstairs to feed Purr, then she flung her coat on and left for the clinic.

Miles was waiting in her office when she got there, and she knew there was trouble the instant she saw his face. "What's wrong?" she asked breathlessly. She had run practically all the way around the pond.

"You haven't heard the news?"

"No, I . . . I didn't have time."

Without another word, he handed the morning newspaper to her. "Here. Read it and weep."

One glance at the sports section headline told her why Miles was so upset. Groaning, she sat down behind the desk and spread the paper out. There, in black and white, but thankfully without a picture, was the story of Mimi's outing yesterday. She read the article through once and then looked helplessly up at Miles.

"Did you know about this?" he asked quietly.

She nodded unhappily. She knew why Miles was so upset; the slant of the article indicated that in some way the clinic had been remiss. The writer never really came right out and said so, but the implication was that if they had been attending to business, America's little skiing darling wouldn't have had her accident. The tone was almost, but not quite, libelous.

But she couldn't be concerned about that—not yet, anyway. Miles would straighten it out, and in the meantime she had to explain. "Yes, I was at the Duncan's when Jack called from the hospital," she said, and felt even more guilty. She realized now that she should have called Miles last night, if not from the hospital, certainly when she brought Mimi back to Stonebridge again. She would have called, if she and Yale hadn't . . .

But there was no use thinking about that right now, either. "Look, Miles," she said hastily, "I know I should have called to warn you, but I really didn't think there'd be this much of a fuss."

He gave her an incredulous look that made her feel even worse. "About someone like Mimi Duncan?"

She flushed and glanced away. "Yes, well, but she wasn't hurt," she said defensively, and glared down at the newspaper. "This article makes it sound as though we're back to square one."

"Are we?" he asked quietly.

"No. I talked to the doctor in Rutland, and unless they find something else today when Yale takes her in for another checkup, he seemed to feel that she didn't do any new damage."

"Wonderful," he said, with barely concealed sarcasm. "What was she doing out there in the first place?"

Kira sighed. "I don't know, Miles. Trying to prove something to herself, to me, to her father—who knows?"

"I think it's time we found out," he said heavily. "I really don't care to have a repeat of this. She might not be so lucky next time."

"I know," Kira said unhappily. "I'm sure her father is going to talk to her."

Miles stood. This wasn't a morning for coffee and doughnuts and a comfortable chat, she saw, and felt even worse. "I'm sorry, Miles," she said again. "I should have called you, I know. But there wasn't time when I heard, and then later there didn't seem much point. It was so late by the time Hilda and I got Mimi settled again that I didn't want to wake you. I thought we could talk about it this morning." She glanced distastefully at the sports section again. "I didn't dream I'd be upstaged."

Miles was silent, but when she looked at him pleadingly, he finally relented. "All right," he said. "But next time—"

Kira shuddered. "Let's hope there won't *be* a next time."

He nodded grimly to that, and went to the door. As soon as it closed behind him, she sagged against the chair with relief. It hadn't gone as badly as she'd thought it would when she first walked in, but she knew Miles was still annoyed with her, and that he probably had every reason to be. She felt now that she hadn't handled this situation as well as she could have, and she decided to do the month's budget for him this afternoon when she finished with her patients. Miles hated to do the budget almost as much as she did, but it could be her penance.

Eight hours later, as she was diligently working away over the columns of figures, someone knocked on her door. Thinking it was Betsy, or Noreen, or one of the assistants, she called permission to enter without looking up.

"I'll be right with you," she murmured, toting up the cost of the gauze pads and Ace bandages they had used that month.

"Take your time," a familiar voice said, and followed that by tossing three airplane tickets on top of her desk. "Calculate these in while you're at it, will you?"

Surprised, she looked from the tickets up to Yale's handsome face. He was smiling that wonderful smile of his, and she felt herself blossoming under it. Flushing slightly, she glanced down at the desk again. "What are these?"

"What do they look like?" he asked in amusement, and closed the door. Coming around to the back of the desk where she was sitting, he grasped her shoulders and pulled her to her feet. Before she could protest, he was giving her a deep kiss.

"Yale!" she exclaimed, when he released her. Her eyes flew to the door. "What if someone came in ... What if they—"

He grinned. "Are you ashamed?"

"Of course not! It's just—" She saw that she wasn't going to get anywhere with him in this mood and decided she couldn't wait for him to tell her. Trying to ignore the tingling of her lips from that kiss, she said, "I was going to call you about Mimi, but I didn't know what time her appointment would be. Did you take her to the doctor today?"

He sobered. "Yes. It's as you said. There's no new damage."

Kira let out a sigh of relief. "Thank goodness for that."

"But the doctor did say that he thought she should get away for a while."

She was instantly alarmed. "For how long?"

"Oh ... about a weekend," he said innocently.

Her glance went to the airline tickets again, and she felt deflated. "Oh," she said, trying not to show her disappointment. "And you and Mimi and Hilda are going. I see."

"You don't see anything at all," he said, grabbing her by the shoulders again. His eyes were a deep, hypnotic blue as he stared down at her. "Mimi and I want *you* to go, not Hilda."

"Me!"

He laughed. "You make it sound like the idea's inconceivable."

"Well ... but ... it is!" she stammered, and wondered why it should be. She didn't know the answer to that; she just felt that things were moving too fast. Already her head was spinning, and she had no idea what to say. She couldn't just go off for a weekend with him; she didn't know what would happen. Yes, she did, she thought hastily. She just wasn't sure yet if she wanted it to.

"Yale, I can't go," she said quickly. "I've got work—"

He raised an eyebrow. "On the weekend?"

She flushed. "Of course not. But...but there are other things."

"Such as?" He grinned. "If you're worried about your cat, I'll ask Hilda to feed him. Not that he needs it. A two-day fast might do him a world of good. Improve his mood, too."

"Yale, this is no joking matter!"

He sat on the edge of her desk, casually swinging one loafered foot back and forth, amused at her distress. Then he stopped smiling and stood again, his expression somber. "I'm not joking, Kira," he said quietly. "After what happened last night, I think it would be a good idea to get away."

She faltered before that piercing blue gaze. "You mean because of Mimi's accident," she said faintly. "And all the publicity."

He put his hands on her shoulders, his thumbs tilting her head up so that she had to look at him. "No," he said. "I mean because of us."

"Yale..."

He stifled her weak protest. "I'm not sure what's happening to me, Kira," he said softly. "But something is, and I know you feel it, too. I thought this would give us both time to find out what it is. Are you willing to take the chance?"

She didn't answer for a long moment. Finally, she sighed. Glancing away from those hypnotic eyes, she reached down and took one of the tickets. With a shaky smile, she turned back to him and said, ''What time does the plane leave?''

CHAPTER THIRTEEN

MIAMI INTERNATIONAL Airport was busy, but Yale whisked Kira and Mimi through as though he'd been there dozens of times before. Remembering that this was the site of the Orange Bowl and the headquarters for the Miami Dolphins, the professional football team, Kira wasn't surprised. She had learned by now that Yale's client roster was comprised of athletes from every imaginable sport, including one of the favorites here, jai alai. Mimi had confided excitedly on the flight down that Ricardo Renaud, the newest jai alai sensation, had recently sighed with Yale. Kira had gathered from Mimi's awed tone that Ricardo was, to use one of Mimi's expressions, quite a hunk.

But as Yale drove the rented Lincoln onto the Airport Expressway toward Miami Beach, Kira was much more interested in Miami's famous skyline. She had never been here before, and she hadn't realized until Yale explained that the city of Miami itself was on the mainland, while Miami Beach was on an island across the bay. He had made reservations at Bal Harbour's Fontainebleau, but as the plane descended, he had pointed out Miami's downtown, recognizable by the stand of high-rises that included the award-winning Cultural Center and the Southeast Financial Center, the tallest building south of Manhattan.

It was all so exciting and so different from Stone-bridge—from any place Kira had been—that she felt like laughing with pleasure. And every time she glanced across the seat at Yale, she tingled all over. They had all gratefully shed their heavy winter clothes for the trip, and he looked so handsome in his open-necked sport shirt and linen slacks that she had to force herself not to reach out and touch him just to make sure he was real.

Even more gratifying to see was the change in Mimi. Her depressed mood seemed to lighten with each passing minute, and by the time they landed at the airport, she was almost her vivacious, voluble self again. Kira was also glad to see that except for a slight limp, Mimi didn't seem the worse for her skiing accident. They had all carefully avoided the subject on the flight, but she couldn't help remarking on it to Yale when they reached the famous hotel. Mimi had already gone eagerly ahead into the red velvet and chandeliered lobby, and after watching her with clinical interest, Kira turned to Yale.

"Mimi seems none the worse for her experience," she said as he handed the car keys to a valet. A bellman was already waiting on the curb with a rack for their luggage, and Yale glanced at the doorway where Mimi had disappeared.

"I hope you're right," he said somberly, watching the removal of their bags from the trunk. "I had a long talk with her before we left, and I don't think she'll be that foolish again."

Kira didn't reply to that, but she couldn't help wondering if Yale and his daughter had really worked things out, or if things had just been smoothed over again. Then she was ashamed of herself. She had no reason to be suspicious, and if Mimi's present attitude was any indication, she had learned her lesson. Or at least she hoped so, Kira thought. Mimi had been lucky this time, but they couldn't count on her being so fortunate again.

Once inside the hotel, though, she stopped worrying about Mimi and was awed by the grandeur of the place, instead. According to the brochure she picked up while Yale was registering, the Fontainebleau was the largest hotel in the Miami area, with a one-acre pool, cabanas, gym, solarium, restaurants, bars, night clubs, meeting facilities, drug store and just about everything else anyone could imagine. With the lighted tennis courts and boutiques and a bowling alley, it was like a city in itself, and once registered, a guest never needed to leave. It seemed that anything anyone could possibly want could be found right here.

Kira was even more amused when she discovered that Yale had reserved a connecting suite for the two of them, with a separate room for Mimi. "Did you think you were being discreet?" she murmured.

He gave her a surprised look, and when she gestured with her head to Mimi, who was grinning openly at them, he reddened. "I keep forgetting she's not a child," he muttered back, and tried to avoid the mischievous look in his daughter's eyes as they went up in the elevator.

"Wow," Mimi said, when the bellman opened the door. She turned to him with an excited expression. "Dad, can I stay in here with you? This is fabulous!"

Yale reddened again. "You can if you want to, Sprite," he said bleakly. "But I thought you'd prefer your own room."

Obviously enjoying herself, Mimi wandered around, gawking at the luxurious furnishings. The view from the vast windows was spectacular, and after pausing there a moment to gaze out, she finally turned back to her father. "I guess you're right," she said with a broad grin. "I would rather have my own room. That way I can order room service whenever I want, and stay up all night if I like. Right?"

Boxed neatly into a trap, Yale gave Kira a helpless look. She had to smother her laughter when he said weakly, "Right."

"Great!" Standing on tiptoe, Mimi gave him a quick kiss on the cheek before she flitted off to her own room. As soon as she was gone and they were alone, Kira collapsed in laughter on the couch.

"Boy, you really handled that one well," she said, her eyes dancing at his discomfiture.

He sat down beside her. "Yeah, I did, didn't I?" he said with a grimace. He glanced at her. "Were we that smart at her age?"

She looked wry. "Somehow I doubt it."

"Well, at least we're here," he said with a grateful sigh, and put his arm around her shoulders, drawing her close. She caught a whiff of that spicy lime scent he wore, and closed her eyes in pleasure. "And we've got a whole two days to relax and do nothing but laze around and..."

She looked up at him. "And...?" she prodded mischievously.

He kissed the tip of her nose and drew her even closer. "And whatever comes naturally," he murmured.

She had just raised her head for his kiss when there was a quick knock on the door, followed immediately by "Dad? Guess what? I found the most exciting thing!"

Yale and Kira looked at each other, and when she saw his expression, Kira burst out laughing again. Pulling away from their intimate embrace on the couch, she smoothed back her hair and said, her lips twitching, "Don't you think you'd better answer it?"

"No," he said, looking exasperated and amused at the same time. "Maybe she'll think we've gone down to the pool or something."

The knock came again, louder and more exuberant this time. "Dad?"

With a sigh, Yale got up to answer the door. Mimi burst in, waving a fistful of brochures. "Guess what?" she cried. "If we hurry, we can see all these things before we leave tomorrow. What do you say?"

Kira couldn't say anything; she was trying too hard not to laugh at the look on Yale's face.

In the end, they made a tour of Miami and environs that day that would have put a travel guide to shame. Every time Mimi excitedly suggested another stop on her itinerary and Kira saw Yale's reaction, she felt like laughing again. Like Mimi, she was having the time of her life.

Kira had never enjoyed zoos; she had always felt that the animals would be much better off in their natural habitats. But Mimi insisted that a visit to Miami wouldn't be complete without at least a quick tour of the Metrozoo, which had gained a national reputation as one of the best cageless zoos in the country. Once they were there and saw the famous white tigers roaming on a grassy island with a Siamese temple as a backdrop, even Kira had to admit it was worth the visit.

From the zoo they went to the Monkey Jungle, where the visitors were the ones in the cage. Kira had never seen so many apes in one place at a time, and it was a disorienting feeling to see them running free outside while she and Yale and Mimi were confined to a screened-in walkway.

"Do you think there's something symbolic in all this?" Yale murmured. Kira laughed and agreed there might be.

When they stopped for lunch—Yale insisting that he would not go another step until he had fortified himself—Mimi was quiet for about two seconds as she pored over her brochures. Then, "We can go to the Everglades next," she said eagerly.

Yale groaned. "Oh, Sprite, not today!"

"Of course not!" Mimi exclaimed. "Today we go shopping!"

Two malls later, Kira was amused to see that Mimi was an inveterate shopper. When Yale collapsed on a bench and she commented on Mimi's inexhaustible energy, Mimi turned to her and said blissfully, "Oh, I love shopping when I have time! Dad, are you ready now?"

They'd sat there exactly two minutes, and Yale groaned. It was late afternoon by that time, and they had already visited the Falls, a mall built around a winding waterway and actual waterfall, and were facing what Mimi enthusiastically told them was the Miracle Mile, a four-block-long street of shops that sounded endless to Yale.

"I've got an idea," he said cajolingly. "Why don't we go back to Bal Harbour instead? I've heard they've got a Neiman-Marcus and Ungaro and Rive Gauche and a Martha there."

Mimi's eyes gleamed. "Rive Gauche?"

Yale nodded wearily. "I'll buy you one thing—just one," he said warningly, "and then we'll go back to the hotel. If I don't get some rest before dinner, I'll probably fall asleep right in the soup."

"Oh, Dad," Mimi said with a giggle, and led the way to the Bal Harbour Shops, the most exclusive shopping mall in the area.

Two hours later, Kira and Yale supported each other inside the hotel while the tireless Mimi rushed off to her own room to try on her purchases: the beaded and fringed Western shirt whose price had made Kira gasp, the two pairs of boots made of leather so soft Kira could hardly believe it was real, and the three pairs of jeans with the distinctive label on the back pocket, each so tight-fitting that Yale had wondered how Mimi had tried them on without help. Inside the suite, they both collapsed on the sofa again, too tired to move.

"I'd get you a drink, but I don't think I can make it to the bar," Yale said.

"That's okay," Kira replied, resting her head against the back of the couch. "I don't think I'd have the energy to drink it if you did."

He nodded gratefully and let his head fall back, too. After a moment, his eyes closed and he smiled. "Well, I don't think Mimi is depressed anymore, do you?"

Kira grinned, deciding to tease him a little. "Oh, I don't know. Today was a beginning, I guess."

He raised his head. "What do you mean—a beginning?"

Her smile became even more mischievous. "Well, there's still the Everglades tomorrow."

He groaned and threw his head back again. "Thanks for reminding me. Until now, I'd forgotten about that."

She leaned over, snuggling against him. "Oh, come on. You'll enjoy it once you're there."

His arms went around her. "I can think of other things I'd enjoy more," he replied, his voice suddenly husky.

She raised her head. "What?"

He looked down at her and kissed the tip of her nose. "Oh . . . just things," he said, and smiled.

Her eyes sparkled. "Isn't this where we came in? As I recall, we were talking about something like this this morning. You don't want to start something only to be interrupted again, do you?"

He hugged her more tightly. "Why do you think I bought her all those clothes?" he murmured.

"I knew you had an ulterior motive," Kira murmured back, and laughed as he picked her up and carried her into the bedroom.

The big bed was soft as he carefully set her down, and when he settled himself beside her with a sigh, she was glad the mood was slow and languid. They had time to explore each other this time; there was none of the frenzy each of them had felt when they'd made love before.

Not that she didn't desire him as much, she thought; gazing into his handsome face, she realized she desired him even more. But before, their hunger had been an insatiable thing, a power that ignited desire, like a flash fire, sweeping them along mindlessly, neither of them having the will to wait.

Tonight was different. With the lights of Miami Beach beginning to twinkle so far below them, they lay in the big bed and just gazed at each other.

"Are you glad you came?" he whispered finally. His finger traced her face, and she took his hand and pressed her lips against his palm.

"Yes," she whispered back, and moved closer to him. "I never thought it could be like this."

"Nor did I," he said with a sigh, and carefully put his arm around her, drawing her to his side. She lay her head against his chest, listening to the strong, steady beat of his heart under her ear, and when she finally slid her fingers under his shirt and touched his skin, he drew in a breath and turned toward her again.

One by one, he undid the buttons of her blouse and slowly slid the material off her shoulders. She was wearing a suggestion of a bra, a flimsy thing of satin and lace, and when he slipped the straps of that down her arms, too, then ran his tongue over the swell of a breast, her breath caught. Gently pushing her back, he did the same to the other breast, and then his head dipped lower. She felt his fingers at the waistband of her slacks, and then the tug as he tried to pull them down. She helped him by raising her hips, and gasped as he reached for her bikini panties. Naked, she lay on the bed, one of his hands holding her gently down, the other separating her thighs so that he could caress her there. When he lowered his head and used his tongue on the sensitive flesh between her legs, she moaned and tried to bring his head up to hers again.

"No," he murmured. "Let me..."

She had no choice. His caresses, his stroking and his kisses in that most sensitive of all places, drove her wild, and one second she knew she couldn't stand it, and the next, she didn't want him to stop. A flooding warmth was spreading through her body, every nerve felt on fire, every inch of her skin so alive that it was almost an agony.

"Yale..." she groaned and grabbed frantically for him. "Please..."

He was breathing hard when he flung himself off the bed and stripped. When he returned to her, naked, she could see that his arousal was complete. He lay on top of her, but instead of guiding him inside her as he wanted, it was her turn to please him. Pushing him over onto his back, she lowered her head. He uttered a hoarse sound when she teased him with her tongue; when she took him in her mouth, he groaned.

She hardly heard him; she was lost in sensations of her own. His body felt strong and lean and hard under her seeking hands. The very maleness of him was exciting to her, and she felt flushed. Sweat broke out on her skin, and for some reason it added to the sensations she was feeling. He was so powerful; she couldn't get enough of him.

But her body betrayed her at last. Responding to the throbbing she felt herself, she climbed on top of him. His face was contorted with desire when she guided him inside her, and she arched her back with pleasure. He ran his hot hands from her hips, up her torso, to her breasts, squeezing, kneading, pulling her toward him so that he could suck one, then the other. His body moved powerfully under hers, lifting her with each thrust, and with every pulse, her desire for him swelled. Their mouths met, hungrily, fiercely, and they clung together, their bodies moving as one.

She felt that surge of pleasure and wanted to hold on to it, to delay for another blissful moment, to prolong the anticipation, but she was helpless against the tu-mult.

"Yale!" she cried.

"I'm here," he gasped, and went with her.

Some time later, Kira lifted her head. They were still sprawled on the bed, too exhausted to move after that cataclysmic bout, and when she saw what time it was, she sat up.

Yale felt her movement and groaned. He was face down in the pillow, and he groped blindly for her. "What's the matter?"

"Nothing, it's time to get dressed," she said. "Mimi will be here any minute."

He groaned again. "Tell her I changed my mind."

"You tell her. I'm going to go get dressed."

Blearily, he raised his head. "Do you have to?"

"Yes," she said firmly, and gave him a push. "And so do you."

"You're a hard woman, Dr. Stanfield."

"You'll thank me for it in the morning," she said with a grin, and went through the connecting door into her own room.

They went to the Palm, an offspring of the same in New York, and one of Miami Beach's more elegant dining spots. Kira was surprised at Yale's choice, for Mimi had been raving about Mr. Clyde's, a rib place with supposedly the best barbeque sauce in the world, until they were seated inside. Adorning the walls of the dining room were caricatures of local and national ce-lebrities, and when Mimi saw a drawing of herself, she didn't know whether to be flattered or embarrassed.

"Did you know about this, Dad?" she demanded, her cheeks pink.

Before Yale had a chance to answer, the maître d' came up, along with two waiters. All asked for Mimi's autograph, and as she signed, her cheeks reddened even more.

"Oh, Dad," she demurred, when they had gone. But Kira could tell she was pleased, and she gave Yale a private glance to which he shook his head. She smiled, thinking what a thoughtful gesture it had been, and allowed Mimi to grandly order the house delicacy for all of them: lobster that was flown in daily from Maine and Iceland.

After dinner, they took a stroll to help burn off the rich meal before they returned to the hotel. As Kira walked with Mimi on one side of her and Yale on the other, she thought that it had been a long time—longer than she could remember—since she had been this happy. All the doubts she'd ever had about the wisdom of a relationship with Yale seemed to have vanished, and every time she looked at his handsome profile, she felt a thrill.

Her euphoria lasted until morning.

Although it had been an effort of will to get up early after a night in Yale's arms, Kira had forced herself out of bed at eight. She didn't want to be blatant about their affair, and with Mimi excited about the Everglades expedition that day, she especially didn't want to be caught in bed with him if Mimi unexpectedly popped in.

So, feeling dazed and sated and decadently lethargic after that magical night, she dragged herself off to a shower. As she stood under the spray, she lifted her face to the warm needles of water and closed her eyes luxuriously. She hadn't dreamed that she could experience more with Yale than she already had, but last night he had proved her wrong. She'd lost count of the times they had made love after saying good-night to Mimi, and she smiled to herself as she reached for the soap. Many more nights like that, and she wouldn't be worth a thing. Even now, she felt drugged; it was an effort just to stand and let the water flow over her.

Somehow, she dressed. During dinner, they had managed to dissuade Mimi from something ominously called a 'wet walk' through the swamps in favor of a more sedate ranger-guided canoe trip, and Kira was looking forward to it by the time she entered the sitting room of the suite. Yale had awakened and ordered room service, and when she heard him on the phone in the bedroom, she poured a cup of coffee and wandered to the window to enjoy the view until he was finished.

When she heard him hang up and come into the room, she turned with a smile that disappeared the instant she saw his face.

"What is it?" she asked quickly. "Is something wrong?"

He seemed uncomfortable, unable to hold her gaze. "I've got to go meet a client," he said finally.

She felt relieved. For a moment, she'd thought that something had happened to Mimi. Thinking that the client was here in Miami, she said, "All right. Mimi and I will wait for you here."

As though he needed something to do with his hands, he poured a cup of coffee, gesturing toward the one she held with the pot.

"No, thanks." She could tell by his face that something *was* wrong. Tentatively, she said, "Yale? You do plan on coming back in time to go to the Everglades, don't you?"

He set the coffee down without tasting it. "I...um...I'm afraid not," he said.

She stared at him. "What?"

He jerked his head in the direction of the bedroom. "That was Wally Kozinski on the phone," he said, avoiding her eyes. "My service put him through, and I've got to meet with him...today." He took a breath. "In California."

"California!"

Hearing her shrill tone, he tried hastily to explain. "I know it's bad timing—"

"Bad timing!"

He winced. "Yes, bad timing. But I've been working on this guy for months, Kira. Can I help it if he's finally decided he wants me to represent him?"

"If he's waited this long, why can't he wait one more day?" she demanded. "Why do you have to see him *now*?"

Yale looked more uncomfortable than ever. "Because I promised him I'd come today. He might change his mind, and—"

She couldn't believe she was hearing this, that they were even having this ridiculous conversation. What difference did one more client make to Yale? He had more than he could handle right now!

"What about the promise you made to Mimi?" she exploded. "You told her you'd take her to the Everglades today, remember? Isn't your daughter more important than another client?"

He reddened slightly. "Mimi will understand."

She looked at him incredulously. "And what if she doesn't? If I'm having a difficult time understanding this, how can you expect a fifteen-year-old to accept it?"

His flush had become a red stain that was working its way up his neck. "Because Mimi knows about my work. She'll understand that this is important."

"What's so important about Coski, or Kozelli, or whatever his name is?"

"Kozinski," Yale corrected, sounding angry now himself. "And don't tell me you've never heard of him. He's the new running back who's been in the papers lately."

"No, I—" she started to say, and stopped. "Kozinski," she repeated. Her eyes narrowed in recognition, and then widened with disbelief. "You don't mean Big Wally Kozinski! The one who drives his car into plate glass windows and starts fires in hotel rooms? *That* Wally Kozinski?"

Yale was almost crimson now. "Wally told me this morning that those stories have been exaggerated."

"Exaggerated! How can you possibly exaggerate driving through a window, Yale? What in heaven's name are you thinking of?"

"He said it wasn't his fault!" Yale said sharply.

Her sarcasm was withering. "Oh, I suppose the car drove itself up the curb and right into that store window. He didn't have a thing to do with it!"

"Something was wrong with the steering!"

"Yes, the man at the wheel!"

"He said it was an accident!"

Her eyes flashed. She remembered the stories she'd read about Kozinski now. "Like the fire in the hotel room was? As I recall, it was right in the middle of the floor, under the bedspread he had put up as a teepee when he was playing Indian."

Yale was beet red by this time. "He didn't know what he was doing. He'd had too much to drink."

"And that makes it all right?" she said incredulously. "My God, Yale, do you actually intend to represent this... this person? How can you possibly want your name linked with his?"

"Because he *has* a name, that's why!" Yale exploded. "Because he's highly marketable, because he's hot right now."

"Hot!"

"Yes, hot! Do you know how many endorsements I can get for him, how many—"

"And all at a percentage for you, right?"

"Yes, at a percentage for me!" he shouted. "What's wrong with that?"

She was too furious now to care what she said. "I should have known you hadn't changed, Yale. You're just like you always were—out to make a fast buck. You don't care who you step on to do it, who you hurt!"

"That's not true!"

"Isn't it?" she said scornfully. "I knew you when, Yale, remember? I knew you when you'd do anything to further your career, even taking kickbacks under the table!"

The veins were standing out on his neck by this time. He looked angry enough to smash something, but Kira didn't care. She was angry enough to throw something, too. Oh, she should have known this was all a pipe dream; she should have realized that sooner or later it had to end. She and Yale would never agree; they didn't share the same standards, the same beliefs, the same morals or ethics or opinions. It had been impossible from the first, and this latest argument proved it. If Yale had been the man she wanted him to be, he never would have cut short his holiday with his daughter to sign up an irresponsible football player, just because he had a *name*. Money and prestige and power had always been more important to him than any relationship, and if she ever needed proof of that, she had it right now. She had practically begged him to stay, and he had refused. Didn't that demonstrate clearly exactly where his loyalties lay?

"You never did understand, did you?" he said bitterly. "You were always such a damned little prima donna. I don't think you ever had to struggle for anything in your life!"

She was furious at that. "That's not true!"

"Isn't it? Oh, it was so simple for you, back then. Kira Blair, the Faerie Queen! If you needed new blades for your skates, Daddy bought them. If you needed a new skating costume, Daddy was right there to pay for it. Well, it wasn't like that for me, Kira, and you had no right to look down from your ivory tower and judge me! You did it then, and you're doing it now!"

"And you're not?" she flared. "*You* were the one who called me a coward and a quitter, remember? *You* were the one who said I just didn't have it in me when the chips were down!"

"Ah, that's what this is all about, isn't it? You're still festering about that fight we had, after all these years!"

"You're damned right I am!" she cried. "You just said I had no right to judge you, that I didn't understand. Well, I understood, all right. You didn't want that gold medal because of the honor it would bring you or the sport, or even because it would prove you were the best at what you did. You wanted it because of the money it would bring you. The money! That always was the most important thing to you!"

"And what was important to you?" he flung back. "Everything was okay when you were winning, but what about when the pressure was on? You couldn't handle it, Kira, remember? You were falling apart. I always did wonder if you threw that axel purposely. If you couldn't skate, you couldn't lose!"

"How dare you say that to me!"

"Is it true?"

She was so furious she didn't even realize what she was doing. They were standing face to face, shouting at each other, and without even thinking, she drew back her hand and slapped him as hard as she could.

Yale rocked with the force of the blow, but he didn't raise his hand to touch the red marks she had made on his cheek. After a tense moment of silence, when Kira didn't know whether to apologize or burst into tears or run out of the room or what, he said, very quietly, "You know what I think is wrong with you? You're jealous of any sports figure who becomes prominent. You could have been right up there with the best, Kira, but you gave it away. I don't think you've ever forgiven yourself for that."

Her face was white, her stark green eyes the only color. "And I don't think you've ever forgiven yourself for not winning that gold medal, Yale," she whispered, her voice shaking with anger. Later, she would wonder why this had happened, why they had hurled all these terrible accusations at each other, but right now she was too furious to care. How could he do this to her? How could he do it to his daughter? Her chin lifted and she looked at him contemptuously. "That's why you're so obsessed with your work, Yale," she said. "That's why you can't see how much your daughter needs you. What are *you* trying to forget? That you're an also-ran...like me?''

Without waiting for him to reply, she turned and left the room. She didn't know what he said to Mimi; she didn't care. It was all she could do to retain her precarious composure as they checked out of the hotel and drove to the airport. With the subdued Mimi beside her, she flew back to Vermont. Yale had left directly for California.

And good riddance, she thought, resting her head against the back of the seat. As far as she was concerned, she never wanted to see Yale Duncan again.

CHAPTER FOURTEEN

KIRA HAD PROMISED Mimi the night of her skiing accident that she would take over her therapy sessions again herself. She hadn't been influenced at the time by the possible publicity, or what the press might say if they discovered their star skiing attraction wasn't receiving the attention of the head of the department; she'd been more concerned about the patient herself. Even before Mimi had clung to her and begged her to help that night, she had already decided to take over again, but now it was the morning after that ignominious return from Miami, and as she waited for Mimi to arrive at the clinic, she wondered if she'd made the right decision, after all. As the clock inexorably approached the hour of Mimi's appointment, she still didn't know how to handle this awkward situation, or what she should say. Wishing she wasn't too embarrassed to confide in someone, she paced her office and thought about that awful trip back to Vermont yesterday.

Mimi had been mercifully silent during the tense flight, her head buried in a teen magazine with garish pictures of rock stars wearing outrageous makeup and even more unbelievable hairstyles. Trying to dredge up her courage to explain their hasty departure, Kira had glanced at a few of the more incredible photos and was distracted by the question of why anyone would voluntarily want to look like that. *I must be getting old,* she'd thought, and put her head back against the seat. It was true; she did feel as though she had aged a century in the past two days, and without realizing it, she'd fallen into an exhausted sleep. She woke as the plane landed, and she never had found an opportunity to explain things to Mimi. By the time they arrived in Stonebridge, it seemed too late for explanations, and finally she had just dropped Mimi off at the house and went wearily home herself.

But she couldn't avoid Mimi any longer. She had an appointment this morning at the clinic, and as Kira stood at the office window, sipping a cup of coffee, she still didn't know what to say when Mimi came in. She couldn't just pretend everything was fine; she had seen the sidelong glances Mimi had given her on the way to the airport, and it had been obvious that she knew something other than her father's sudden business trip was wrong. Chagrined at the thought that she owed Mimi some kind of explanation, Kira wished now that she knew what Yale had told his daughter. Mimi hadn't said anything, and she'd been afraid to ask.

She was still reluctant to broach the subject, and as she finished her coffee, she wondered if it might just be best not to say anything at all. Then she sighed. That was the coward's way out. She was reluctant to talk about this because she still wasn't sure how she felt about the situation herself.

Her lips tight, she glanced down at the empty coffee cup. She knew one thing, and that was how angry she was with herself for ignoring all the danger signs. She had known from the beginning that she shouldn't get involved with Yale again, but because she'd allowed her attraction for him to overwhelm her good sense, she had convinced herself that it didn't matter that they had never worked things out from the past. Blinded by him, she had been as ready to gloss over their problems as apparently he had been, and now she was paying the price for her foolishness.

Wondering what Yale was thinking this morning, she looked out the window again, her glance straying toward the Duncan house. They were both to blame, she thought. They never should have gotten involved again if they weren't ready to work out their differences, if they weren't ready to admit that they had serious problems in the first place.

Or maybe, she thought glumly, neither of them had wanted to bring up the past because they had both known instinctively that things wouldn't work out. How could they, when she and Yale came from such different backgrounds?

Remembering the argument they'd had, the accusations he'd hurled at her about being a prima donna, about living in an ivory tower, Kira felt her face flush. Maybe it was true, she thought—or had been, then. But could she help it if her father had been able to support her skating and his family, too? Was she to blame because she hadn't had to struggle for every penny?

Was it Yale's fault because *his* father hadn't been able to provide? Was *he* to blame because he had been forced to accept help from outside sources? He wasn't the only one who had done it. She hadn't been so self-involved at the time that she hadn't heard rumors about other athletes, about the money that changed hands, about the funds that were funnelled through skating or skiing or hockey—or any of a dozen other clubs. She'd known about that, but it had never really affected her... until she'd found out about Yale.

Pressing her hands against her hot cheeks, Kira closed her eyes. She had known that Yale's father was a construction worker and that his family rarely came to his races, but she hadn't really given it much thought. Embarrassed, she had to admit that she'd never given much thought at that time to anything but her skating. What difference did it make to her what anybody else had to do to participate in a sport? She was America's little darling, the country's hope for another gold medal; as long as she could go on competing and winning, she didn't care about anything. She'd been so wrapped up in her own little world that nothing else had mattered.

Then she had found out about Yale, and the blinders had been torn from her eyes. She was forced for the first time to face reality, and the ugliness of it had horrified her. She'd been so angry at him for making her see what was real. She'd been so... so disappointed in him for being a part of it. It was a shock to realize that her knight had a chink in his armour, and she'd been furious with him for letting her down.

Or maybe that had only been her excuse. Chagrined at the thought, she tried to thrust it away. It was all so long ago, she told herself, what did it matter now?

"If you couldn't skate, you couldn't lose! I always did wonder if you threw that axel purposely."

Yale's voice rang in her head, and she closed her eyes in pain. She had tried to drive that terrible accusation from her mind, but it returned to haunt her now, making her face another question. Maybe she hadn't really been angry with Yale for accepting outside support. Maybe the problem was that she had been jealous of the fact that he'd gone out and won his medal, while she . . . she'd been afraid even to try.

A cry escaped her, and she put a hand to her mouth. No, it wasn't true, she told herself desperately. She couldn't have competed, not with that ankle! She remembered, she remembered so well. Her ankle had been so swollen that even if she'd been able to lace her skate around it, it never would have withstood the stress. If it wouldn't bear her weight in practice, the strain of her long program would have been impossible. She had four double jumps planned for the competition; she would have fallen on the first one.

But you could have tried.

The ghostly voice rose at the back of her mind again, and she turned abruptly from the window. The clock struck nine just then, and she drew in a deep breath. She wouldn't think about it anymore. She couldn't change the past even if she tried. Setting her coffee cup down, she left the office and went down the hall toward the therapy room.

Mimi was there when she arrived, already changed into the T-shirt and shorts she wore during her workout. Tense herself, Kira didn't ask why Mimi was so quiet; she suspected it was the same reason she felt discouraged herself. Still, they had to try to get through this somehow or the session would be wasted. She knew how a patient's state of mind affected progress, and even though she had tested Mimi before they left for Miami and discovered that she hadn't lost much ground because of her accident, after all, she knew they still had a lot of work ahead of them.

Deciding that a cheerful approach would be best, Kira determindedly put aside her own depressed feelings and said brightly, ''Which shall it be first today—the bicycle, or the trampoline?''

Mimi didn't even look up. She was sitting on one of the therapy tables, swinging one foot, apparently absorbed in the movement. Shrugging, she muttered, ''I don't care.''

Suppressing a sigh, Kira glanced at her clipboard. This was going to be more difficult than she had anticipated, and she wondered if she should say something now about the quarrel she and Yale had had in Miami. Glancing covertly again at the girl, she knew she didn't have the courage just yet, so she said, ''All right, then, how about the bike? Have you already warmed up?''

She had given Mimi a set of stretching exercises so that her muscles wouldn't be stiff before she started her workout, and Mimi nodded listlessly. ''Yeah, I did everything I was supposed to.''

''Fine, then. Shall we begin?''

Her steps dragging, Mimi moved to one of the stationary bicycles. Everything seemed an effort for her today, and when she hauled herself up to the seat and began to peddle unenthusiastically, Kira knew she had to say something.

''Mimi, what's wrong?''

Looking down, Mimi shook her head. Her shoulders were bowed, and she was gripping the bike handles so tightly her knuckles were white. ''Mimi?''

The bike pedals slowed, then stopped, but still Mimi didn't look up. When Kira realized the girl's shoulders were shaking, she immediately set the clipboard down and put her arm around her.

''Mimi, what is it?'' She was really alarmed now, afraid that the girl was in pain and hadn't told her.

Mimi finally looked up. Before she could say anything, she burst into tears. Flinging herself off the bike, she threw her arms around Kira and held on tightly. "Oh, Kira," she cried. "I'm so afraid!"

Trying not to feel helpless, Kira held her tightly and patted her back. After a moment she tried to lift Mimi's face so she could look into her eyes, but Mimi buried her head in her shoulder and shook with sobs. They were alone in the therapy room, but Kira wasn't sure how long that would last, and finally, she said, "Would you like to go to my office?"

Mimi shook her head. She had her face covered with her hands now, and Kira reached under the table where they kept various supplies. She found a tissue and handed it to her. "Tell me what's wrong, Mimi. Is it that your father had to cut our Miami trip short?"

Mimi shook her head.

"What is it, then?"

The blue eyes were tragic when Mimi glanced up again. "I'm never going to ski again, that's what's wrong!"

Kira was startled. "That's not true!" she exclaimed. "Why, you're making excellent progress, even after your accident last week." She wanted to say something about that, but instinctively she knew that now was not the time. "You'll be back on skis in no—"

Mimi shook her head violently. "No, you don't understand!" she cried. "I won't! I'll never be able to ski again! I tried, and it didn't work!"

"What do you mean—it didn't work?"

"Don't you see? Why do you think I went skiing with Jack and Alison? It wasn't a prank, Kira. I knew I shouldn't go, but I had to. I had to see if I still had it, if I had the guts to go all out. And I didn't, Kira—" Mimi's voice broke, but it was as though once started, she had to go on. "I stood at the top of that hill and looked down, and I was more afraid than I'd ever been in my life. I knew I wasn't going to get down without falling, and I didn't. I didn't! Do you know what that means? I've lost it. I'll never be able to ski again!"

Kira listened to this outpouring with increasing horror. There was no doubt that Mimi meant what she said; even in the telling, her voice vibrated with remembered fear. But before she could think of something to say, Mimi was rushing on.

"I'll never forget how it felt," Mimi said with a shudder, her eyes wide and straining as she relived it all in her mind. "I can remember rolling over and over again and crashing into those bales of hay, and cartwheeling some more. I thought I was never going to stop, and then I thought I didn't want to stop because I knew that once I did, I'd be dead. And now I can't get that picture out of my mind. Every time I think about skiing, I get afraid and I know I'll never be able to do it again and I—"

"Stop it!" Kira said sharply. She knew she had to put an end to this before Mimi became completely hysterical, and she placed her hands on the girl's shoulders and shook her, forcing that blank look to retreat from her eyes, forcing Mimi to focus on her. "Now, listen to me," she went on. "I know you're scared, and I understand. You took a terrible fall. No one would blame you if you didn't want to ski again."

Mimi stiffened under her restraining hands. "But I have to, don't you see? What will my father say if I don't?"

Kira didn't hesitate. Despite her own conflicting feelings for Yale, one thing she was sure of was that he loved his daughter. He might not show it all the time, but she knew he did. "Your father only wants what's best for you, Mimi," she said fiercely. "He wouldn't think less of you if you never skied again."

"You still don't understand!" Mimi shrilled. "I only started skiing in the first place so that he would notice me! I thought that if I was good enough, he'd want to be with me more than he did his clients. But now that will never happen. I'll never be the skier I was before, and he won't want to stay home with me because I'm not famous anymore!"

Horrified, Kira watched as Mimi crumpled into tears again, drawing her knees up and huddling into a ball. She wondered how Mimi could think such a terrible thing, and then was struck with the knowledge that this was what had been wrong all the time. This was the reason Mimi had been so obsessed with skiing; this was the reason why she was so anxious to return to her sport. Mimi *did* think that skiing was the only way to get her father's attention; Kira had been right all along. Somehow, the knowledge brought no satisfaction.

"Mimi," she said quickly, "listen to me. Your father is proud of your accomplishments, but he cares more about you. I'm sure if you explained—"

"No! No, I'd never tell him! And you have to promise not to tell him, too! Please, Kira, if you do, I'll never forgive you. I'll... I'll run away!"

Normally Kira would have ignored such melo-drama, but one look at Mimi's face told her that the girl meant what she said. "All right, all right," she said soothingly. "I won't tell him."

"You promise?"

"I promise."

Mimi let out an explosive breath of relief, slumping from her taut position. "Thanks," she said shakily.

Kira didn't want to say it, but she had to. "Mimi, you can't hide this from your father forever."

Immediately agitated again, Mimi looked up with those stricken eyes. "Yes, I can! I'll think of something, I will!"

"But—"

As though suddenly realizing how much she had said, the deep fears she had confessed, Mimi jumped down from the table. "I thought you'd understand!" she cried. "I thought of all people, you'd be on my side! After all, *you* never returned to competition after you were injured. I thought you'd understand why I can't!"

Kira felt as though she'd just been slapped. "It's not the same thing, Mimi."

"Isn't it?" Mimi shrieked. Her face was blotched with tears, and her hands were clenched into fists. Alarmed, Kira tried to reach for her, but she moved away. "Oh, forget it!" she cried. "Just forget it. I want to go back home to California and never ski again. Go ahead and tell him if you want! He'll know soon enough that I'm a failure. He might as well hate me now!"

"Mimi!" Kira cried, horrified. But before she could reach for her again, the girl turned and ran from the room.

Somehow Kira managed to get through the rest of the day. But she was preoccupied and distant, and the staff, sensing that she was troubled about something, kept out of her way. Even Miles left her alone, though she was tempted several times to confide in him and ask his help. In the end, uneasily remembering her promise to Mimi, she said nothing, but she was still disturbed when she left the clinic that night and walked slowly home.

Should she tell Yale what Mimi had said? She wasn't sure. He had told her before in no uncertain terms that he knew his daughter better than she did, but it was obvious now that he didn't know her as well as he thought. Would he be glad she had broken her promise to Mimi, or angry that she had tried to interfere? She worried the problem as she fixed a dinner that she couldn't eat, and she was still mulling it over when she gave the scraps to Purr and listlessly cleaned the kitchen.

I thought of all people, you'd be on my side! After all, you never returned to competition after you were injured....''

Mimi's accusation still rang in her ears, and she bit her lip. She'd told Mimi it wasn't the same, but was it? Maybe, deep down, she'd been glad that lack of money had prevented her return to competition; maybe she had been relieved that she had an excuse not to make a comeback. What would she have done if her father hadn't died, and the funds were still there? She would have been in the same situation Mimi faced now. Could she have conquered her fear?

For she had been afraid, she had to admit it now. Yale was right when he'd accused her of being afraid to fail; he'd been right when he said that the pressure had been too much. Everyone in the world, it seemed, had been waiting breathlessly for her to come through with a gold-medal winning performance, and even now she could remember that bone-chilling fear. What if she failed to do it?

"If you couldn't skate, you couldn't lose!"

Was it true? Had she subconsciously given herself an excuse? *Had* she thrown that axel?

Mimi was wrong, she thought suddenly. She *did* understand how Mimi felt. She knew the fear, and she knew the reluctance to return to something that had hurt you. But how to tell Mimi that? How to show that she wasn't alone with that fear?

The idea came out of nowhere. Or maybe it had been there all along, lying in wait at the back of her mind. She had always comforted herself with the notion that her injury had prevented her from competing for the gold, but she wasn't injured now. The winter carnival was a week away. Could she do it in that amount of time?

She had to, she thought grimly, and went into the bedroom to get her skates. Her hands shook as she opened the case and looked inside, but she had known the die was cast the instant Mimi accused her of not understanding. Snapping the locks shut on the case again, she knew that it was time to show Mimi—and herself—that it was possible to perform in spite of fear. Fortunately, there was a rink in Manchester, and she decided to use it so she could practice in private. As she went out to the car with her skates, she thought about having seven days to prepare for the competition she had never completed. Tossing the skates into the car, she got behind the wheel. It was time she finished what she had begun all those years ago, she decided, and started the engine.

YALE STOOD at one of the windows of his big condominium in Huntington Beach, and stared somberly out at the night. He had a drink in his hand, but it was untouched; he'd only poured it to give himself something to do. He didn't know why he'd gotten the bright idea to stop by the condo; he supposed it had something to do with checking the place to make sure the plants hadn't died or the pipes hadn't backed up while they were all away in Vermont.

Then he knew that wasn't true. He paid the manager quite well to make sure that everything was all right in his absence. The simple fact was that he hadn't wanted to go back to Stonebridge, not just yet. He'd concluded his business with Wally Kozinski, and even though he'd had time to catch a return flight, he'd delayed long enough to miss it. He needed to stop somewhere, and think.

Sighing, he thought that it seemed as though that's all he had been doing since he left Miami. That argument he'd had with Kira had been going around and around in his mind until he thought he'd go crazy. It had even affected his meeting with Wally. He'd taken one look at that giant hulk and all he could think of was what Kira had said. Was a man who smashed his car into plate glass windows for fun more important than his daughter? After meeting with Wally, he wondered why he had ever come. But then, he was wondering about a lot of things these days, and it was all Kira's fault.

Frowning, he thought that he never should have suggested that trip to Florida. He should have known something would go wrong. As much as he hated to admit it, Kira had been right about one thing. It seemed that he couldn't even take two days away from business now, what with all the demands on his time. But, damn it, she didn't understand. Being a sports agent wasn't a nine-to-five job; his clients depended on him to be there when they needed him. Was it his fault that they seemed to need him all the time?

His frown deepened. Sometimes he thought that he was nothing more than a glorified babysitter, required to be there no matter what his personal feelings were, when someone needed to hold his hand. This business with Wally Kozinski was a perfect example. The man had called, and he'd immediately dropped everything to rush to California and sign him before he changed his mind.

What are you trying to forget, Yale? Why are you so obsessed with your work that you can't see how much your daughter needs you?

Kira's angry voice rose in his mind again, as it had been doing for the past two days, and he winced. That accusation she had flung at him had hurt more than the slap she had dealt him across the face. Was it true that he couldn't forgive himself for not winning the gold? Was that why he'd become so obsessed with work?

Grimacing, he turned away from his unseeing contemplation of the night. Of course it was true, he thought; it was pointless to deny it. After losing out on the gold, he had vowed that he would never again be second best. Never again be an... also-ran. Kira had been right about that, too, but was that a fault? What was the harm in wanting to be the best? Wasn't that what it was all about?

Muttering a curse because he knew that wasn't what it was about at all, and because his churning thoughts wouldn't leave him alone, he threw himself into a chair and wearily rubbed his eyes. He'd been wondering for days now if Kira hadn't been right about Mimi. She'd been right about so many other things, why not that? *Had* he been so obsessed with his work, with getting ahead, with financial success, that he hadn't really listened to his daughter? Oh, he had heard her assurance about understanding why he had to be gone so much; he had heard her assertion that it didn't matter because she was away so much of the time herself. But had he really listened to what she was saying? Maybe all these years he had only heard what he wanted to hear. And maybe Mimi had told him those things because she knew he wouldn't have heard anything else. Had she said what she had because she wanted to please him?

Dropping his hand, he stared broodingly in front of him. Kira had asked him once if he knew why Mimi was so avid about skiing. Did he know? Was he sure? Or was that another thing Mimi had learned to please him, too?

Without warning, he remembered a strange incident in the ambulance right after her accident at Lake Placid. He'd gone with her, of course, sitting right by the cot, holding her hand, terrified to let her go. His head had been filled with those terrifying images of his daughter careering down that mountainside, and he'd been brushing away tears when she suddenly looked up at him. The attendants had given her something to relax her, and he'd thought until then that she was asleep.

"What is it?" he'd asked quickly when he realized she was staring at him. "Are you in pain?" He'd been ready to grab one of the paramedics by the collar and compel him to do something when Mimi shook her head.

"I'm sorry, Dad," she said with a sigh. "I let you down."

He was appalled that she thought such a thing. "Oh, no, Sprite," he'd said, tightening his grip on her hand.

He was afraid to touch her anywhere else until they'd reached the hospital and the specialist had examined her thoroughly. "How could you think that? You didn't let me down at all."

He was chagrined to see the look of hope that leaped to her eyes. "Really? Do you mean that?"

"Of course I do, darling. How could you possibly think anything else?"

The anxious look returned, and she searched his face. "Then you're not disappointed in me?"

"Of course not. I could never be disappointed in you, Mimi. I love you."

She continued to look at him, but he could see whatever medication she'd received working again, for her eyelids drooped heavily. At last, her voice a sigh, she said, "Then you won't leave me?"

"Never," he'd assured her, and bent forward to kiss her gently on the forehead. She'd fallen asleep then, and he watched her until they reached the hospital, willing everything to be all right. It hadn't been, of course, and he'd forgotten about that conversation until this moment. But now he couldn't help wondering...

He'd thought at the time that when she asked him not to leave she meant that she didn't want to be left alone at the hospital. But now he wondered if she had meant something else. Did she really think that he'd abandon her if she couldn't ski?

At first, he rejected the idea as absurd. But the more he thought about it, the more convinced he became that that was exactly what she had meant. Galvanized, he bolted upright and reached for the phone. He had to call her; he had to make sure she understood how ridiculous that was. He had to reassure her...

He had dialed the first four numbers before he realized what time it was. It was after eleven here, too late to call. Mimi would be asleep, and she'd be alarmed if he woke her to babble something about never leaving her. She'd think he'd lost his mind.

Maybe he had. Maybe he was the one who was being absurd. His head in his hands, he groaned. He didn't know what he thought anymore. Kira had him so turned around that he couldn't think straight about his own daughter, much less about her.

The thought startled him, and he raised his head. What *did* he think about Kira? he wondered, and knew the answer immediately. Even though they'd had so little time together, Kira had made him realize how much he'd been missing in his life. Even after that blazing argument they'd had—maybe because of it—he wanted her more than ever. She was the other half of himself that he'd been searching for without even knowing it. Along with Mimi, she was a reason to come home. Somehow he had to convince them both of that, the two women in his life; somehow he had to convince them that he was willing to change, that he *had* changed. The only problem was how.

He sat in the chair for a long time, staring unseeingly at the floor. Finally, just when the first fingers of dawn were exploring the dark sky, he stirred. Sometime during that long night of introspection, he had found the answer.

CHAPTER FIFTEEN

OPENING DAY of winter carnival dawned clear and cold and fair, and started with a flourish by Miles, who was especially proud that the governor had come. When he grandiosely presented the distinguished silver-haired man, the applause was genuine. The governor was a popular man who didn't believe in long speeches.

"You don't want to listen to me when the parade's about to start," he said after a few opening remarks, and to the delighted laughter of the crowd, raised his arms as a signal for the carnival to begin.

As always, one of the most popular events was the annual sleigh parade, modeled after St. Paul's famous winter carnival. Stonebridge couldn't boast a participation of sixty or more of the old-fashioned sleighs and their smaller counterparts, the cutters, as St. Paul could, but everyone enjoyed the exhibition to the fullest. Cheers competed with the jingling of bells as the half-dozen vehicles glided down the main street of town, and bets were taken as to which was the most authentic. Since both drivers and their horses were outfitted in the appropriate attire from a century or two ago, the competition was extremely difficult to judge, and when Elmer and his two Belgians, their manes and short tails beribboned and belled, won pulling a refurbished hundred-year-old draft wagon, the applause swelled.

Then it was time for the ice sculpture contest, which this year had produced a wonderful array of modern and traditional ice art. The favorite turned out to be the huge Mickey Mouse sculpture Mr. Hepplewhite had whimsically carved in front of his little store, and he excitedly offered free hot cider to everyone when he won.

Kira had found out from Miles that Mimi had taken part after all in hiding the treasure medallion, helping to compose clues that had appeared in the Stonebridge newspaper for days now. When Tad McAlister, her youthful admirer from the hayride, triumphantly handed over the medallion from its hiding place in the stone lion's mouth in front of the library, he received more than he bargained for. Along with the twenty-five-dollar finder's check, Mimi gave him a kiss on the cheek that made the crowd laugh in delight as he blushed crimson.

Then it was time for the hockey tournament and the speed skating. Watching from the sidelines, Kira tried to cheer with the rest when the home team scored, but she was too anxious to enjoy herself. Now that the day was here—worse, that the hour was almost at hand—she wondered if she'd lost her mind. She wasn't ready for this; she knew she wasn't. She was going to go out there and make a complete fool of herself.

"Nervous?" a voice murmured in her ear.

When she turned and saw Miles smiling at her, she nearly clutched him in relief. Because he was the chairman of the carnival, she had told him what she intended, but he was the only one who knew. It had been announced that there would be a surprise event later in the day, and speculation was buzzing all around her about what it would be. She was sure everyone she saw was wondering if she was involved, and by the time late afternoon rolled around, she was a wreck.

"Nervous?" she repeated, and stifled the urge to laugh hysterically. "Heavens no. What makes you think that?"

He laughed and patted her shoulder. They were standing some distance away from the hockey spectators, but mindful of the secret, he leaned closer to her. "You haven't changed your mind, have you?"

Oh, she was so tempted to say that she had. "No," she muttered, glancing covertly at the cheering crowd. The final minutes were ticking away on the clock, and she looked nervously back at Miles. "Just promise me that you'll come out and throw a blanket over me if I fall, all right?"

He laughed again. "Do you want me to leave you out there?"

"Will you?" she said hopefully.

He shook his head and patted her again. "You won't fall," he said, and winked at her. "Don't you remember? The Faerie Queen never fell in competition, not once."

She looked heavenward. "Trust you to remember that."

He gave her a little push. "Go on, you'd better get ready. The game's almost finished, and it will be dark soon."

"Good," she muttered. "Maybe no one will see me."

He tried to hide his smile. "Don't worry about that. Elmer spent three hours last night wiring floodlights."

She gave him a sour look. "Be sure to tell how much I appreciate that."

"I will. Now go. I'll announce you as soon as I see you come out to the pond."

He turned to leave, but she grabbed his arm. "How's Mimi?" she asked. Ever since that traumatic day when Mimi had run out of the clinic, Miles had taken over her therapy. Kira had briefly told him what had happened, but not what Mimi had said, and they had agreed that it might be best for him to work with her for a while. She hadn't talked to Mimi since, and though she had seen her around today and tried to catch her eye, Mimi had studiously ignored her. She hadn't seen Yale, either, but that was no surprise; Miles had found out that he was still out of town. She'd been relieved when she heard that. She wasn't ready to talk to Yale yet. Not until she had succeeded—or failed—at this.

"Physically, Mimi is doing fine," Miles said in answer to her question. His eyes sought out that bright red hair in the crowd. "As to her emotional state..." He shook his head and looked at her again. "I wish you had let me tell her about this, Kira."

She had debated about that, but in the end, she had decided not to say anything about her participation in the carnival. She wasn't sure why, exactly. Perhaps it was because she had to prove something to herself first.

"She'll understand soon enough," she said, and hoped it was true. Trying to smile, she added, "Well, I guess I'd better go get ready," and then was struck by an awful thought. "I did give you the music, didn't I?"

"Yes, you gave me the music," he said solemnly. "I've got everything I need... except you."

There was nothing to do then but go inside and change. She had never really known why she had saved her skating dresses all these years; perhaps because they were so beautiful. Crafted by one of the most famous designers of the time, every one was a gorgeous creation of sequins and beads and chiffon and lace. She hadn't expected any of them to fit, and had been surprised when she had tentatively tried one on the other night. Except for a little tightness across the bust, the brief dress fit perfectly, and when she had pirouetted in front of the mirror, she'd been taken back years. This beautiful white costume, with the gold and silver beads and sequins in a glittering spray over one shoulder and spilling diagonally down across her waist, was the dress she had decided to wear for her final program. As she'd taken it off and hung it up again, she'd thought how apt it was that she would use it for this.

"Ladies and gentlemen!" Miles called over the microphone. His voice rang out into a sudden silence as the crowd around the pond turned toward the rostrum. They'd been told to expect a surprise, and it was obvious that everyone wondered if this was it. A sound of excitement rippled through the spectators as Miles paused to make sure he had their attention, and Kira shivered involuntarily under the cape she wore to disguise her costume. True to his word, Miles had begun his announcement when he saw her step to the edge of the pond. The hockey players had departed, and the ice had been swept. Elmer's floodlights had just been turned on, and under their glare, the surface of the pond looked…expectant. Shivering again from nerves, Kira looked toward Miles and willed him to go on.

He did. "I'm sure by now you've all heard about the surprise guest we have with us today." He smiled at the renewed murmur that rose up to meet him, and went on, his voice suddenly choked. "And I just want to say how honored we are to have her. It's been fifteen years since any of us last saw her perform, and the skating world has been a dimmer place with her absence."

People were starting to turn toward her now, but Kira ignored them. She knew she'd lose what little courage she had if she met anyone's glance, so she kept her eyes firmly glued to Miles.

"I know how anxious you all are," Miles continued, his voice booming out over the loudspeaker, "so without further ado, it is my pride and pleasure to present to you a three-time National Champion, twice World Champion, America's own Faerie Queen...Miss Kira Blair Stanfield!"

In a sudden deafening silence, Kira stepped to the edge of the ice and threw off her cape. The sequins on her dress glittered in the spotlight Elmer turned her way, and in the instant she paused a sound started. Softly at first, almost reverently, then swelling with excitement and abandon and awe. It was the sound of applause, and for a moment, Kira was so overcome at the welcome that she didn't move. She couldn't go out there, she told herself frantically. What if she disappointed them? What if she failed?

The sequins flashed again, sending out sparks and rainbows of light as her heart started to pound with fright. Her legs were shaking, and she had completely forgotten her routine. Even the blades on her feet felt foreign; she couldn't remember how to skate!

Then, from behind her, came strong hands supporting her waist and a voice she would never forget. "You can do it, Kira. I always knew you could."

Startled, she looked around, directly into Yale's face. When she saw the glitter of tears in those deep blue eyes, she forgot everything else. He knew how difficult this was for her, she thought. He understood!

"It's your moment, love," he said hoarsely. "You've waited a long time for this. Go take it."

Somehow, without realizing it had happened, she found herself stepping out onto the frozen surface of the pond and gliding to the center, where she struck her opening pose. Miles started her music, and with the first bars, Kira forgot her fear. As she had before, so many years ago, she burst from the pose to balance delicately on the point of a blade, one leg straight behind her, her head up, her arms lifted like wings. She looked like a beautiful creature, poised for flight.

Except this time she wasn't going to run, not like she had before. She might not be the champion she once was, her body might not be capable of doing the intricate movements she had practiced so endlessly all those years ago, but she could still create the magic that had earned her the title of Faerie Queen. She knew it; she could feel it as she whipped around in a three turn and started a series of backward crossovers to build up speed. The music flowed with her, building to a fortissimo that propelled her into a long back outside edge, then into a forward inside mohawk, and from that into the axel she had missed during that long-ago practice. Vaguely, she heard the gasp of the crowd, but she had already landed as light as a feather, and was moving forward into a combination of a waltz jump, half loop, and then into a salchow. She landed each one with the grace and poise that had made her famous, and before the swelling applause of the spectators could subside, she was into the first of two split jumps, leaping into the air so high that she looked as if she was floating. She continued with a falling leaf jump and went right into a flying camel, her torso and her extended leg absolutely perpendicular to the ice. The roar of applause was so deafening that she could hardly hear her music, but it didn't matter. She knew that music by heart; she had practiced hours and hours and hours to it, and as she started around the perimeter of the ice in a series of traveling toe turns, or chenais turns, it was as though she was flying. The crowd went wild when she stepped into a bauer, that graceful move with one leg stretched behind and the other knee bent in front, and with her back arched, she traveled the length of the pond on a diagonal, her arms lifted in graceful counterpoint. The noise from the cheering, shouting crowd was one long sustained sound, music to her ears.

Then, too soon, it was time for her final move. She caught a glimpse of Mimi's awed face as she rushed by, but she didn't have time to do more than smile. This was the move she was famous for, the move that had been named after her, and she had to do it right. Slowly, her back bent into that incredible arch that had never been duplicated, her head dropped back, her arms wafted up, and the crowd went mad. No one had ever been able to do the Blair Layback the way Kira had. It had been years since anyone had seen it performed with such grace and precision and utter beauty, and for a few seconds, there was absolute, awed silence when she came out of it and dropped like a butterfly onto the ice into a deep bow.

Then the applause exploded again, a swelling sound of cheering and hoarse shouting and whistling that resounded throughout the town. Kira stayed where she was for a moment, her head bowed, her shoulders shaking, but not from exhaustion. When she finally looked up, the spotlights caught the glitter of tears on her face. She had done it. She had performed that final program at last. Then she looked over and glimpsed Yale standing with his daughter. When she saw the look of awe and admiration in their eyes, her joy was complete.

"WASN'T SHE GREAT, Dad?" Mimi breathed, watching as Miles ran out to throw his arms around Kira and present her to the still-applauding crowd.

"Yes, Sprite, she was," Yale said, and blinked rapidly. He knew what this had cost Kira, and he was so proud of her that he felt like cheering. He took a surreptitious look around and saw that he wasn't the only one with tears in his eyes. What Kira had just given them would be a memory everyone here would treasure.

Mimi tugged at his arm. "Can we go talk to her, Dad?"

Yale looked out and saw Kira immediately surrounded by admirers, nearly lost in the press of the crowd as she came off the ice with Miles. He smiled. That was the way it used to be, he thought; oh, he remembered it well. He always had had to wait his turn. Then, as now, her fans had been legion.

"I think we'll wait awhile," he said, deciding to let Kira have her moment. She had waited a long time for this; she deserved to enjoy every second of it. He glanced down at Mimi again. "In the meantime, I'd like to talk to you, Sprite. Do you mind?"

Mimi hesitated. He'd come home this morning in time for the opening of the winter carnival, the first time they'd actually been together in a week. She looked for a minute as though she expected him to say he was going off on business again, and her voice was low when she said, "Sure, Dad. What about?"

The crowd was clearing, spectators heading toward the town hall where a huge potluck had been set out as a finale to the carnival. But there were still scattered knots of people around, and Yale didn't want to say what he had to say where anyone could hear. Glancing over to the copse of pines a short distance from the pond, he remembered a bench inside the clearing there and led Mimi toward it. Once under the sheltering trees it was as though they were completely alone, but now that they were, and Mimi was sitting on the bench gazing expectantly at him, he wasn't sure how to begin.

"I've been doing a lot of thinking lately, Mimi," he said finally. "And I wonder how you'd feel if I wasn't gone so much."

Mimi's face lit up before she could stop herself. But that bright look vanished as quickly as it had appeared, and she said warily, "Gee, I don't know, Dad. I haven't thought about it before."

Yale was silent, studying her. Kira had been right all along, he thought, and saw his daughter with new eyes. She was telling him what she thought he wanted to hear, and he wondered how he could have been so blind.

He cleared his throat. "Haven't you, Mimi? Haven't you really thought about it before?"

She glanced away. "I don't know what you mean," she muttered. "You've always been gone a lot. It's the nature of your business."

"It was," he said carefully. "But I don't think it's going to be that way anymore."

She looked up quickly. "What do you mean?"

"Mimi," he said hesitantly, "I think it's time for us to be honest with each other, don't you?"

She hesitated. "Sure," she said finally. "I guess."

He took a deep breath. He had never told anyone—not even Kira—this story before, but sometime during the past week he had finally come to grips with it himself. Oh, he'd done a lot of thinking since he and Mimi had come to Stonebridge, and it was all due to Kira. She had made him see things he had never seen before; she had made him realize what he'd been running away from for years. He knew he was going to have to face her after this, but right now, he had to square things with his daughter.

"Mimi," he said, and sat beside her on the bench. Before he lost courage, he plunged in. "I'd like to tell you why I've been so involved in my work all these years. I'd like to explain—"

"You don't have to, Dad," she said quickly.

He reached for her hand. "Yes, I do. I want to. As I said, I think it's time for us to be honest with each other...."

And so he told her—about his father, the grandfather she had never known because he died right before she was born. Ross Duncan had been a carpenter, a man who had worked hard on construction all his life, a man who had been a hard drinker, and who had wanted both his sons to follow in his footsteps. Rory, Yale's older brother, had obeyed his father's wishes, and Yale had believed he was destined for the same life, too—until he'd gone on a skiing trip with some friends. After that, things had never been the same.

He'd known from that point on that skiing was what he'd been meant to do. He was a natural—like Mimi—and nothing could keep him away from the sport. Because his father wasn't going to give him money for "that damnfool sissy skiing business," he had worked odd jobs after school, saving every penny he could so that he could rent equipment and buy lift tickets and spend as much time as he could on the slopes. He took lessons from the local pro and soon surpassed him, but when he tried to talk to his parents about training seriously, his father was furious. Skiing was a rich kid's sport, a waste of time. If he pursued this stupid pipe dream of his, he couldn't expect any help from him.

He'd accepted that, he told Mimi, because despite his father's scorn, he had to ski. He left home, scrimping and saving and working at odd jobs along the way to train. And he started to win. And win. Then when it began to look as though he was actually in contention for an Olympic medal, he became determined to get it. He had vowed to show his father that he'd made the right choice; the medal would prove that he had done something valuable with his life.

And then he lost the gold by a hundredth of a second. Ross Duncan called him the night of the race and told him he'd always known it was all for nothing. To him, Yale would always be second-best.

"And that's when I decided no one would ever say that about me again," he finished painfully. "I became a sports agent, because sports were what I knew. But I became obsessed with financial success." He looked sadly at his daughter. "And somewhere along the line," he added softly, "I think I lost track of my priorities. I'm sorry, Mimi...."

Mimi had listened to the story in wide-eyed silence. Now tears sprang to her eyes, and she threw herself into her father's arms. "No, I'm the one who's sorry, Dad! I didn't know. I never realized!"

He held her away from him. His expression somber, he gazed into her eyes and said softly, "That's my story, Sprite. What's yours?"

Mimi gulped. But her father's confession had freed something inside her, and once she started, she couldn't seem to stop. It all poured out of her: how she thought it was her fault that he was gone so much, how she had decided that if she became famous enough, he'd want to be with her instead of his clients. She loved to ski—the desire was in her, too. But always, at the back of her mind, was the desperate desire to win, to hold on—not to a title or an award or medal—but to him.

"And when I thought I'd never be able to ski again, I was so scared, Dad," she ended. "I thought...I thought..."

She couldn't finish, but there was no need. Enfolding her in his arms again, Yale hugged her tightly. "Don't you know that the only thing that matters to me is you, Mimi?" he said. "I don't care if you never ski again. I've always been proud of your accomplishments, but I'm more proud of you. You're the most beautiful daughter a father could ask for."

Mimi drew back a moment to search his face. Then, with a sigh, she snuggled against him again. "Oh, Dad," she breathed, wrapping her arms tightly around his waist. "I love you."

"I love you, too," he said roughly, and for the second time that day, blinked back tears. "We're a pair, aren't we?"

"Yes, you are," Kira said, and stepped into the clearing.

When Yale and Mimi looked up in surprise, Kira tried to find the words to explain her appearance. She had finally been able to escape her newfound fans, and when she had seen Yale and Mimi heading in this direction, she had followed. Now that her performance was over, she had to talk to both of them. She'd been concerned for days about Mimi, and she and Yale had unfinished business. She hadn't meant to eavesdrop, but Yale's painful story held her captive until the end, and the only thing she could think of when he finished was what a fool she had been. If only she'd known! she thought, and wondered how she could ever have judged him.

It was obvious to Yale that she had overheard their conversation, but instead of being angry, as she half expected, he looked relieved. "You heard," he said simply.

"Why didn't you ever tell me, Yale?"

"Because you wouldn't have understood."

She forced herself to hold his gaze. She knew it was true, and after a moment, she nodded slowly. "You're right," she said. "But I do now. And I want you to understand about me."

"You don't—"

She interrupted him. "Yes, I do. You see, everything was always so easy for me back then. I never had to struggle for what I won, I was a natural, just like you. But unlike you, Yale, my family smoothed the way. They allowed me to concentrate solely on my skating, and after awhile, that's all I saw. I loved it—I loved being on the ice. It was the only thing I could do well, and because of it I felt so free. It seemed to me that I had the world in the palm of my hand...."

She paused a moment, blinking back the memories that came crowding in. "Or at least I felt that way until the pressure was on. Suddenly it wasn't enough to enjoy skating or practicing; suddenly I had to win.

Even when I got hurt, everyone felt I had to go out there and give it a shot, even if I never walked again afterward. It was as though a medal had somehow become more valuable than I was as a person, more important than me.''

Mimi stirred. Her eyes big in her pale face, she whispered, ''Was that why you didn't skate your final program?''

Kira hesitated. But this was a time for honesty, and she said, ''I don't know, Mimi. I always told myself that my injury prevented me from getting that gold medal, but now I wonder if it was just an excuse. Maybe I was just afraid to fail.''

''But you didn't fail today,'' Yale said quietly.

''No,'' she said. ''I didn't.''

Mimi left her father's side and came to look into Kira's eyes. ''You did that for me, didn't you?''

Kira reached out and touched that bright cloud of hair. ''I did it for all three of us,'' she said softly.

Mimi looked at her a moment longer. ''Thanks,'' she whispered, and moved away. Glancing from one to the other, a twinkle came into her eyes. ''You know, I think I'll leave you two alone for a while, and go find Tad.''

Yale smiled wryly at the resilience of the young, but his eyes never left Kira's face. ''Fine,'' he murmured. ''We'll be along in a minute.''

Mimi had become her irrepressible self again. ''Only a minute?'' she teased. ''Is that all the time it's going to take to convince Kira to marry you?''

They both looked at her in dismayed surprise. ''What?'' Yale exclaimed.

''Oh, come on.'' Mimi giggled. ''You both couldn't have been more obvious if you'd tried!''

"Mimi—"

"I'll see you later," she said, and ducked under the trees. They could hear her merry laughter as she sped away in search of her own conquest, and when the last gay notes had faded in the distance, Kira and Yale finally looked at each other.

"It seems my daughter knows me better than I know myself," Yale said wryly.

Kira laughed. "And here I thought we were being so subtle."

"You were never subtle," he teased. "Champions aren't, I've found."

"You should know."

"So should you."

They were silent again for a moment, then Yale moved toward her. Without touching her, he murmured, "So what do you think, Kira? Is Mimi right? Do you think we can mend a few dreams, or is it too late?"

"I found out today that it's never too late to mend a dream," Kira said softly, and reached up to touch that beloved face.

EPILOGUE

"GOOD AFTERNOON, sports fans," the announcer said excitedly, his handsome face filling television screens in millions of homes across the country. "And welcome to our coverage of World Cup skiing! We're in Grenoble, Switzerland today, and this race promises to be one of the most exciting of the circuit. As some of you are no doubt aware, the top contender in the women's competition is our own Mimi Duncan, the sixteen-year-old wonder who has come back stronger than ever after a bad fall at Lake Placid just last year. Here with the story is Chad Devane, our expert commentator on the scene. Chad...?"

Far below the announcer's booth, the mini-cam swung to the red-cheeked Chad. He was muffled to the chin in a thick down parka, and his gloved hand shook with cold and excitement as he held the microphone up to his face. "Thank you, Kent," he said, "and quite a story it is! As you recall, we were at Lake Placid when Mimi took that fall, and wondered with the rest of the world if she would ever ski again. Now, after surgery and extensive therapy, she's back on the slopes in better form than ever, and if she wins today the World Cup title is hers. We interviewed her yesterday, and she insisted that most of the credit belongs to two special people in her life. We just happen to have them on hand...." At a signal from the director, the cameraman drew back to widen the shot, bringing Yale and Kira into view. "And here they are. Ladies and gentlemen, the former silver medalist in the Downhill, Yale Duncan, Mimi's father, and the beautiful Kira Blair Duncan, our own twice World Champion in Ladies' Figure Skating. Yale, Kira—what do you think of Mimi's chances today?"

Looking more handsome than ever in his thick cable-knit sweater and ski pants, Yale stood with his arm around Kira. Without cracking a smile, he said. "Oh, I think she's got a pretty good shot at it."

Chad looked startled. "A pretty good shot, did you say?" he repeated, and blinked. "What do you think, Kira?"

Trying to hide her amusement at Yale's uncharacteristic modesty, Kira thought back over the past ten months since Mimi had come to the clinic. So much had happened since then, and the wedding ring on her finger proved it. Glancing down at the wide gold band with the single-carat solitaire diamond, she smiled. She'd been ecstatic the day she and Yale had gotten married, but she still believed that the happiest time the three of them had ever experienced was the day Mimi had successfully completed the Stanfield Marathon, that final test of endurance and strength that Kira gave to all her graduating patients. Mimi's spectacular and determined performance meant that she was ready to get back into training, and though it had been hard letting her future stepdaughter fly off to training camp, she and Yale couldn't deny her the chance.

"I want to do this," Mimi had said fiercely, "for myself!"

And so they had let her go. But she had flown back briefly to be the maid of honor at the wedding, and to tease her father about his new office. Yale had bought the storybook house he'd leased when they first came to Vermont, and had converted the den.

"If I'm going to stay home so much of time," he had declared, "I might as well have it the way I like it."

He had given up his superstar clients and was now working hard to establish grants for amateurs. Any talented athlete without financial support could qualify, and his new business was already a success. But then, Kira thought with a private smile, she had always known how persuasive Yale could be, and his contacts in every field seemed endless.

As for her, Miles had been delighted that she planned to continue working at the clinic, and the only sad note was the departure of Hilda Trent. Kira and Yale had begged her to stay, but she had smilingly declared her old bones wouldn't take another Vermont winter, and that California was the place for her. However, she wouldn't be averse to a visit now and then.

Realizing that the sportscaster was still waiting for her reply, Kira leaned toward the microphone. "I think she's got a pretty good shot, too," she said with a mischievous glance up at Yale.

"Oh, well, thank you both," Chad said uncertainly, and seemed about to say something more. But just then there was a quickening among the crowd that lined the course, and he placed a hand to his ear. Kira and Yale were already moving to a spot that had been reserved for them by the finish line, and Chad said excitedly into the camera, "I've just received word that we're about ready to begin the competition, so we'll switch now to our cameras at the starting gate."

"Three . . . two . . . one . . . and go!"

At the finish line, Yale reached for Kira's hand. Mimi was the first competitor, and as his fingers tightened around Kira's, she imagined that she could see that blur of crimson at the top of the steep mountain. She closed her eyes. This was always the hardest part for her: it had been this way with Yale all those years ago, and now it was the same with Mimi. She wouldn't be able to breathe until Mimi crossed that finish line.

They knew she was coming long before they could see her, for the excited shouting of the crowd lining the course rose like a wave. It was obvious from the roar that she was making good time, and Kira dared a quick glance at Yale. His eyes were riveted on the mountain, and his fingers tightened again on hers as he said, "Here she comes...."

Kira looked up. Mimi was a blur as she rounded that last curve and crouched into that "egg" position, shooting like an arrow toward the finish line. When she crossed it, the crowd went wild. The noise became a tumult, the shouting and yelling and whistling and screaming so deafening that the announcer's voice was drowned as it came over the loudspeaker, announcing the time.

Had she won? Was her time good enough to beat all the others who would follow? Surrounded by those screaming fans, Kira and Yale shared a private glance. Arms around each other, they looked over to where Mimi had raised her ski poles in triumph. As far as they were concerned, this time they had all won the gold.

FOLLOW THE RAINBOW...

Sally Garrett
RAINBOW HILLS SERIES

If you enjoyed *Weaver of Dreams*, Book One of Sally Garrett's trilogy celebrating the inspiring lives of three strong-willed American farm women, you're sure to enjoy Book Two, *Visions*, even more. Abbie's cousin, Eileen, discovers strength and courage she didn't know she had when she becomes a single parent struggling to save the family farm. And in time she makes the greatest discovery of all—broken hearts do mend when healed by the transforming power of love!

Coming from Harlequin Superromance next month, is *Visions*, Book Two of Sally Garrett's Rainbow Hill Series.

Harlequin
Superromance

COMING NEXT MONTH

Take 4 best-selling love stories FREE

Plus get a FREE surprise gift!

An intriguing story
of a love that defies the boundaries of time.

BEVERLY SOMMERS

Time and Again

Knocked unconscious by a violent earthquake, Lauren, a computer operator, wakes up to find that she is no longer in her familiar world of the 1980s, but back in 1906. She not only falls into another era but also into love, a love she had only known in her dreams. Funny...heartbreaking...always entertaining.

Available in August or reserve your copy for July shipping by sending your name, address, zip or postal code along with a check or money order for $4.70 (includes 75¢ for postage and handling) payable to Worldwide Library to:

<u>In the U.S.</u>

Worldwide Library
901 Fuhrmann Blvd.
Box 1325
Buffalo, NY 14269-1325

<u>In Canada</u>

Worldwide Library
P.O. Box 609
Fort Erie, Ontario
L2A 5X3

Please specify book title with your order.

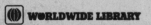 **WORLDWIDE LIBRARY**

TIM-1